Hook, Line, and Murder

A *Murder, She Wrote* Mystery

Hook, Line, and Murder

A *Murder, She Wrote* Mystery

A NOVEL BY JESSICA FLETCHER,
DONALD BAIN & RENÉE PALEY-BAIN

Based on the Universal Television series created by
Peter S. Fischer, Richard Levinson & William Link

BERKLEY PRIME CRIME
New York

BERKLEY PRIME CRIME
Published by Berkley
An imprint of Penguin Random House LLC
375 Hudson Street, New York, New York 10014

Copyright © 2016 by Universal Studios Licensing LLC
Murder, She Wrote is a trademark and copyright of Universal Studios. All rights reserved.
Penguin Random House supports copyright. Copyright fuels creativity, encourages
diverse voices, promotes free speech, and creates a vibrant culture. Thank you for buying
an authorized edition of this book and for complying with copyright laws by not
reproducing, scanning, or distributing any part of it in any form without permission.
You are supporting writers and allowing Penguin Random House to continue to
publish books for every reader.

BERKLEY is a registered trademark and BERKLEY PRIME CRIME and the B colophon
are trademarks of Penguin Random House LLC.

Library of Congress Cataloging-in-Publication Data

Names: Fletcher, Jessica, author. | Bain, Donald, 1935- author. |
Paley-Bain, Renée, author.
Title: Murder, she wrote : hook, line, and murder / Jessica Fletcher,
Donald Bain & Renée Paley-Bain.
Other titles: Hook, line, and murder | Murder, she wrote (Television program)
Description: First edition. | New York : Berkley Prime Crime, 2016.
Identifiers: LCCN 2016019626 (print) | LCCN 2016031274 (ebook) |
ISBN 9780451477835 (hardback) | ISBN 9780698411692 (ebook)
Subjects: LCSH: Fletcher, Jessica—Fiction. | Women novelists—Fiction. |
Women detectives—Fiction. | BISAC: FICTION / Mystery & Detective /
Women Sleuths. | FICTION / Media Tie-In. | FICTION /
Mystery & Detective / General. | GSAFD: Mystery fiction.
Classification: LCC PS3552.A376 M276 2016 (print) |
LCC PS3552.A376 (ebook) | DDC 813/.54—dc23
LC record available at https://lccn.loc.gov/2016019626

First Edition: October 2016

Printed in the United States of America
1   3   5   7   9   10   8   6   4   2

Cover art: *Lake* © Songquan Deng/Moment/Getty Images
Cover design by Katie Anderson

Hook, Line, and Murder

A *Murder, She Wrote* Mystery

Part One

Chapter One

The big white banner with the blue letters flapped across the front of Town Hall.

CABOT COVE DERBY DAYS HAVE ARRIVED.
CATCH 'EM WHILE THEY'RE BITING.
TROPHIES! CASH PRIZES! REGISTER HERE.

"I suppose you've already signed up, Mrs. Fletcher," Seth Hazlitt said as we descended the steps of the downtown municipal building where we'd attended an early-morning meeting.

"As a matter of fact, I have," I said. "Got my fishing license, my derby permit, reserved a guide, and I convinced Jim Shevlin to rent me one of his cottages out on Moon Lake for the week."

"Isn't the mayor participating in the derby himself?" my physician friend asked.

"He said he may—if he can convince his wife, Susan, to give

up one of her summer weekends. But she says she'd rather camp out down in Kittery at the outlet stores. Anyway, Jim has two cottages on the lake property, so he can always bunk in the other one if he wants to fish in the derby."

"Who's going to be your fishing partner this year?"

"I haven't got one. Since I'm camping out for the whole week—I'm making a little vacation out of it—I figured it was better to sign up as a singleton this year."

"Sure you'll be comfortable all alone in a cabin in the woods? No phone? No TV? Sounds a tad boring if you ask my opinion, which I know you haven't."

"Sounds heavenly to me," I said as we made our way down the dock at the end of Main Street. "I have a pile of books I've been meaning to get to, and when the derby is over, I'll fish just long enough to catch something to eat, then climb into the rocker on the porch and spend the rest of my week reading."

"But what'll you do when the sun goes down? The electricity there is spotty at best. Barely enough to run the plumbing."

"I'll have a flashlight and a lantern, and there are always candles. I'm not afraid of the dark."

"Isn't it rash to be going by yourself? You never know who could be wandering in the woods looking for trouble."

"I'm actually looking forward to being by myself."

"You spend enough time by yourself at home. I think you should invite someone to keep you company, help you handle the camping chores. I'd join you myself, but I already have patients booked for the week."

Seth held open the door to Mara's Luncheonette for me. "I've never been concerned about roughing it," I said. "Besides, I can't think of anything nicer than getting up with the birds, going out on the water, and throwing in a line when the fish are hungry for breakfast."

"I'm not serving any fish for breakfast this morning," Mara said as she carried a tray past us, the aroma of eggs and bacon trailing behind her.

"Speaking of breakfast," Seth said, sliding into a chair at an empty table, "fancy some blueberry pancakes?"

"Not for me but you go ahead." I took the chair opposite his and picked up Mara's menu. I don't know why I bothered. I knew it by heart.

Mara slid two mugs of coffee onto the table. "What made you think of fish for breakfast?" she asked. "You can get smoked salmon on a bagel, but that's the extent of my marine offerings this morning. It's local; I got it straight from the smokehouse."

"I'll have that," I said.

Seth tucked a napkin in his collar. "Mrs. Fletcher here has gone and signed herself up for the fishing derby. She plans to camp out in the woods with the wolves."

"We don't have any confirmed sightings of wolves in Maine," I said. "You must be thinking of coyotes."

"Nevertheless," Seth said, ignoring me, "if she's smart, she'll pack some of your bagels so she has something to eat in the morning in case the trout aren't biting. I'll have the short stack with maple syrup, none of that artificial stuff."

Mara pulled herself up tall. "And when have I ever served you 'artificial stuff,' Dr. Hazlitt? I have some maple butter if you want a change of pace from maple syrup."

"The syrup is fine with me. I like to stick with what Mother Nature provides."

I waited until Mara had left to remark that I didn't recall having heard that Mother Nature ever made pancakes.

"You're changing the subject," he said.

"What subject?" I asked.

"You. Alone in the woods. What happens if you come across a bear or get chased by a moose? What if you sprain an ankle or worse, break a bone?"

"Good heavens, Seth, you'd think I'd never gone anywhere by myself. I just came back from New York City. There's more danger there than in the forests of Maine."

"I thought you said the crime rate was down in the city."

"It is, but that doesn't mean it's gone entirely. Anyway, I'll be fine in Jim's cabin. I booked a fishing guide for two days, so someone will be checking on me."

"For two days."

"Yes, for two days. Why are you such a worrywart all of a sudden?"

He shrugged. "Just don't like the sound of it. A woman alone—if you'll pardon my sexist view—is puttin' herself in harm's way."

"And a man alone wouldn't?"

Seth harrumphed. "Don't go planting words in my mouth. I believe in the buddy system. Two people can look out for each other. Safer that way. And remember, you don't even drive. How are you supposed to get home in an emergency?"

"I'll have my bicycle and my cell phone."

"If there's even service up there. If you take my advice—"

"Okay, Seth, I'll give it serious consideration."

"That just your way of tellin' me to mind my own business?"

"Did it work?"

"Mebbe, but only for the moment," he said as Mara placed our orders in front of us.

While I spread cream cheese on half my bagel, Seth made circular designs with the maple syrup in the center of his pancakes and carefully cut into them to keep the syrup from dripping onto the table.

Cabot Cove Derby Days is an annual fly-fishing competition that takes place on local lakes and streams. Instead of a weigh-in, contestants are invited to place the fish they catch in a measuring trough together with their derby permit—showing the number—and take a picture before releasing the catch back into the waters. Prizes are awarded by type of trout, and the photographs of the winners are displayed at Nudd's Bait & Tackle for all to admire.

We were halfway through our breakfast when Sheriff Metzger came in with his wife. "May we join you?" Maureen asked, pulling out a chair.

"Of course," I said, moving my mug to make room on the table.

"I saw you coming from Town Hall," she said, fluffing her red hair and stealing a look at her husband, who frowned down into a menu. "Did you sign up for the derby, Jessica?"

"As a matter of fact, I did," I said, smiling.

"Jess and I were just talking about it before you came in," Seth said.

"Seth," I said, shooting him a cautionary look.

He shifted his gaze to Mort. "You plan on entering the derby, Sheriff?"

"Someone has to hold down the fort at headquarters," Mort replied. "Two of my deputies have asked for the weekend off so they can take part in it. We can't have the whole department on the water and nobody keeping an eye on the town."

"So when will it be your turn?" Maureen Metzger asked, batting her eyelashes at him. "I'm dying to try it, but he always has to be on duty whenever anything fun is taking place." She faked a pout, then smiled up at Mara who came to take their orders. "I'll have the Veggie Benedict, please."

"What's that?" Seth asked.

"Sautéed vegetables on an English muffin with hollandaise sauce," Mara rattled off. "It was Maureen's suggestion and it's pretty popular."

Maureen grinned.

Mort set aside the menu. "I'll have the usual: fried eggs, bacon, and home fries."

Maureen shook her head. "I keep telling him he has to eat a green thing every day, but he doesn't listen."

Mort rolled his eyes but gave his wife a warm smile.

Maureen was our sheriff's second wife. His ex, Adele, had opted to return to New York City where Mort had been a member of the police force before abandoning the Big Apple for Cabot Cove's more quiet life. But that was not what Adele had in mind, and after trying out Cabot Cove for a few years she decided it was not for her.

Though they parted amicably, Mort had been a little lost until he'd met Maureen, a fiery redhead who threw herself into every project with joy and enthusiasm. Her first passion was cooking. She was a devoted fan of all the shows on the cooking channels and had transformed her kitchen into a laboratory for experimental cuisine. At many a dinner their friends were guinea pigs for her culinary inventions, some of which were—

putting it politely—difficult to stomach. But she'd kept at it, and we all had to admit that a lot of her recent creations were delicious.

"Hear anything about that guy who escaped from the state prison last week?" Seth asked Mort.

"Jepson? Not a word."

"How'd he escape?"

"The paper said he hid under a pile of dirty linen. An easy disguise for him. When the laundry truck left the prison, he left with it."

"Well, that was clever," Seth said, "but if he was still in one of those orange or yellow prison uniforms, he shouldn't be hard to spot."

"He probably ditched those clothes first thing," Mort said. "My contacts at the state troopers' office figure he must be hiding out somewhere along the Canadian border."

"That's a lot of miles to cover," I said.

Mort nodded. "There was a report he was sighted in Calais across the bridge from New Brunswick, but the border patrol was on alert, making it tough to get past them. They're figuring if he hitched a ride up U.S. One, he could be near Quebec by now. They alerted the Mounties in both provinces. Anyway, not our problem anymore."

"Wasn't he a local boy?" Maureen asked.

"Yeah," her husband replied, "but a long time ago."

"An angry young man," Seth said. "I seem to remember him threatening his attorney and everyone associated with the case."

Mort made a face at Seth and shook his head, darting his eyes at his wife.

"Oops! Sorry," Seth said, taking a big forkful of pancake.

Maureen seemed to have missed the exchange. "Why was he in prison?" she asked.

"He killed a man in a robbery," I said.

"They had him dead to rights on the store's security tape," Mort said. "He pleaded not guilty, but the jury saw right through him, through both of them, in fact."

"Don't start, Mort," I said.

"I know you believe the other guy's story, Mrs. F., but you can't convince me."

Seth cleared his throat loudly. "You ever fished in a derby before?" he asked Maureen.

She looked curiously from her husband to me before answering. "I never have. I was hoping Mort would teach me so we'd have a hobby we could do together. He doesn't like to cook."

"I like to eat," Mort pointed out. "Don't I always appreciate what you make?"

She winked at him. "You do, even when I'm not certain the dish came out the way it was supposed to."

"Well, that's okay," Mort said. "You worked hard at it."

"Mrs. Fletcher here doesn't have a partner for the derby," Seth said, studiously avoiding my eyes. "Just mebbe *she'd* be willing to teach you."

Maureen's eyes lit up. "Oh, Jessica! Would you? I'd be so grateful."

"Well, I—"

"I've been dying to learn how to fish, and Mort just doesn't have the time. I know what equipment I need to buy, and Charles Department Store is running a special on fishing gear ahead of the derby."

"You didn't tell me about that," Mort said.

"You didn't ask," his wife replied. "Jessica, I'll be the best company. I won't talk too much and scare away the fish. I'll even bait the hook if I have to, even though I always feel sorry for the worm when I watch those fishing shows on TV. And for the fish, too."

"You've been watching fishing shows?" Mort asked.

"Actually, the derby is for fly-fishing. No bait is used and no harm comes to the fish," Seth put in before the conversation was dragged in another direction.

"Yeah?" Mort said. "I didn't know that."

"Ayuh. You just take a picture of the fish and put it back in the water. Everyone turns in their photos at the end of two days and the winners are announced. Isn't that right, Jessica?"

"Yes, Seth."

"Then it's settled," he said, sitting back with a smile. "You sign up for the derby, Maureen, and the sheriff here can drop both of you off at the mayor's cabin on Moon Lake."

"Wait a minute, Doc. I'm not sure Mrs. F. even wants company at the lake, and Maureen's never been fishing before. There's a lot to learn before you enter a competition. Besides, what about my—?"

"Oh, you," his wife interrupted. "You can manage being a bachelor again for a few days. Half the town will be out fishing, so you shouldn't have too much to do. Mara will be happy to cook up some dishes for you to take home."

"Did I hear my name being taken in vain?" Mara said, bearing two plates bound for our table.

"If I sign up for the Cabot Cove fishing derby, you'll make sure Mort won't starve in my absence, won't you, Mara?" Maureen asked.

"Was kinda thinking of entering the contest myself," she said, setting down the dishes.

Seth guffawed. "You weren't!"

"What's so funny about that, Seth Hazlitt? I know how to fish."

"So you're going to close this place for the weekend?" he asked.

"Bite your tongue! It's summer, my busiest season. I'm not about to miss out on all the tourists looking to eat." She eyed Seth's half-eaten pancakes. "You finished with that?"

"Keep your hands off that plate, woman!"

"Thought so," she said, walking away.

Maureen picked up her fork. "I saw the cutest fishing vest in Charles's window. It's got all these little pockets. I could put my lipstick in one, my wallet in another, and there was even a pocket for my cell phone. It was really reasonable and I probably wouldn't even need to carry a handbag if I had that vest."

"Just how 'reasonable' was this vest?"

"Now, Sheriff, your wife has to have the proper equipment if she's entering the derby," Seth said, slicing the last of his pancakes into small pieces. "She can rent a fly-fishing rod if they're not all spoken for, but she'll need her own waders."

"I already bought the waders," Maureen said, focusing on dabbing a bit of asparagus in the hollandaise sauce.

"Is that the big box I saw in the back of the hall closet?" her husband asked. "I wondered what you were hiding there."

"I wasn't hiding anything." She addressed Seth. "The man at Nudd's Bait & Tackle said he'd put aside a fishing rod for me, but what do I put on the hook for bait?"

"You have to use dry flies—not real flies," Seth said. "You

need the kind made with feathers and thread. I'm sure I have a couple I can give you, and Jessica can lend you whatever else you need, or your husband can spring for an assortment."

"Thanks for offering to spend my money, Doc."

"Well, you want your wife to fish like a pro, don't you?"

There was a moment of silence as food was consumed.

I used my napkin to wipe my lips. "Is anyone interested in what I have to say?"

Two sets of eyes turned my way, but I noticed that Seth continued swirling around the remains of his pancakes in the leftover syrup.

"I've actually rented Mayor Shevlin's cabin for a full week, but"—I looked at Maureen—"if you would like to stay with me just for the weekend of the fishing derby, you would be welcome."

"Oh, Jessica, thank you so much."

"Don't thank me yet. It's pretty rustic up there. There's barely any electricity, no phone, no running water. I don't want you to get up there and be disappointed by the lack of amenities."

A small smile played over Maureen's lips. "You probably don't know it, but I went to Girl Scout camp. I can start a fire and build a wickiup. I actually won an adventurer patch. I'm pretty sure I can handle whatever's there. And I'm so excited to learn how to fish. I know some great trout recipes, but I know the derby is—"

"Catch and release," three voices said in unison.

"All right, all right," she said. "I'll pack a picnic basket."

Back home, I paused in reviewing the manuscript for my latest mystery and the notes my editor had sent to ponder how my good friend Seth Hazlitt, Cabot Cove's favorite physician, had maneuvered me into agreeing to have Maureen Metzger along for the derby days portion of my vacation. If I wasn't careful, he'd find a way to have someone else drop in to check up on me the rest of the week, and there would go my plans to escape to a cabin in the woods. While I appreciated his concern for my safety, I was as much looking forward to private time relaxing by the lake and catching up with my reading as I was to catching a fish to enter in the competition.

What I eventually ended up catching, however, was something else altogether.

Chapter Two

From the *Cabot Cove Gazette*

GROCERY KILLER STILL AT LARGE

HUNT FOCUSED ON UPSTATE BORDER

THIS YEAR'S DERBY DAY NUMBERS TAKE A HIT

Sheriff Mort Metzger encouraged a nervous citizenry today to go on with their regular routines and not to worry about a convicted murder who recently escaped from the state prison in Warren, assuring the local population that the fugitive is thought to be hours away, somewhere along the state's 611-mile border with Canada.

"I've been in touch with state police every day and the troopers assure me that they're closing in on their man," Sheriff Metzger told the *Gazette* at a hastily assembled press conference at Town Hall. "All twenty-four land border crossings are under surveillance, and federal and state agents are fielding myriad calls about sightings and are concentrating their manpower in the northern part of the state. Cabot Cove is not within the search environs."

Mayor James Shevlin called for the public announcement after learning that registrations for the upcoming Cabot Cove Derby Days were off by a wide margin over last year's numbers. The mayor said he didn't know if the jailbreak was the reason there seemed to be less interest in the annual fishing competition, but just in case it was, he asked the sheriff to restore public confidence in the security of the town's outdoor recreation.

Metzger declined to answer questions about Darryl Jepson, who lived in Cabot Cove before being incarcerated for the knife killing of Stanley Olberman, who operated the mini-mart on North Main. Instead the sheriff ended the press conference on a light note.

"Not only will you be perfectly safe going up to Moon Lake for the fishing derby," the sheriff stated, "you're liable to have one of my deputies in the next boat. A couple of my men have asked for time off so they can participate, too."

Mayor Shevlin said that the recreation office in Town Hall would remain open after hours to accommodate any late entrants in the derby.

Metzger closed the discussion by thanking Shevlin for the use of one of the mayor's Moon Lake cabins and issued a jocular warning to local fly-fishing enthusiasts. "If you decide not to sign up for the competition, that'll mean a better chance for my wife, Maureen. She's fishing in her first derby and promises to haul in the biggest rainbow trout. So, all you other fishermen, you're being put on notice."

The *Gazette*'s coverage of the press conference, and the conference itself, was intended to ease the concerns of Cabot Cove's citizenry. Whether it did depended on each individual's outlook and level of apprehension. Everyone, of course, was concerned to a greater or lesser degree about having an escaped murderer roaming loose in Maine, ostensibly far north of us according to our sheriff. For me, and for Maureen Metzger, it was something to think about but not to the extent that we would even consider postponing our fishing plans on Moon Lake. "Fish on!" was our operative philosophy as we arrived at the cabin that would be our home for the next few days.

Maureen clumped up the front steps of the cabin in her chest-high waders and lurched through the door. The floppy hat she wore and the size of the ice chest she was carrying made it difficult for her to see where she placed her feet, and I was amazed that she managed to stay balanced.

I hurried over to relieve her of the load and hauled the cooler up onto the wooden picnic table. "Why are you wearing your waders?" I asked. "The derby doesn't start until tomorrow, and we'll be spending most of our time in a boat."

"They didn't fit in my suitcases." She collapsed on the bench next to the table, let out a big sigh, and fanned her face with the hat.

"Suitcases?"

"They're halfway down the path. Mort got a call on the way

up here. I told him he could just drop me at the bottom of the hill. He did and took off."

"What was the call about?"

"Oh, the deputy said something about somebody on a boat. Anyway, Mort didn't wait around to help me up the hill. I don't think he's happy with my being away for the weekend." She sighed again.

"I'm sure he'll muddle through," I said. "You rest. I'll go get your luggage." I walked outside and trotted down the steps. The day was cloudless and warm, the hum of insects the only sound apart from the rustle of leaves in the trees when a brief breeze blew by. Ahead on the grassy path down to the dirt road—the only access to the cabin's location unless you came by water— were matching red roller bags, one larger than the other. I grabbed both handles and hauled them behind me up the hill.

I had arrived an hour earlier—delivered by Dimitri's Taxi Service, Cabot Cove's trusty cab company—with my only luggage a well-worn duffel bag, as well as my fishing gear, bicycle, and two paper bags' worth of groceries. I knew Jim Shevlin usually stocked his shelves with an assortment of canned goods and fresh water for guests in addition to a selection of silverware, plates, and pots. A magnetic rack held a knife, spatula, and serving spoon.

The cabin was a two-room affair—a main section with a picnic table, woodstove, and a kitchen cabinet for the sink, hand-operated water pump, and hot plate; and a bunk room off which was a minuscule bathroom. Shelves and pegs on the log walls accommodated whatever equipment and supplies were brought in, while a pair of wooden rocking chairs on the porch could be pulled inside when it got dark or the weather was bad.

Moon Lake was about thirty miles northwest of Cabot Cove on the fringe of the town limits. Mayor Shevlin often invited visiting dignitaries from Augusta to come up to one of his cabins for the day, claiming that the relaxing atmosphere enabled him to negotiate better deals from our representatives in the state capital. Regardless of whether they were male or female, fishing fans or landlubbers, the smell of the pines and the view of the sun striking sparks off the shimmering water worked magic on bureaucratic minds, and our town reaped the benefits.

Maureen came out of the cabin and met me halfway. "Oh, I didn't mean for you to get stuck with both my bags. Let me get one of those."

She grabbed the handle of the larger suitcase, lifted it up the steps, and rolled it across the porch and into the front room. I followed with the other bag and deposited it in the cabin's small bunk room, which held two cots—my duffel bag sat on one—separated by a single nightstand. A socket holding a bare bulb was affixed to a rafter. It was the bunk room's only illumination, and its match hung above the sink in the main room.

Maureen peered through the door at the spartan accommodations. "Don't make fun of me, Jessica. I know I overpacked."

"Perhaps," I said. "We don't usually dress for dinner."

She giggled. "And you don't have to worry. I'm not planning to spend the week. I wasn't sure what I'd need, so I took it all. After this weekend I'll have a better idea what to bring next time."

Next time. Selfishly I hoped Maureen wasn't planning for this weekend to be repeated. Even though I enjoyed her company, I wasn't ready to commit to an annual derby date. "Why don't you get settled and then we can take a walk down to the lake and talk fish," I said.

"Talk fish! Ooh! I'm excited already."

There was a knock on the screen door and a voice called out, "Halloo. Anybody there?"

Maureen gasped, her eyes wide. "Who is that?" she whispered.

"It's probably our guide," I said, squeezing around her. "Is that you, Brian?"

"Yup." A slim man in his early thirties, wearing a white T-shirt, cargo shorts, and a ball cap, waved at me through the screen door. "Hi there, Mrs. Fletcher. Nice to see you again. Have a good trip up?"

"I did. Come on in, Brian. How's Alice? And your little girl? She must be a big girl by now."

"Emma's nearly four. Pretty as her mother." Brian wiped the rubber soles of his ankle boots on the mat outside and opened the screen door.

"Please say hello for me when you see them."

"Happy to," he said pulling the cap from his head as he entered.

"I'd like to introduce you to my friend." I looked around. "Maureen? Where did you go?"

"I'm right here." Maureen exited the bunk room, red-faced. "I wasn't expecting anyone else to see me in these rubber overalls," she said, plucking at the vinyl leg of her waders.

"Those look like a great pair of waders," Brian said, extending his hand. "I'm Brian Kinney."

"I'm Maureen Metzger," she said, shaking his hand.

"The sheriff's wife?"

"Yes. Do you know Mort?"

"Sort of." There was an awkward pause, and then Brian

cocked his head at Maureen's waders and asked, "You have a belt for those?"

"Do I need a belt?"

"Yes, you do," I said. "If you wade into the water to fish, the rocks can be slippery."

"A belt keeps the water out in case you accidentally fall in," Brian added. "We don't want you to drown. But you won't need waders or a belt tomorrow. I'm going to be guiding you ladies on the water. I have an electric motor rowboat. Nice and stable. You'll still need a PFD; that's a personal flotation device."

"In other words, a life jacket," I inserted.

"That's right, but you can leave your rubber overalls at home."

"So I don't get to wear these?" Maureen asked.

"Not tomorrow," Brian replied, "unless you want to stand in the lake to fish, but I wouldn't recommend it."

"Why not?"

"The water near the shoreline is warmer. The advantage of a boat is that we can find the cold spots the fish like best."

"The trout like cold water?" Maureen asked, forgetting her initial embarrassment.

"Yes, ma'am. Trout are cold-water fish. If the water gets too warm, they huddle in the coolest spot they can find. Harder to catch, then. But not to worry, I know where they hide."

"If I'm not wearing these, what should I wear?" Maureen asked me a little uncertainly.

"We can review your wardrobe choices after dinner tonight," I said. "I'm dying to see what you packed in those bags. I'm sure you'll be the best-dressed fisherwoman on the lake."

"What time would you ladies like to start?" Brian asked.

"We'll follow your recommendation," I said.

"The best time is just before dawn, so I'm wondering if you want to go out as early as five."

"A.M.?" Maureen asked, horrified.

Brian scratched the back of his neck. "Guess not, huh? Okay, how about we fish from seven to nine or ten. Take a break, and get back on the water at three—that's when the bugs come out and they're biting."

"Who's getting bitten?" Maureen asked. "Not us, I hope."

Brian laughed. "Nope. The trout are the ones biting the bugs, so it's a good time to confuse them with an artificial one."

"And we have repellent to keep the bugs off us," I said.

Maureen was quiet for a long time after Brian left. I had busied myself seeing what we could rustle up for dinner from our joint grocery contributions when I realized my guest was not with me. I found her sitting on her cot, paging through a book.

I sat on the bunk opposite her. "Is it all too overwhelming?" I asked.

Maureen sighed. "I hope I haven't made a mistake, Jessica. I don't want to mess up your vacation."

"Why would you think you've made a mistake? You haven't even tried fishing yet. And don't worry about my vacation, I have all week. You're only here for two and a half days."

"I know, but this book made it sound all so romantic and thrilling, and then Brian came in and talked about drowning and getting bitten by bugs, not to mention dragging myself out of bed before the sun comes up. I don't even know how to tie on a fly." She ended on a groan.

"Maureen," I said, taking her hand, "you are not a delicate flower. You are a strong, capable woman, one who braves the unknown and takes on new challenges."

"I am?"

"What did you know about cooking before you decided to become a great chef?"

"Nothing."

"And how did you go about it?"

"I'm not really a great chef."

"We'll leave that aside for now. What did you do to learn the culinary arts?"

"Well, I studied all the cooking shows and read all the cookbooks I could find and experimented in the kitchen." She blushed. "You know that. You got to sample my disasters."

"And your triumphs," I said. "You are going to love fishing. I guarantee it. Don't worry about the parts you don't know. Like cooking, it takes time to learn. We can practice tying knots if you want, but if we leave it to Brian, it will go a lot faster and we'll lose fewer flies."

She gave me a watery smile. "Thanks, Jessica."

"No thanks needed," I said. "What we need is something to eat, and I can't figure out what you intended to make with all those condiments."

"Oh, let me show you."

Between my groceries and the contents of Maureen's cooler, we fixed ourselves a nice meal, washed our dishes in cold water, sealed our garbage in bearproof containers, and strolled down to the water while it was still light, passing the stone-ringed campfire pit.

Maureen took a deep breath and let it out. "Oh, it's so beautiful here—and peaceful."

"It is lovely," I said, watching a great blue heron spring into the air and fly across the lake.

"I feel like I could stay here forever. Do you think the mayor would let me rent his other cabin for a week or two?"

"I don't see why not if he isn't using it. But you may want to see how you feel after two days of rustic living before you commit to a longer stay."

"Don't you think I'm up to it? I was a Girl Scout, remember."

"I think you can do anything you put your mind to. I'm only saying that I've found that camping is fine—wonderful even—in short spurts, but after a while you begin to miss reliable electricity and hot running water and other luxuries we've grown accustomed to."

"Like computers?"

"Like computers and refrigerators and coffeemakers and air-conditioning and nearby shops and—"

"Okay, I see what you mean. But maybe I could get Mort to come with me for a week. He has vacation days he hasn't taken. Do you think he would?"

I tried to imagine Mort free of all the electronics that ruled his life. "You know him better than I," I said.

Maureen laughed. "What am I saying? That man can't spend five minutes without a walkie-talkie on his shoulder, a phone in his hand, and his ear to a police radio."

I smiled. "Maybe get him up here for a day and see how he handles it."

We walked back to the cabin and settled in the rocking chairs on the porch. "Speaking of Mort, that reminds me," I said.

"What reminds you?"

"You said he got a call before he dropped you off and rushed away. You said the call was about somebody on a boat. Do you remember what exactly?"

"I never listen to that radio, but Mort said he had to get down to the dock. Now that I think about it, it may not have been about somebody on a boat."

"No? What was it then?"

"Maybe it was some *body* on a boat."

"That's quite a difference. And certainly an emergency."

"Not really. I think the deputy told him that whoever it was, was already dead. At least that's what I think I heard him say."

Chapter Three

"Think, Maureen. What else did you hear?" I said, looking at her with surprise.

"They found some old guy submerged in the water next to his boat," Maureen said. "They thought he must've tripped and hit his head when he fell overboard and drowned."

"How awful. Do you know who it was?"

"I didn't recognize the guy's name. Wes Carters or Caraghers, maybe. Car-something anyway."

"Not Wes Caruthers?"

"That sounds right. Did you know him?" Maureen slapped a hand over her jaw. "Oh, me and my big mouth! I'm so sorry, Jessica, if he was a friend of yours. Here I go, just blurting it out. That's why Mort tells me never to discuss his cases. He'll be angry if I tell him I told you."

"Nothing to worry about. Wes Caruthers wasn't a friend at all, but I did know him, or know of him."

Caruthers was an attorney, most of whose cases were assigned by the courts. He was rarely successful in exonerating his clients, some of whom accused him of not doing enough to prove their innocence. One of them was Darryl Jepson. A few threatened to sue, but obtaining another lawyer when you didn't have enough money to pay for the first one was difficult to say the least. Most of Caruthers's clients remained in prison for the full length of their sentences, too poor to mount an appeal.

"Let's sort out your wardrobe," I said, more to distract Maureen from her distress than out of interest in her purchases. "We have to get up early, and it'll be helpful if we've set out our clothes the night before."

"Okay! I can't wait to show you my convertibles."

"Convertibles?"

"You'll see."

Maureen spread out all her purchases on the cot and reviewed the piles of clothing, weighing one outfit against another before finally selecting a peach-colored, button-down shirt.

"David at Charles Department Store told me this fabric *breathes*." She drew out the word as I was certain David must have, too. "He said it blocks UV rays and dries really fast if it gets wet. Plus I think the color goes great with my red bandana. What do you think?"

"They're lovely together. I think you'll be the best-dressed angler in the boat."

"But wait, there's more, as they say in the TV ads." She pulled out a pair of pink rubber clogs to go with her convertibles, which turned out to be a pair of lightweight khaki pants the bottoms of which could be zipped off above the knee to become shorts if the weather got hot.

"Isn't this the greatest?" she said, holding up her prized fishing vest, the pockets already bulging with items she was convinced she couldn't do without. She hung it up on a peg and hooked a long-handled fishing net onto the tab at the back of the vest.

"There! I'm all set to go," she said, grinning.

"It's a nice feeling."

"Now what are *you* going to wear?"

I unzipped my duffel bag and pulled out my fishing clothes, some of which also doubled as my gardening attire.

"I think I'll wear my vintage cargo pants," I said, holding them up. "I'm not sure if they're retro, but they're definitely old. And here's my hand-decorated T-shirt last used to paint the back porch, and this elegant piece." I dangled my light blue chambray shirt in the air.

"Jessica, I think you're making fun of me."

"Maybe a little, but I love your enthusiasm."

I was going to look like a dull moth next to her butterfly, but with only Brian as a fashion judge it didn't matter. At least we wouldn't waste time in the morning deciding what to put on. I set my travel alarm, and after taking turns washing up at the kitchen sink, we plugged our cell phones into the only two electrical outlets and climbed into bed.

Maureen was too excited about the upcoming fishing competition to fall asleep right away, and she babbled to me in the darkness about the videos and television shows she'd watched to prepare for the derby.

"You won't believe this guy. He caught a catfish with his bare hands. Ew, I don't think I could ever do that, could you? And another time, he hooked this giant fish the natives were convinced was eating people alive. And you know what? It was true."

I made appropriate listening noises, but my mind was busy remembering what I knew about the late Wes Caruthers, and one case in particular where his client paid a steep price for the lawyer's incompetence.

The case involved two young men of limited means and with too much time on their hands. From what townspeople would call the wrong side of the tracks, the young men, high school dropouts, were well known to local law enforcement for a variety of misdemeanors—fishing without a license, being drunk and disorderly with their buddies, "borrowing" a bicycle, and setting off a cherry bomb in the high school gym early one Sunday, among other offenses. One of them, Darryl Jepson, liked to play with knives. A part-time gas jockey, he spent his off hours playing mumblety-peg with his friends or practicing his knife throws on a scraggly pine behind the filling station. Many other trees in town had scars from the blade of Jepson's knife, so it was no surprise, when a local grocer named Olberman was stabbed during a robbery and later died from his injuries, that the authorities pulled Jepson in for questioning. A security tape showed him pocketing items from the store the day of the robbery. Caruthers was assigned to take his case, but those who attended the trial said he did a terrible job of defending Jepson, who was convicted of murder and sent away. His friend was accused of being an accessory, and despite limited evidence, the jury found him guilty as well.

But Jepson's friend had not appeared on the security tape.

His conviction was based on witnesses who swore they saw two men running from the scene of the crime and a tip from a questionable source. Because of his association with his knife-wielding pal, the young man spent seven years behind bars—repeatedly denied parole because he wouldn't admit his guilt in the robbery and murder. But he used his time productively, getting his high school diploma, studying the law, and spending many hours writing letters seeking help until finally finding a receptive ear at the Innocence Project. A young lawyer from that volunteer organization—which is committed to helping those wrongly convicted—prevailed upon a judge to reopen the case, citing unreliable eyewitness reporting, a snitch with a grudge, and the complete lack of video or other forensic evidence. Plus, the young man had an alibi—dismissed during the trial—that he was with his girlfriend, Alice, at the time of the crime.

While his buddy remained incarcerated, the young man was released, came home to Cabot Cove, married his girlfriend—much to the chagrin of her well-to-do father—and settled down to become a productive citizen. But despite his acquittal, many people in town still suspected he was guilty, and they turned their backs on his efforts to find employment and establish a life for himself, his wife, and their daughter.

That's when the young man, Brian Kinney, our guide, took the only road he saw available, becoming a Maine guide, chiefly for tourists who'd never heard his name before and for the likes of a number of us—like me—who believe in giving an innocent man another chance to make good in his hometown.

Whether Darryl Jepson was also innocent, I didn't know, although I suspected the sheriff's office had arrested the right man. Jepson had chosen a different route to get out of jail: breaking out of the state prison by hiding in a laundry cart. And now authorities were hunting for clues to his whereabouts along the Canadian border.

Despite her groans at the prospect of our early start, Maureen was up before the alarm. She was still in her pajamas, sipping a cup of tea, sitting on one of the rocking chairs on the porch when I came outside at six o'clock.

"Oh, good, you found the tea and mug I left out for you. Is Earl Grey okay? I hope you like a cranberry scone."

"One of my favorites," I said, sliding into the other rocker and blowing on the tea to cool it before taking a sip.

"It's such a beautiful morning that I just wanted to take it all in. I never knew the sun rose so early. I think I saw a fox playing with a grasshopper. Do foxes eat grasshoppers?"

"I'm not sure what a fox's regular diet consists of, but it wouldn't surprise me. Clearly the fox didn't see you or it would have run away."

"I tried to sit very still when I saw him. I don't think I would have been as calm if I'd seen a bear. Are there a lot of bears up here?"

"Some. And moose, too. We're in the woods. Wildlife encounters are definitely possible, as you've discovered this morning. The best thing to do is to keep our distance and let them move on."

"I'll remember that."

Maureen and I were both dressed and waiting on the porch when we saw Brian's rowboat and heard the soft whoosh in the water as he cut the engine and eased up to the dock.

"Good morning, ladies," he called. "Ready to catch some trout?" We walked down to the dock carrying our fishing rods.

"How can we be sure that trout is the only fish we catch?" Maureen asked. "Aren't there other fish in the lake?"

"Yes, ma'am, and if we're lucky enough to hook a good-size pike, we'll get a nice lunch out of it. They're bony but taste great when you know how to make 'em."

"Oh, do you cook?" Maureen asked, immediately warming to our guide.

"My skills are limited to campfire cuisine, but I make a mean fried fish," he said, sliding our rods along the bottom of the boat under the seats. He stood and offered his hand to help Maureen aboard.

She stepped down into the rowboat, hesitated, then chose the narrow seat in the bow. I followed and took the center seat.

Brian waited until we were settled before raising his hand to get our attention. "I always do a little checklist before we push off. Do you have your fishing licenses?"

"Yes, sir," I said, pointing to the plastic pouch pinned to my shoulder.

"Derby permits?"

"Check!"

"Sunscreen?"

"Right here," Maureen said, extracting a tube from one of her vest pockets.

"I already put mine on," I said.

"Hats?"

Two pairs of hands reached up to be sure our hats were secure.

"Bug spray?"

"Check."

"Water? Snack?"

We were only going to be out for three hours, but I had prepared a little care package with bottled water, some fruit, and three sandwiches in case we weren't able to catch our lunch. I handed it to Brian, who stowed the insulated canvas bag in the stern, under his seat.

"I have something to contribute to your goodies," he said, pulling out a plastic container. "Emma insisted on baking chocolate chip cookies for you."

"Is that your daughter?" Maureen asked. "How sweet! It's wonderful that she's learning how to cook."

"She's not much of a baker at three and a half but she loves to make cookies with her mom. And her dad loves to eat them."

"And share them," I added.

"Yes, but only occasionally," Brian said with a fake scowl, and we all laughed.

He handed us both life jackets, and I slipped mine over my blue shirt. Maureen had a little difficulty fitting hers over the bulging pockets of her fishing vest, but once she was enveloped in it, we looked up expectantly and Brian pushed off, starting up his electric motor and aiming the bow of the boat toward the center of the lake.

Some odd feeling made me look back at the cabin, but I didn't notice anything out of the ordinary. I snugged down my hat to shade my eyes and turned around. Had I kept my gaze on the shore, I might have seen an uninvited visitor climb up to the porch.

Chapter Four

Moon Lake is one of Maine's six-thousand-plus lakes and ponds, many of them unnamed. Next to deep-sea fishing, which I also enjoy, fly-fishing on a lake or stream is among my favorite pastimes, whether part of a derby or not. While deep-sea fishing is like wrestling a brawny competitor, fly-fishing is more peaceful and contemplative. At least it is for me. I know how to tie an artificial fly onto the fine filament of fishing line called a leader. I know how to cast upstream and watch the line float past me, taking up the slack as it does. And I know the satisfaction of feeling a tug when a hungry trout mistakes my fly for an honest-to-goodness insect. Whether or not I net a catch, the best part of fly-fishing for me is simply standing in the water or sitting in a boat on a beautiful summer day, communing with my surroundings—listening for the call of the loon, watching dragonflies and damselflies circle their territories, and hearing the burble of the water. It calms my soul and renews my energy. It makes me sigh just to think about it.

I wasn't sure what Maureen Metzger's expectations of fly-fishing were, but I doubted they had a lot to do with nature appreciation.

"How will we know when we get where we're going?" she asked.

"Some of the other guides said they had good luck over at Martha's Pond," Brian said, "so we'll start there and move on if they're not biting."

"Why couldn't we fish right near the cabin?" Maureen asked, clapping her hand on her hat to keep it from flying off in the breeze as the boat sped up.

"Water's too shallow there," Brian replied. "Great for swimming, less so for fishing. We have to go where the fish are."

Fifteen minutes later, Brian slowed down and guided the bow into a narrow inlet using one of his oars to push aside reeds that arched over our boat until we emerged into another body of water. "Look over there," he called, pointing.

Near the shore standing knee-deep in the water was a bull moose with a broad rack of velvety antlers. He raised his head, a stream of weeds dripping from his mouth, peered at us for a moment, and went back to grazing, pushing his snout under the water.

"Ooh, wait till I tell Mort that I saw a real moose," Maureen said, her eyes gleaming.

"Haven't you ever seen one before?" Brian asked.

"Once, when one crossed the road when we were driving out of Bangor, but that doesn't count."

"Why not?" I asked.

"Because it wasn't really in its native habitat, more like a suburb."

"Moose were probably there before the houses. Human beings have been encroaching on moose habitat for years," Brian said.

"Lucky for them it's a big state so there's still plenty of room for wildlife," I added.

We rounded a curve in the pond and spotted two men in a canoe. Brian slowed the boat and waved. "Any luck?" he called.

One of the men gave him a thumbs-up. "Two brookies so far," he yelled.

"Okay!" Brian said, pumping his fist and pointing the bow across the pond.

"Are we close?" Maureen asked.

"Soon," Brian replied.

"It's warmer than I thought it would be," Maureen said, rolling up the sleeves of her shirt and fanning her face with her hat.

"Maureen, did you put on your sunscreen yet?" I asked.

"Not yet, but I will," she said as she unzipped her convertibles.

"Don't think you can only get a burn at midday," I said. "The sun rises early and it's plenty strong now."

"It is, isn't it? I didn't realize it would be this hot."

"Okay, ladies, see that?" Brian pointed to an area of water shaded by tall trees leaning over the bank. The water was stippled and there was a cloud of insects hovering over the surface.

"What is it?" Maureen asked, making a sour face.

"Caddis fly hatch. Yummy eating for trout," he replied. He picked up Maureen's rod and tied an artificial fly on the end of her leader. "Have you ever tried casting before?"

"I practiced with a piece of cork on the line before I left home," she said.

"Good! So you already know about 'two o'clock and ten o'clock.'" He demonstrated with her pole, tipping it behind him and casting forward, stopping when the rod made about a sixty-degree angle with the water, and slowly lowering it until the line landed gently on the surface. "Okay, now reel it in and you try." He handed Maureen her rod and looked at me. "Mrs. Fletcher, do you need any help?"

"I already have an elk-hair caddis fly tied on. What do you think?"

"I think that sounds perfect. Why don't you try it?"

We spent the next half hour casting into the area of water where the insects had been swarming over the surface. Maureen's line slapped the water more often than landing gently, but she concentrated on improving her casting technique, with gentle instructions from Brian.

I knew that Mort was not aware that our fishing guide was his former prisoner, one he was still convinced had been let out of prison on a false pretext. I had purposely left out that information, trusting that when Maureen got to know Brian and saw what an upstanding citizen he'd become—and told her husband—that Mort might soften in his antipathy to the former convict. At least I hoped so.

Fishing is a sport that requires a good deal of patience, a trait that was not one of Maureen's strongest points. Several times she got excited when the weight of the line felt a little heavy, but her face fell when she realized that she'd hooked a weed and not a fish.

"I think there's a fish on my line," I said minutes later, feeling a familiar vibration.

"Keep reeling it in," Brian said, watching the curve of my

rod. "I believe you have something there. Now give him a little slack and pull up sharply."

I followed Brian's instructions, Maureen cheering me on, until Brian took up the net and scooped it under the fish as it flopped on the surface near the boat. "That's a pretty good-looking rainbow," he said. "Where's your camera?"

"Hooray for you, Jessica! You caught the first fish," Maureen said, bouncing up and down on her seat.

"Hold the excitement till we get this guy measured," Brian said, deftly extracting the trout from the hook and laying it in a measuring trough. "Sixteen inches! He looks like a good one. Where's your derby permit, Jessica? We want to put him back in the water as soon as possible."

"Right here," I said, handing it to him. "And I have my cell phone camera ready."

I took a picture of my rainbow trout and e-mailed it to the derby judges. Brian slid the fish back in the water and wiped off my damp permit on the knee of his pants before returning it.

"You might have a winner right there. That guy must have been a two-year-old," Brian said.

"Okay! Now it's my turn," Maureen said, facing the pool under the trees with renewed enthusiasm.

We fished there for another half hour and Maureen did reel in a fish, but it was a yellow perch, not a trout.

"They're good eating, too," Brian declared, and dropped the fish into a bucket of lake water. "See if you can find some of his relatives and we'll have a nice lunch."

All told for our morning of fishing we netted four trout (another rainbow for me and two brown trout for Maureen) and two more perch. Brian guided the boat away from shore and we headed back toward our cabin for a midday break and a light meal.

"I can't wait to call Mort and tell him about the fish I caught," Maureen said, climbing onto the dock and holding out a hand for me.

"Why don't we leave the rods in the boat for this afternoon's session?" Brian said, handing me up our canvas bag and the box with his daughter's cookies. "You ladies relax and I'll get started on a campfire and clean the perch."

Maureen stumbled onto the porch and collapsed into the nearest rocking chair. "I'm beat but it was wonderful." She raised her arms in the air and swayed from side to side.

"I told you, you'd love fishing," I said, laughing at her seated happy dance. "I'm going inside to wash up. Would you like a cup of tea or a bottle of water?"

"Not this second," she said, hopping up. "I'm going to watch Brian make the fire and see how he plans to cook up our perch." She skipped down the steps.

I pushed open the cabin door and looked around. There was an odd smell in the air. I checked the bunk room and small bathroom. Everything seemed to be where we'd left it. I noticed some crumbs on the floor, probably from our morning scones. *I'd better remind Maureen we need to be careful with our food or risk inviting wildlife inside.*

I swept up the crumbs and took them outside to spread under a tree for the birds.

"Jessica, you have to see this," Maureen called out, waving to me from the lake.

I walked toward the dock where Brian was cleaning the fish. "What is it?"

"Footprints. I mean paw prints. Brian found bear prints in the mud next to the lake."

"Really?"

"It looks like a mama and her cub stopped by for a drink," Brian said, coming over to where we stood admiring the prints. "Don't go near them if they come back. A mama bear can be real trouble if she thinks someone is threatening her cub."

"I'm going to take a picture of the paw prints to show Mort before we cover them all up with our own." She pulled out her cell phone and stepped around the prints already on the beach to get the best angle for the ones made by a bear and her cub.

I frowned down at the prints and looked back up at the cabin. We'd been careful with our garbage last night, wrapping it up in a bearproof container, but had this ursine pair smelled good things to eat here anyway? Was that strange odor I detected *eau de bear*? I decided that the next time we left, we'd lock that cabin door just to be sure we didn't get any unwanted visitors.

Chapter Five

S itting on logs around the campfire, eating a leisurely lunch including sliced peaches and Emma's chocolate chip cookies for dessert, Maureen and Brian and I spent a comfortable hour discussing fishing, the Boston Red Sox, and the relative merits of cornmeal versus flour when cooking pan-fried perch.

"I use both," Brian declared. "You mix them together, a cup of flour for every half cup of cornmeal. Dip the fillets in buttermilk, maybe add a little garlic powder and fresh ground pepper, and fry 'em up. Delicious, don't you think? Works for the pike, too, but with pike you gotta be careful of the bones."

"Do you ever cook the perch with the skin on?" Maureen asked.

"I don't. I think you get a more delicate flavor with the fillets. If I'm home, I might soak the fish in the buttermilk for a while."

"Plain yogurt works, too, if you don't have buttermilk," I put in. "But after a couple of hours on the water, who wants to wait that long to eat?"

"I'm going to try this when I get home," Maureen said. "I bet it'll work with other fish as well."

"Of course any fillet will taste delicious if it's served in a restaurant as beautiful as this," Brian said, waving a hand at the lake and the trees.

"True," Maureen said. "You can't beat the atmosphere."

After lunch, as Maureen and I watched him, Brian cleaned out our campfire, making sure the fire was smothered by pouring a coffee can of lake water over the embers. He stirred the ashes with a stick, adding handfuls of dirt and plucking out bits of aluminum foil left by previous campers and depositing them in the can to dispose of later.

"What are you doing?" Maureen asked as he pulled out some stones and reset them.

"Checking under the stones to make sure there are no embers left, and that the stones are set correctly," Brian responded.

"I never knew they could be set incorrectly. I thought you just make a ring of stones and put on a grate and that's all you need."

Brian smiled. "Not quite all," he said. "A fire pit has to be set up where there won't be any danger of a forest fire. On public lands, the Maine Conservation Corps checks to make sure they're in the right place. But on private properties, we usually just site them correctly for our clients."

"Fishing guides do that?"

"The ones I work with do. You can tell people how it's supposed to be done, but most of the time it's easier doing it yourself."

"How did you get to be a fishing guide, Brian?"

Brian shot me a look. I shrugged as if to say, "It's your decision."

"As a kid, I was always interested in the wilderness," he said, carefully patting the mud-pie concoction he'd made out of the fire. "I knew all the woods around Cabot Cove. Used to hide from my old man in them when he was on a bender. Me and my friends would pretend to be Indians and see if we could live off the land. We would go fishing and hunting until the game wardens chased us away for not having a license. Those were good times."

"Did you work at anything else before you became a fishing guide?" Maureen said.

Brian snorted. "I got a little experience in the upholstery trade, thanks to the government."

"I don't understand."

"Maureen, I think maybe we should let Brian finish up," I said.

"That's all right, Mrs. Fletcher. She's going to find out sometime."

Maureen looked from Brian to me. "I'll find out *what*?"

"I was a prisoner over in the state pen in Warren."

"Oh."

He stirred the muddy water without saying anything more.

"Brian, you can't just leave it there," I said.

Brian stood. "You tell it, then," he said, gathering up our plates and walking down to the shore.

"I shouldn't have been asking so many questions," Maureen said, watching him sadly. "Mort always says I'm as bad as you in asking questions. Oh, I didn't mean that the way it came out. Mort has such respect for you. You know that, right?"

I smiled. "Yes. And I respect him as well."

"What did Brian want you to tell me?"

"Brian was convicted of a crime he didn't commit and went to prison."

"Oh, how awful. Didn't he try to get Mort to help him?"

"Mort was the arresting officer, Maureen."

"That was before Mort and I met," she said. "I didn't know anything about it. Mort never said anything."

"Mort doesn't know which guide I hired."

"How come you didn't tell him?"

"You wanted to fish with me in the derby."

"Do you think he wouldn't have let me come if he'd known?"

"I don't know what his reaction would have been, but I decided it was best not to mention it."

Actually, that wasn't strictly true. I had a pretty good idea that Mort would have hit the ceiling had he known Brian was our guide, and I didn't want him to create a scene in Mara's Luncheonette. I also thought that if Maureen got to know Brian without prejudice, she might convince her husband to give him a second chance.

"Do you think I shouldn't tell Mort about Brian?"

"I would never ask you to withhold information from your husband. That would be unfair of me."

"But Brian got out of prison. He's served his debt to society, right? We shouldn't keep holding it against him."

I could have given her a big hug, but I didn't want to embarrass her.

"Thank you, Maureen. Yes, he served a debt to society, but it was one that he should not have had to serve. He had an alibi."

"If he had an alibi, how come he was arrested at all?"

"He was out with his girlfriend, Alice, who is now his wife. Her father didn't approve of him, and Brian thought that he was protecting Alice by not coming forward with the truth right away. When Alice realized he wasn't telling the police that they'd been together at the time of the crime, she went to the authorities herself. But by then the trial was halfway over, and the prosecutor accused her of lying to protect Brian."

"How could she prove she wasn't lying?"

"She couldn't at the time."

"So Brian was found guilty, but what was the evidence against him?"

"He was friendly with the other young man who was also convicted, Darryl Jepson. And witnesses were sure they saw both of them at the scene of the crime."

"But they couldn't have seen Brian if he wasn't there."

"Exactly."

"How long was he in prison?"

"Seven years."

Maureen let out a long sigh. "Boy, that's a long time to be in prison when you didn't do anything wrong." She looked down at the water, where our guide squatted by the shore rinsing our tin plates.

I knew those years had weighed heavily on him. I had followed the trial in the local newspaper but hadn't known both defendants before they were sent to Warren. After a frustrating year of fighting the prison system and only getting punished more for his efforts, Brian changed his approach. I was one of the first people he reached out to even though he knew me only by reputation.

At the time, I couldn't say whether his claims of innocence were true, but I advised him to become a model prisoner and to use his spare hours to make a legal case for himself. Was there any proof he'd been with Alice during the hour when the grocer was stabbed? Were there gaps in the testimony given against him? Was his lawyer competent? (I already knew the answer to that in general, but I didn't know if the late Wes Caruthers had made egregious mistakes in Brian's trial.)

I also put him in touch with the Innocence Project, an organization I have great respect for and with which I have worked on occasion.

Forensic science has made leaps and bounds over the years, especially in the area of DNA testing, a far more reliable source of evidence than eyewitness reports, which have been found to be faulty in many cases and for which there have been no best practices or standardized procedures in place to make them more trustworthy. In fact, one study found that seventy-five percent of cases later revealed to be wrongful convictions were based on eyewitness accounts. Brian's was one of them.

"If you ladies don't mind, I'm going to check in at home before we go out again. I can't get any reception on my cell phone up here."

"Is anything wrong?" I asked, hoping our earlier conversation hadn't upset him.

Brian smiled shyly. "Not at all. It's just Alice has been having a little—what do you ladies call it?—morning sickness, except hers seems to last all day. It's kind of tough when you have to take care of a three-year-old who doesn't understand why Mommy can't play. I just want to make sure she's okay."

"Of course. Please give her my best."

"Will do, Mrs. Fletcher. Thanks for understanding."

Brian left us at the cabin promising to return by three for our afternoon session on the water.

The sun was high as well as the temperature when Maureen and I retired to the cabin, where the air inside was only minimally cooler than outside. I hung up my long-sleeved blue shirt and fanned myself with a fishing magazine I found in a box of kindling next to the woodstove.

"Do you mind if I take a nap?" Maureen asked. "We got up so early."

"I don't mind at all," I said. "I have lots of reading material with me. Would you like me to wake you a half hour before Brian is due back?"

"That would be great, only Jessica?"

"Yes?"

"Can I ask you a question? It's about Brian."

"What's your question?"

"How did he finally prove he wasn't at the grocery store when they said that he was?"

"He got help from the Innocence Project."

"What did they do?"

"One of their lawyers who had been corresponding with Brian sent a request to the presiding judge, asking her to reopen the case."

"Did he have new evidence?"

"Yes and no. He pointed out the fact that unlike his friend, Brian wasn't seen on the store's security videotape. In fact, the only evidence linking him to the scene were reports from the eyewitnesses who saw two men running away."

"But how could they identify someone from behind?"

"They claimed they knew who they were based on the clothing they were wearing."

"Why would the jury believe them?"

"Juries can only base their decisions on what's presented to them, Maureen. They had witnesses who identified Brian."

"Even if they were wrong."

"Yes. And they also didn't know that the tipster who swore that Brian had been one of the robbers had once accused Brian's father of cheating him at cards."

"Oh, boy. I wouldn't believe that guy."

"He certainly wasn't an unbiased source."

"And what about Alice?"

"Alice and Brian had gone hiking in the woods that day."

"But they couldn't prove it."

"No."

"How awful. Didn't anyone else see them?"

"Someone actually did. They came across a man using a compass to find his way, stopped to ask him what he was doing, and discovered he was in training to become a Maine guide."

"Cool! Maybe that's what inspired Brian to become a guide."

"Perhaps, but they didn't know the man's name or where to find him again."

"Nuts! Did they ever find him?"

"They did. Or at least the lawyer from the Innocence Project did. He sent e-mails to all the wilderness organizations asking them to poll their members to see if any of them remembered talking to a young couple on the date in question about the training needed to become a guide."

"And someone came forward."

"Yes. He completed an affidavit the lawyer presented to the judge, who reversed the verdict and Brian was let out."

"So at least it's a happy ending."

"Almost," I said.

"Why almost?"

"Brian had to give up many years of his life for no reason."

"Of course. I didn't mean to make light of that."

"You also have to remember that once someone has been in prison, even if he was there for a crime he didn't commit, people look at him differently."

"You mean they don't trust him anymore?"

"Don't trust him or don't believe he was really innocent."

"Maybe they're just afraid of how that experience may have changed him."

"Whatever their reasons, it's a blemish that is hard for Brian and others like him to escape."

"That's not fair."

"There's a lot that's unfair in this world."

Chapter Six

"I think I got a little sunburn," Maureen said, resting a hand on her red knee as Brian guided our boat into new waters. "My skin feels hot."

"Did you forget to put on sunscreen this morning?" I asked.

"I remembered to put it on my face and the back of my hands, but forgot my arms and legs when I rolled up my sleeves and unzipped my convertibles. What can I tell you? It's the story of my life. I'm a redhead. We always burn."

"That's not a good thing," I said. "If you're uncomfortable, we can go back to the cabin. I'm sure I packed some witch hazel. That will help a little, and Jim Shevlin always leaves a first-aid kit under the sink."

"Oh, no, you don't! I'm not missing my chance to catch a big fish just because of a little sunburn. I want to see if I can net a rainbow as big as yours."

"Listen to her," Brian said, chuckling. "She's talking like a real fisherman now."

"I am?" Maureen said, her pink cheeks becoming even pinker. I studied her face. Whatever sun protection factor she'd used this morning hadn't kept her from getting a burn. Her cheeks, nose, and chin were glowing, and her neck was red. "I think you might want to put on some extra sunscreen now if we're going to be out for another three hours."

Maureen fumbled in the pocket of her vest and withdrew a half-squeezed tube. She squinted at the small writing on its side. "The SPF is fifteen. It's what I use most of the year."

"Most of the year you aren't sitting on a boat with the sun's rays hitting you from above and reflecting off the water," I said.

"Okay. Okay. I'll put it on now." She squirted out a blob of white cream, rubbed her hands together, and swiped them over her face, leaving streaks of cream on her cheeks and around her nose. She patted more on her already-red knees and up her arms.

"Do you feel all right?" I asked, cocking my head at her.

"I'm fine, just a little hot."

Brian took a thin towel from the duffel under his seat, dragged it in the water, wrung it out, and handed it to Maureen. "Here, wrap this around your neck. It should make you feel better."

Maureen grinned. "Ooh, that feels good. See all the tricks I'm learning, Jessica?"

"The trick is not to get burned in the first place," I said under my breath as Maureen twisted around in her seat to face the direction in which we were heading.

We passed several other boats either anchored near a promising pool or drifting along under the shade of tall trees.

"Aren't there any big fish in this lake?" one of the fishermen called out. "All I can catch are eight- or nine-inchers. Not even big enough for a good-size sandwich."

Brian laughed. "Keep trying," he yelled. "This lady reeled in a sixteen-inch rainbow this morning." He pointed at me.

"I thought they're not supposed to eat the trout," Maureen whispered to me.

"I think he was kidding," I said.

"I caught two brookies," Maureen called out.

"How big?"

Maureen held her hands up to show the size of her fish and kept moving them father apart. She grinned and shrugged.

The fisherman laughed and gave her a thumbs-up.

"Just how big can a brook trout get?" she asked Brian.

"A twelve- to thirteen-incher is a pretty good size. Depends on the lake. Bigger lake, bigger fish, but the rules for this derby keep us restricted to a specific geographical area. Where we're fishing most of 'em average out around ten inches."

"So my guys from this morning are only average?"

"Or girls," he said smiling. "It's hard to tell the sexes apart when they're young."

"And when they grow up?"

"When they spawn in the fall, there's a color difference you can see."

Brian found a cove the other fisherman had missed—or perhaps had already abandoned.

"This looks promising," he said, allowing the boat to float toward the shore while he pored over a tray of artificial flies trying to decide which one to tie onto Maureen's rod. "What do you think about a Royal Wulff?" he asked me, holding up a fuzzy fly with an abdomen of bright red thread.

"I like that one," Maureen chimed in.

"Royal Wulff it is," Brian said.

"I think I'll try an ant this time," I said, choosing a fly made out of three beads of black foam rubber.

"Ick! That looks a little too real," Maureen said.

"I hope the trout feel the same way," I said, smiling as we cast our lines.

The location proved disappointing, and we moved several times before finding the perfect spot—an outcropping of rock shaded by long branches of a swamp maple—that yielded our best catches of the day: a rainbow for Maureen, pretty close in size to the fish I'd caught; three brook trout; two more perch, which we released; and a good-size pike Brian decided to keep for dinner, either ours or his.

We returned to the dock by six thirty, tired, sweaty, and with the distinct aroma of fish on our clothing. Brian offered us his pike, but we encouraged him to take it home to Alice.

"Not sure her stomach is up to eating fried fish," he said, "but Emma and I will have a nice dinner. You guys have enough to eat?"

"Without doubt. My friend here could stock a small grocery from her cooler," I said, smiling at Maureen.

We bid Brian good-bye and said we'd see him bright and early the next day.

"How's about seven thirty?" he said. "Give this lady a chance to sleep in." He nodded at Maureen, whose cheeks were an alarming shade of red.

Once Brian had pulled away, Maureen collapsed into one of

the rocking chairs on the porch and promptly fell asleep. I changed into a bathing suit and took a dip in the chilly waters of the lake, glad to wash off the day's combination of sunscreen, perspiration, and fish. When I checked on her an hour later, she was still sleeping, her fishing hat covering her face. I opened a can of chicken noodle soup and poured it into a small pot to heat on the hot plate, sliced some tomatoes using the knife from the magnetic rack, and put two pieces of whole-wheat bread on a plate.

I went outside and shook her shoulder. "Maureen? You won't sleep tonight if you take too long a nap."

She mumbled something, turned her head, and her hat fell into her lap. Maureen's face was scarlet, her eyes swollen, and her lips chapped.

"Maureen, come on. We've got to put some first aid on that burn or you're going to be hurting a whole lot."

She squinted up at me.

"I don't want you to get sunstroke. Come inside and let's treat this right now."

Maureen stumbled into the cabin and went straight to the bathroom. "I don't look too great, do I?" she said when she came back to the main room.

"I'm less concerned with your looks. How do you feel?" I said.

"I have a little headache."

"I'm not surprised," I said, rinsing a towel under the cold water from the pump. "Here, put this on the back of your neck."

"Mmm. Feels good."

I opened the cabinet under the sink and pulled out a metal box. "There should be a bottle of ibuprofen in this first-aid kit."

"It'll fade by tomorrow. It always does. Then I peel and turn white again. Never could tan."

"Can you take this?" I asked, handing her the bottle of pills and a glass of water.

"I'm not allergic, if that's what you mean."

"Ibuprofen is an anti-inflammatory. It reduces the swelling and the redness and can keep the burn from getting worse."

"Thanks! This water is so nice and cold."

"Don't drink too quickly. Take sips. You want to stay hydrated, but you don't want to overdo it."

Maureen took the pills, and I put a bottle of Vitaminwater and a bottle of witch hazel on the picnic table next to her.

"Don't confuse these, please."

She giggled. "Can you imagine if I drank the witch hazel by mistake?"

I took the towel from her, rinsed it in water again, and poured a capful of witch hazel onto the cloth. "Let's keep this away from your eyes," I said, patting her swollen cheeks with the witch hazel–laced towel. "You'd better take off your ring in case your fingers get swollen, too. Sometimes it takes four to six hours before all the sunburn symptoms show up."

Maureen removed her wedding band and tucked it into one of the many pockets on her fishing vest. She snapped the pocket closed and yawned. "Can I go to bed now?" she asked in a little-girl voice.

"Not yet. I'm heating up some chicken soup. You need something to eat, and the soup is also liquid."

"Yes, Mama," she said, smiling at me. "I tried to wink at you but my eye isn't working right."

"Your eyes are swollen. Let's hope you can open them in the morning."

"That bad, huh?"

"That bad," I agreed.

We ate our simple meal in silence while I kept a close watch on Maureen, popping up to keep her towel cool by running it under cold water and wringing it out. Sunburn is enough of a problem, but sunstroke can be a medical crisis. I thought of Seth's warning about being isolated without means of help should there be an emergency. We already knew our cell phones were not reliable in an area with spotty service at best. If Maureen became light-headed or disoriented, if she felt weak or nauseated, or had a seizure or trouble breathing, we'd be in big trouble. I counted the ways I could get help. I could tramp through the woods to Mayor Jim Shevlin's second cabin on the other side of the lake and hope that the cellular phone service was better over there. I could take my bicycle, parked around the side of the cabin, and ride down the dirt road in hopes of finding another resident or a roadside store. But either option would be difficult in the dark. Or we could stay put until Brian arrived in the morning and send him for help.

After our light dinner, I helped Maureen undress and apply a soothing cream to her arms, legs, neck, and face. I placed a towel on her pillow and rinsed out the one we'd used earlier that was no longer cold. There are several places on our bodies where blood vessels are near the surface of the skin. Behind the neck is one, and a cold-water compress there can make your whole body feel cooler.

Maureen fell back on the cot with a sigh. "You know, I haven't had a bad burn since I was a teenager. My friends used to slather baby oil on themselves and use a reflector to get tan faster. Stupid kids, huh? We didn't worry about skin cancer, never mind wrinkles." She lifted her head to flip over the washcloth so the chilly side was against her skin. "I usually avoid the sun at all costs because I know I can burn. I just wasn't paying attention. I was so excited to learn to fish and to catch a good one for the derby. I did it, too, didn't I?"

"You certainly did," I said. "Your rainbow trout was bigger than mine."

"Oh, you're just being kind," she mumbled and sighed. "If it is, it's probably because I used a Royal Wulff fly. I love that name. How did such a fluffy little fly get such a serious name? Does Queen Elizabeth use it when she goes fishing?"

"It's possible, but I don't know how we'd go about researching what flies the queen uses." I added a second wet towel to her forehead.

"You missed your proper profession, Jessica."

"I did?"

"Mmm-hmm. You're a great nurse. I feel better already."

"I'm glad."

"But I think I'll go to sleep anyway. Got to be ready in the morning for when Brian takes us out again," she said, her voice trailing off.

"Let's see how you feel tomorrow. You may want to rest up in the morning and just go out in the afternoon."

But my advice fell on deaf ears, or at least sleeping ones. Maureen's soft breathing reassured me, and I tiptoed into the main room and sank down on the picnic table bench, relieved for the moment.

Camping always requires more work than you anticipate, and I spent the next hour cleaning up. I washed our soup bowls, dried them, and stacked them on a shelf alongside the bread plates. I rinsed out the soup can, gathering leftover pieces of chicken and noodles to add to our bearproof garbage bag hanging from the laundry line outside, and made certain any food stuffs were properly stored away. I set out two more ibuprofen pills for Maureen and made a note of the time she could safely take the medicine again. My clothing from the day's fishing required more than a night's airing, but that was all it was going to get under the circumstances. At the end of the derby I'd give our clothes a good wash in the sink and hang everything on a line to sun-dry.

As I gathered up Maureen's things, which I'd left on my cot, I heard the sound of a car heading up to the cabin from the dirt road. I hurried to the door and looked out to see Brian climbing from his Jeep holding a brown paper bag.

I stepped out onto the porch. "What are you doing back?" I asked in a low voice, not wanting to disturb Maureen's sleep.

"Just checking up on you," he said. "Mrs. Metzger looked like she got a bad burn today."

"She did, and I'm grateful for your concern. I was wondering how to get help if her sunburn became sunstroke."

"Do you think it will?"

"I'm hopeful it won't. She's sleeping now, but I'm afraid she'll be hurting tomorrow."

"Alice told me to give you this aloe vera cream. She swears by it, calls it her miracle cure." He handed me the paper bag he'd been carrying. "I think she put in some extra cookies, too."

"Ooh! That was so kind of her. Please thank Alice. Are we depleting your supply?"

He shrugged. "Don't matter. She can always make more." He shifted from one foot to the other as if he had more to say but couldn't find the words to put together.

"Can you keep me company for a little while, or do you need to get right back to Alice? We haven't really had a chance to catch up."

An expression of relief passed over his face. "Sure. Alice won't mind. She's the one who insisted I come up here."

"Let's sit on the porch so we don't wake Maureen. Would you like a bottle of water, or I could make a mug of tea?"

He shook his head. "I have a bottle of water in the Jeep, but I wouldn't mind one of those cookies."

I laughed and passed him the paper bag after we'd settled in the rockers. He dug out a packet of aluminum foil, unfolded it, and took a cookie. "Want one?"

"Don't mind if I do."

We chewed in companionable silence for a moment before he asked, "Do you think Mrs. Metzger will be okay to go out tomorrow?"

"She says she's eager to fish again. I'm not sure it's the best idea. Maybe you can help me convince her to take the morning off—if she'll listen."

He chuckled. "I'm not very good at convincing anyone of anything," he said. He handed me back the paper bag. "I have something else for you."

"Oh? What is it?" I opened the bag. I could feel the shape of the bottle of lotion and knew there was a packet of cookies in there but wasn't able to see its contents in the dark.

"No. Not in there." He sighed, then pulled a rolled newspaper from the back pocket of his jeans. "Alice thought I should give you this."

"It's not easy to read by moonlight. Can you tell me what's in it?"

"It's about Stinky. I mean Darryl."

"Was that Jepson's nickname? The prisoner who escaped?"

There was enough moonlight for me to see Brian nod.

"Have they found him?" I asked.

"Not yet, but they don't think he's trying to sneak into Canada anymore."

"Why not? Where else do they think he'd go?" I asked.

"They think he's coming to Cabot Cove."

Chapter Seven

"Coming to Cabot Cove?" I repeated.

"Or maybe he's already been here," Brian said.

"Why would they think that?"

"I don't know if you remember our lawyer."

"Wes Caruthers."

"You heard?"

"I understand that he fell off his boat and drowned."

Brian shook his head. "I can't believe it."

"Maureen told me the sheriff's office thought he hit his head when he fell and may have knocked himself out."

"That's what they said at first, but now they're thinking someone may have clocked him, that it wasn't an accident after all."

"That's a very different story. Does the newspaper say Darryl Jepson is suspected of murdering Caruthers?"

"Not in so many words. They called him a 'person of interest,' but the murder took place right after he broke out of prison. Caruthers had been our lawyer and Jepson blamed him for doing a lousy job, so they immediately thought of him."

"But you don't believe it?"

Brian heaved a sigh. "I don't know what to believe. We haven't talked since I got out. My new lawyer advised me not to keep in touch with him. Not that we were ever that good friends, but the murder trial brought us together. Only thing was, I wasn't there when the grocer got stabbed and he was. And he never told the cops that I wasn't with him."

"Did he say he was innocent, too?"

Brian snorted. "Everyone in prison says they didn't do it. That's why they didn't believe me. And why should they? We were all a bunch of losers."

"But you really didn't commit the crime," I said. "You weren't even there."

"I almost was."

"What do you mean?"

"We had arranged to meet up—me, him, and a couple of the guys—at the market. He wanted to boost some food and then we'd all get together down at the railroad tracks and have a picnic. I'm ashamed to say we'd done it before."

"But you never made it there?"

"No. And I can thank Alice's old man for that."

"Really?"

"He always brought out the worst in me."

"Tell me about that day."

"It's ironic, really. What happened was . . ."

*　　*　　*

Brian told me in detail what had transpired that day.

His father, Tom, staggered to the door of the trailer, leaned out, and roared. "Brian Kinney, get your butt in here."

"What do you want, Pop?" Brian said, using an oily rag to wipe his hands. "I'm trying to get this stupid engine started."

"I want you to go down to the package store and get me a fifth of gin."

"I can't drive anywhere if the car won't start, and they're not going to sell me a bottle anyway. The sheriff took away my fake ID the last time I tried."

"You tell 'em it's for me. They'll let you take it. Here." He waved a twenty-dollar bill at his son.

"Where'd you get that?"

"Never mind where I get my money," Tom Kinney said. "I got it and you're going to buy me my bottle. And bring back the change."

According to Brian, he'd pocketed the twenty and pulled up his bike from where it lay on its side in the tall grass. He was supposed to meet Jepson and two of his buddies at the mini-mart, where each of them would shoplift something for the picnic. Brian looked at the grungy piece of paper his buddy Jepson had stuffed in his back pocket the day before. "Donuts or cookys," it read. *Stinky never could spell*, Brian thought.

"What happened next?" I asked.

"I'd brought potatoes the last time," he told me, a whole bag that the Pelletiers' housekeeper, Helen, was throwing out because the potatoes had eyes growing. The boys had made a campfire near the tracks, dug out the eyes with their fingernails, and roasted the spuds on sticks, laughing when Brian dropped his into the fire and had to fish out his charred lunch with a tire iron.

"Did you buy your father his liquor?" I asked.

"No. I coasted downhill to the main road from the trailer park and sat on my bike at the intersection. If I'd taken a left turn, I would have been downtown where all the stores were, you know, where it ends at the docks. The package store was on the way, just on the outskirts of town. The mini-mart was next door. I figured I could pay for the bottle, stash it somewhere safe, pick up the cookies for the picnic, and get down to the tracks before the others. They'd never know that I'd bought the cookies instead of stealing them, and I planned to pick up the bottle on the way home. By the time I got back my father would be so eager for the drink he'd forget about the change from the twenty, or I could tell him the truth and say I got hungry and bought some cookies. I'd bring back the box to prove it."

"That's a lot of planning for a young man to have to do," I said.

"I know," he said. "Anyway, while I was sitting there at the intersection, a gray Mercedes came down the road. I recognized it immediately as Alice's father's car. I didn't want him to see me, so I pulled on the bill of my cap and ducked my head so her old man wouldn't recognize me. Fat chance! Pelletier knew where me and my father lived. He was always raising it with his kid Alice." He snickered. "Her father never knew that I'd heard him."

"What would he say to her?" I asked.

"Stuff like 'I don't care how nice you think he is. Your mother would have wanted better for you, and I do, too.' He called me and my friends bums, asked her how Alice expected a young man with no future to keep her in the manner she was accustomed to. 'Who's

going to buy you your nice clothes and put good food on the table?'
He kept calling me a loser, just like my father, trailer trash. It went on
and on. He even said I wore dirty shirts. I hated everything he said."

"Where were you so that you could hear him say these
things?" I asked.

"I was hiding in Alice's closet. I remember looking down at my
stained T-shirt. It was one of my favorites, the one with a picture
of Jerry Garcia from the Grateful Dead on the front." His laugh
was rueful. "Jerry's beard had a red splotch on it from when my
father hurled a pot of spaghetti sauce at me for forgetting to bring
home his bottle. It wasn't my old man's fault. He was drunk at the
time and didn't really mean it. He even apologized later, but I never
could get out the stain no matter how many times I scrubbed it."

"I'm so sorry you had to hear that, Brian," I said.

"Alice told me that, too, when her father left the room, slam-
ming the door behind him. I told her that I knew he must have
told her that a million times."

"Did she agree?"

"Yeah, but she told me to not pay attention to him. You know
what she did then, Mrs. Fletcher?"

"What?"

"She kissed me. After that, man, I was hers forever."

"You were saying that you were on your bike when Alice's
father approached in his car."

"Right. His Mercedes sped past me, its wheels kicking up
dust and gravel that sprayed all over me and my bike."

Brian went on to say how much he hated Alice's father back then.
He found it ironic that he lived with his father and Alice lived with
her father, too. Both men had been widowed and were left to raise
a young child alone. Alice had been seven when her mother

succumbed to the flu. Brian was three when his mother died giving birth to a stillborn boy. He said that he often thought about his mother and the brother he never got to see, and thought his father probably did, too.

"How did you and Alice meet?" I asked.

"At school. Maybe we got together because neither of us had a mother. Most of the kids in school had two parents even if they didn't always live with both of them. Not having a mother was rare, I guess, nothing to brag about, but at least Alice and I had something in common."

But their shared experience ended there, according to Brian. Brian lived in a ramshackle trailer park of dirt roads and abandoned vehicles euphemistically named Ocean Heights Mobile Homes. Alice's home was in a neighborhood of manicured lawns with flowering bushes and swimming pools. Pelletier owned a car dealership, forever tooling around in the latest luxury model. Tom Kinney, if he ever worked, did odd jobs for a day's pay and pushed his son to learn to fix their jalopy that sometimes ran and sometimes didn't.

I brought Brian back to when he'd been on his bike and Mr. Pelletier had roared past him in his Mercedes.

"I figured that as long as Alice's father was going into town, it was a perfect time for me to visit her. I could see the guys anytime, and my father could live without his bottle. He probably had another one stashed in the cabinet above the stove, provided he was sober enough to remember where it was. All I wanted was some time alone with Alice without her miserable father cursing me and chasing me out. Spending time with her was going to be a treat, a way to get back at him who thought himself so high-and-mighty."

"Did you see Alice that day?" I asked. "Was she home when you went there?"

"Yeah, she was there. She greeted me at the door. She'd seen me walking my bike up the driveway. She was scared, said that he'd be coming right back, had gone to deliver something to a customer. I said that was too bad because I wanted to buy her lunch. I remember waving my father's twenty-dollar bill at her."

"Did you take her to lunch?"

"No. She said she'd make lunch for us. I knew their house-keeper, Helen, and I asked Alice if she was in the kitchen. She said that she was and warned me that Helen would tell her father if she saw me." He shifted position on the chair and rubbed his eyes. It was obviously painful for him to relive the scene he was describing.

"I thought Helen liked me," he said, "but Alice explained that her father told Helen she'd better report to him every time I was even near the place if she wanted to keep her job."

"So, what did you and Alice do?"

"Alice told me to take my bike around to the side of the house and that she'd grab something for us from the kitchen so we could ride to the lake and have our own picnic."

"And that's what you did?" I asked.

Brian chuckled. "Yeah. I remember thinking that I'd blown off one picnic but was about to have another, and I got to keep my old man's twenty. Anyway, Alice was wearing her backpack, and we pedaled to the long road leading into the wilderness area where there are trails for hiking, lakes for swimming, and plenty of places to lie in the sun and enjoy some privacy."

Brian stopped talking and apologized for having bent my ear.

"Please don't apologize," I said. "I'm flattered that you confided in me."

"I guess the irony of it all," he said, using his toe to set the chair slowly rocking, "is that it never occurred to me that I'd have to prove where I was that afternoon."

"And why should it?" I said. "We all go about our lives without worrying we'll have to provide evidence of our activities to the police."

"You're right, I know, Mrs. Fletcher. If I hadn't been so eager to sneak behind Alice's father's back, I would have gotten caught up in whatever Darryl was doing at the mini-mart."

"Then it was lucky that you made that decision."

He laughed softly. "Boy, when Pelletier heard Alice testify that I was with her the whole time, I thought the steam coming off him would lift the hair right off his head."

"Is he more accepting of you now?"

"Just barely. But Alice told him if he wants to see his granddaughter, he'd better behave. He tolerates me, but I'm sure he still thinks I'm a lowlife." He was quiet for a moment. "I sent her back to his house."

"What do you mean?"

"When I heard about the prison break, I was afraid my old buddy Jepson would come looking for me, and I didn't want Alice and Emma anywhere he could get his hands on them."

"Do you think he'd hurt them?"

"I wasn't going to take the chance. Alice didn't want to go, said we don't live anywhere near the Canadian border and there was nothing to worry about."

"But you said the authorities now think he's headed this way."

"Right. It took some convincing, but I dropped Alice and the baby off at her father's house before I came here."

"Why do you think Darryl would seek you out?"

"He blames me for not being at the mini-mart to back him up."

"But didn't he have other friends there?"

"They were supposed to be, but I wasn't there so I don't know who else showed up."

"You know that witnesses saw *two* people running away from the store after the grocer was stabbed," I said.

"That's what they said."

"Who were the other guys you and Darryl were supposed to meet? Did you ever give the sheriff their names?"

"No. I wasn't about to turn in my friends to protect myself. For all I know the grocer could have been stabbed by someone from out of town. I wasn't there. I didn't see anything. I didn't know anything." His voice had gotten louder as his emotions were raised.

"Brian, a man lost his life in a robbery. Don't you think his family deserves to know that his killer was apprehended and punished for the crime? Wouldn't you want that if it were someone in your family?"

"But it isn't. I'm sorry, Mrs. Fletcher. Please don't ask me to be a snitch."

"Who asked you to be a snitch?"

"Sheriff Metzger. He said if I was really innocent, I would help him put the right guys behind bars."

"He was trying to help you."

"He was trying to help himself."

"And you turned him down."

"And spent seven years in prison, thanks to him."

Chapter Eight

Brian left shortly after our conversation. I was disappointed that he blamed Mort for the time he spent in the state correctional facility, but I understood the bitterness that he felt at having been unjustly convicted. I pushed open the screen door to find Maureen sitting on the bench of the picnic table dabbing away tears with a tissue.

"Oh, my goodness. Are you in pain?" I asked, placing the paper bag Brian had given me on the table. "Why didn't you call for me?"

"I'm okay," she said, sniffling. "I just feel so bad for Brian and I wish he didn't hate Mort so much. He was only doing his duty as sheriff."

"I don't think he hates Mort. Brian's just hurt that people believed the worst of him. And they did. Were you listening the whole time?"

She nodded. "Most of it, I guess. I heard the car and then heard you go outside to greet him. I didn't mean to eavesdrop at first, but when I started listening, I got caught up in the story, and I thought it would be more rude to interrupt than to let him continue talking. Do you think he really knows who else was at the mini-mart that day?"

"I think he knows who was *supposed* to have been there, but he's correct when he says he wasn't there and can't know who showed up."

Maureen groped in the paper bag and pulled out the aluminum foil packet. "I got hungry when I heard you guys eating the cookies."

"They're for us. Finish them up. And Alice sent a bottle of lotion for your sunburn."

"I don't even know her and I like her already."

"She's a good person."

Maureen took a bite of cookie and chewed thoughtfully. "I can understand Brian not wanting to be a snitch. Nobody likes a tattletale."

"Tattletale. Snitch. They're such negative terms," I said, "but that attitude hampers authorities trying to get to the root of a crime. I wish parents didn't teach their children not to tattle. It starts right there."

"But a kid who's always telling on his friends is just trying to make himself look more important at the other kid's expense. Don't you think parents should discourage that?"

"Sure, in those instances, but children need to be taught the difference between a selfish act and a praiseworthy one. It's not only appropriate but important for them to tell an adult when someone else is doing something unsafe or being cruel to another child or committing a crime. We need to encourage trust in the authorities, whether it's a parent, a teacher, or the police."

"That's a hard habit to break," Maureen said. "I mean, you're talking years of thinking it's a sin to tattle on people who are doing something wrong. It's like a code of honor."

"We need to make it a code of dishonor."

"Mort has told me stories of his fellow police officers in New York City who refused to inform on colleagues even when they were breaking the law. It was one of the reasons he wanted to move up to Maine and come work in Cabot Cove. He wanted to be away from the politics and the hypocrisy."

I smiled. "And is he?"

"I guess he couldn't escape all of it."

"I imagine not," I said. "But enough philosophizing. We need to get some sleep if we're to catch the biggest trout in Moon Lake."

Maureen balled up the aluminum foil that had held the cookies and dropped it into the bag.

"Don't forget Alice's miracle cure," I said, handing her the bottle of aloe lotion.

"I'll put some on right now. My skin is feeling a little tight. Do I still look like a tomato?"

"You're not as ripe as you were before, thank goodness."

My travel alarm went off at six thirty the next morning, and I looked over at Maureen to see if her sunburn had gotten any better overnight. Her eyes were still swollen. I thought the tears she'd shed probably hadn't helped improve the situation.

I pulled aside the covers and sat up, slipping my feet into my rubber dock shoes. A peek out the window revealed an overcast sky. Well, that was a blessing. We'd still need sunscreen, but at least we'd escape the worst of the sun's reflective rays.

I dressed quickly and went into the cabin's main room to pump water for our morning beverage. I'd wanted to give Maureen some extra time to sleep, but the squeal of the pump and the rush of the water hitting the sink were so loud she was soon at my side, commenting on the proper method for making tea.

"Did you rinse out the mugs with boiling water first?"

I smiled. "I do that at home, but I don't want to waste any more water here than necessary." I handed her a mug. "English breakfast this morning. Okay with you?"

"Mmm. My favorite," she said taking a sip, sinking down onto the bench, and setting her mug on the picnic table. She'd chosen a short-sleeved T-shirt and was tugging at the neckline with one finger, trying to keep the fabric from touching the tender skin on her neck.

I studied her carefully. "How are you feeling this morning?" I asked, noticing that her face was still red and her cheeks were puffy.

"To tell you the truth, Jessica, I feel foolish. I know how easily I can get burned and should've been more careful. I'm really embarrassed that I was so excited about fishing that I forgot the basics of redhead skin care. I made a serious mistake."

"You're certainly paying the price for not slathering on more sunscreen, but I'm not asking about your mental state," I said, sipping my own tea.

"As for my physical well-being, to quote my uncle Basil, 'It ain't great.'" She pressed both hands to her cheeks. "Still hot, and sore, too. Do we have any more of those pills?"

"We do," I said, pulling down the bottle of ibuprofen I'd left on the shelf and shaking out two for her. "Who's your uncle Basil? I don't remember your speaking of him."

"He was my mother's brother only no one ever met him. She was forever quoting him, but we thought she simply made him up. 'According to your uncle Basil,' she would say, and then invent whatever piece of advice she wanted us to follow."

"What does your uncle Basil say about your sunburn?"

"He would say that I probably should rest in the shade this morning."

"Good advice."

"You wouldn't mind if I stayed behind in the cabin while you went out with Brian this morning? I should be fine by afternoon."

"I don't mind at all. I'll stay behind with you."

"Jessica—"

"We'll let Brian know when he shows up."

"Jessica—"

"He won't be surprised. We talked about it last night."

"Jessica!"

"Yes?"

"I won't stay back if you insist on staying with me."

"But I don't mind, Maureen. I've got all week to fish."

Maureen crossed her arms, then thought better of it and plucked at her shirt. "If you insist on staying with me, you'll force me to go out fishing with you and Brian this morning, and then I'll get an even worse sunburn and I'll tell Mort that it's all your fault."

I laughed. "Maureen, really it's all right."

"It's not all right with me. As Uncle Basil would say, you have to take responsibility for your own actions."

"Well, I agree with that, but what would you do all alone here for hours?"

"I could take a swim. In fact, the idea of cold water on my skin sounds heavenly right now."

"More reason for me to stay behind, just to make sure you're safe."

"If you're going to worry about me swimming, I can go wading or stay out of the water altogether and take a walk in the woods."

"I've been up here before, but you don't know these woods. What if the mama bear came back?"

"I can take a nap, read one of your books, just rock on the porch, figure out a wonderful way to prepare perch for lunch."

"I don't know, Maureen. I don't think Mort would like it if I left you here alone."

"Who was it who told me I was a strong, competent woman?"

"I did."

"A strong, competent woman doesn't need the permission of her husband or her good friend and fishing partner."

"Okay, you win."

"Then that's settled. When Brian gets here, we deliver the news that he has one less fisherperson to guide today."

"One less fisherperson," I echoed, but I wasn't a happy camper.

I went into the bunk room, pulled out a few books that I'd brought with me, and laid them on Maureen's cot. If I could have been sure she would spend her time reading, I'd have felt a lot more confident about leaving her alone. I chided myself for being so uneasy. I had been planning on spending a week all by myself with no "buddy" or partner staying with me, or stopping by to verify my safety. Why was I so concerned with leaving Maureen alone for what might end up being three or four hours at the most?

She lowered herself on the edge of the cot and picked up the books one at a time. "Who do you recommend?" she asked.

"Depends on what you like to read," I said, pointing to each one in order. "Molly MacRae writes about a haunted yarn shop. This Sheila Connolly book takes place in Ireland. And Mary Kennedy analyzes dreams in her mysteries."

"That's going to be a tough choice. But what if I can't finish it today?"

"If you're really nice to me, I'll let you take it home. I also brought my tablet so I can access my books online, that is if we get any Internet service up here."

We heard a knock on the screen door frame. "Ahoy there. Anybody home?"

"Be right there, Brian," I called out. I hurried into the main room, Maureen close on my heels.

"Sorry, I'm not Brian," said a short man standing outside the screen door. "He couldn't make it today. I'm Hank Thompson, filling in for him. Here's my guide ID and fishing license, and I believe you ladies are participating in the Cabot Cove Derby Days."

"But we left our fishing rods in Brian's boat," Maureen said.

"Not to worry. I've got your gear, the measuring trough, extra flies, a bucket for any nontrout fish you want to keep, everything you need."

"Do you cook?" Maureen asked.

"Yes, ma'am. We all have to know how to take care of ourselves in the wilderness."

"Well then, it's all right," she said, looking at me.

"Why was Brian unable to make it today?" I asked. "Last night he was pretty sure he would be here this morning."

"Guess I'm not in the need-to-know category," Hank replied. "All's I can tell you is that he sent me up here to take you ladies out."

"You're just taking Jessica out this morning," Maureen said, handing me my fishing hat and a paper bag of fruit she'd readied the prior evening. "I'm taking a well-deserved rest and I'll join you both this afternoon." She pushed me toward the door. "Leave me some big rainbows to catch later."

Maureen stood in the doorway like a mother waving her children off to school. I looked back several times but she shooed me on. "Be a good girl," she called out, laughing. "Uncle Basil says to have a good time."

I smiled and waved as Hank steered the boat away from the dock, its bow pointed toward the distant shore. And then we motored around a bend in the lake and Maureen was gone from sight.

Chapter Nine

"Maureen, guess what I caught today?" I called out as I trudged up the path from the dock to the cabin, exhilarated and exhausted from the morning's fishing.

Hank and I had fought with a large rainbow trout. When we'd hauled up the fish next to the boat and I'd put our net in the water to scoop it out, the trout had given one last jerk, slipped the hook, and disappeared below the surface.

Talk about the one that got away! That trout had been at least twenty-four inches, maybe as much as six or seven pounds, but, sad to say, I never got to take its picture.

Hank had dropped me off, promising to return at three o'clock for our afternoon session. I'd told him that I couldn't imagine a more exciting time fishing and that if Maureen still needed rest, I'd skip the final hours of the derby and keep her company until her husband came to pick her up.

"I'm paid up for the day," he'd said. "I'll stop by anyway and you can tell me your decision then."

"Maureen? Wait till you hear this fish tale," I said, laughing as I climbed the steps of the cabin and opened the screen door.

The main room was empty. I walked into the bunk room. Maureen's cot was unoccupied, and the bathroom door was open.

"Maureen," I called out, but there was no answer. I looked around to see if she'd left me a note. There wasn't one, but the top of the ice chest was resting on the table; the foil-wrapped ice blocks inside were mushy. *What did she do with the food that was in there?* And there was that smell again, the same odor I'd detected the other day.

Bears?

I hurried out the door, yelling Maureen's name. There was no response. I circled the cabin, looking for something that might indicate where she'd gone. My bike was still leaning against the log wall, the laundry line was still strung out to a tree, and our bearproof garbage bag hung in the center. But there was no sign of Maureen. I strode down to the water and looked to see if any new bear tracks had joined the previous ones but didn't see any. I walked out to the end of the dock, cupped my hands around my mouth, and shouted for her. The only answer was the sound of flapping wings and the alarmed calls of a flock of Canada geese as they lifted off the water and flew away.

Back in the cabin, I pulled out my cell phone and dialed Maureen's number. *Maybe she's just out for a walk in the woods and didn't hear me call her name.*

There was silence until the familiar ring indicated that the call had gone through. I sighed in relief. A buzz from the bunk room caught my attention, and I listened to ringing on the other end of my call as I slowly walked to Maureen's cot. There, peeking out from under her pillow, was her cell phone, vibrating and buzzing quietly until I hung up. I sank down onto her cot and picked up her phone. *Why would Maureen take a walk and leave this behind?*

A million questions flew through my mind. In my imagination's efforts to explain her disappearance I pictured an equal number of possible scenarios, some reasonable and some terrifying. I walked back into the main room holding Maureen's phone and told myself to calm down. There was no reason to believe that Maureen was in danger. So what if she decided to explore the territory and accidentally forgot her cell phone? How many times had I found myself somewhere with my phone either dead or in another handbag? Well, not too often, thankfully, but it was possible.

I dropped her phone in my pocket and began examining the cabin, methodically taking inventory of what she'd brought and what, if anything—other than herself—was missing.

She hadn't packed her clothing yet. Her waders and fishing vest were hanging from two pegs on the wall in the bunk room. I patted the pockets of the vest and could feel the outline of her wedding band in one, but her tube of sunscreen was missing. *That's a good sign*, I told myself. Two out of the three books I'd offered her were stacked on the nightstand. Maybe Maureen took a walk and found a sunny glade in which to read her book and lost track of the time. A good book can do that to you. Look up and it's hours later and you've forgotten to eat or make the calls you'd promised. That was probably what happened. Maureen would come back all excited about the story and full of apologies for being late.

I turned in a circle in the main room, letting my eyes scan all the surfaces. Alice's "miracle cure" aloe vera lotion was standing on the picnic table. My eyes kept returning to the ice chest. Why would Maureen have forgotten to put the top back on? What food had we left in there? Could bears have made off with anything not canned or secured in plastic containers? Maybe Maureen had been out for a walk and on coming back had interrupted the mama bear raiding our food supply. I was pretty sure that she would have taken off at a run. If you meet a bear on a hiking trail, running away is not the best idea, however. A bear can outrun a human on most days, and climbing a tree would have been useless; bears are better climbers than we are. If I remembered my wilderness instructions correctly, the best thing to do would be to make yourself as tall-looking as possible by raising your hands overhead and waving them, speak calmly while backing away, and keep an eye on the bear so you know what it is about to do.

I looked at the ice chest. Wouldn't a bear raiding a cooler have knocked it off the picnic table? Even if it didn't knock it over and simply used its paws to scoop out any food, there would be water on the floor. But the floor was dry and the chest was where we'd left it, even though the top was off. That was peculiar but not necessarily suspicious.

I replaced the top, peered out the screen door, and consulted my watch. Maureen would certainly realize that I should have returned by now. Where was she?

I pulled down a jar of peanut butter and jelly already swirled together. I planned to make two sandwiches. If Maureen was out for a walk, she'd probably be hungry when she got back. Where was that knife? I was sure I'd put it back on the magnetic rack. It was not in the sink, nor on a shelf with the rest of the silverware. I ended up using a spoon to spread the peanut butter and jelly.

I'd give her another half hour before I went out looking for her. Hank, the guide from this morning, was coming back at three and if—I was almost afraid to think about that—if Maureen hadn't shown up by then, we could alert the authorities. What time was Mort coming to pick her up? Did she ever say? Should I call him now? Or wait? If I called now, I might panic him for no reason. Better to give Maureen a chance to show up.

I ate one sandwich and drank a bottle of water while sitting on the porch, alert for any movement or sound that might indicate Maureen was coming back to the cabin. The woods were surprisingly quiet. Every snap of a twig had me jumping to see what had made the noise, but there were few snaps, and no sign of my friend.

After lunch, I went inside, donned my fishing hat, and wrote a note for Maureen, which I taped to the top of the ice chest: "Please stay here until I get back!" I filled a zipper pack with the other sandwich, two bottles of water, the last two granola bars from an open bag, my pocket emergency kit, and a small LED flashlight. I rummaged in my duffel bag for the auxiliary battery for my phone that David at Charles Department Store had convinced me to buy and added that to the bag. I packed for the worst but trusted that I wouldn't have to use any of my supplies, except perhaps the water and sandwich.

Outside, I retrieved my bicycle from the side of the cabin, secured my zipper pack to the bike's basket, and walked down the grassy hill to the dirt road. If Maureen had decided to take a walk and had gotten lost, I hoped that she had the sense to stay put. It's a lot harder to find someone who's lost if they keep wandering about. If she had fallen and injured herself, the same held true. STOP was the order of the day, the initials standing for "Sit, Think, Observe, and Plan." Without her phone, however, she would have a difficult time navigating, and anyone searching for her couldn't take advantage of the phone's global positioning application.

The sky was clear; the sun had burned off the morning's haze, and the rays beat down on my back as I pedaled up the dirt road that followed the shoreline of Moon Lake. I was aiming for Mayor Shevlin's second cabin. I knew there was an abandoned logging road somewhere along here that led to it; I just wasn't sure where it was. From the end of our dock we could spot the float that was anchored off his shoreline, but the cabin itself was hidden in the woods. Even long after the leaves had fallen, the log house was impossible to see thanks to the dense pines that marched down to the water.

A clearing up ahead turned out to be a state-run boat ramp, and I was delighted to see a parked pickup truck and two men wrestling with a motorized rowboat, backing it off its trailer into the shallow water. I hopped off my bike and approached.

"Get that motor up, you gawmy ape, or it'll get stuck in muck."

"Ah'm on it, Newt. Don't get all haired up."

"Well, stop frigging around. Didja 'member the bait tub?"

"Course I did."

"That little thing?"

"We're not goin' after horsefish here."

"I tell ya, Pete. We better not run out."

"If we do, I'll cut up your cap and put it on the hook. There's enough hair oil in that thing to catch a bear."

I cleared my throat. "Excuse me, gentlemen."

Both men looked up. The one called Pete let go of the back of the boat, which dropped into the lake with a splash, setting off a string of curses from his companion.

"No need for such language, Newt. We got a lady present."

"I apologize for interrupting," I said, "but I could use your help."

Newt pulled off his cap and nodded at me. "Sure thing, ma'am. What d'ya need?"

"A friend was staying with me at a cabin back down the road, and now I can't find her. I'm afraid she may have taken a walk and gotten lost. Her name is Maureen. I'm just asking you to look out for her."

"What's this Maureen look like?"

"She's about this tall"—I raised my hand to Maureen's height—"and has red hair. She was wearing a white T-shirt and tan shorts when I left her this morning."

"Why'd'ja leave her?" Pete asked.

"We're fishing in the Cabot Cove Derby, but she got a bad sunburn yesterday and was taking the morning off."

"Yeah? The derby, huh? Yah get any big'uns?"

"Almost," I said.

Newt guffawed and slapped his thigh. "'Almost,' she says. Heah that, Pete? That's what *you* been known to catch. 'Almost.'"

"Very funny, Newt."

"Gentlemen, please. If you see my friend Maureen, would you please help her find her way back? We're staying in Mayor Shevlin's cabin on Moon Lake."

"The one with the dock or the one with the float?"

"The dock," I said, relieved that Pete knew the cabins on the lake.

"Ayuh. We'll keep a lookout for her."

"Thank you so much." I turned my bike around and rode back to the dirt road. It was comforting to know there were now three of us looking for Maureen.

Hopefully, there would be more.

Chapter Ten

Two hours later I rode back to our cabin, eager to see if Maureen had found her way home. On my way I debated whether I should chastise her for making me worry or just welcome her safe return. But there was no choice to make. The cabin was just as I'd left it—empty with no indication of where she might have gone.

She hadn't been at Mayor Shevlin's second cabin, either. After a careful hunt, I'd finally found the rutted track through the woods that led up from the dirt road. The mayor would have to clear some brush if he planned to drive his SUV there any time soon. The log house was shuttered, its only door locked. I tried to open the door and knocked when it wouldn't budge, but there was no response. I looked around outside; it was pretty clear that no car had been up there recently. The long grass was untrampled except for a narrow path where deer or a moose might have wandered by. I'd walked down to the shore and managed to hail a fisherman in a canoe on the lake. He hadn't seen Maureen but promised to pass along a description of her should he come across other anglers or a game warden. I considered taking a shortcut back to our cabin by following the narrow path along the lake, but I couldn't ride my bike on the rough ground and decided instead to retrace my route on the dirt road in case I came across anyone else who could provide assistance.

Hank, the guide from this morning, would be back soon. I could hitch a ride with him to the Maine guide headquarters, and we could alert the state game wardens of our missing person. But first, I had a call to make, one that I had been dreading ever since I suspected that Maureen had lost her way.

I walked out on the porch, where I hoped a direct connection with the sky would make the cellular service clearer, and dialed Mort's number.

"Hey there, Mrs. F. How's the fishing going? Maureen says she caught a big rainbow."

"Yes! She did. When did you speak with her?"

"This morning. She called after you left. Told me about the sunburn. Too bad, but she sounded okay."

"I'm so glad, but Mort—"

"I'm really looking forward to having her back home, I can tell you. We've been running our tails off down here with the manhunt. Haven't had a decent meal in two days. Had to call my deputies back in from the derby when the state troopers shifted their focus to the coast looking for the escaped prisoner."

"Mort, I—"

"You ought to consider cutting your vacation short, too. Might not be safe being up there all by yourself. Listen, I gotta go. I don't have a lot of time to waste. Tell Maureen to be packed and ready by four."

"I can't."

"What do you mean, you can't?"

"She's not here."

"Well, then tell her when she gets back."

"That's just it, Mort. I'm not sure when she's getting back."

He laughed. "Don't tell me you lost her."

"That's exactly what I'm telling you."

"What? Say that again."

"Maureen wasn't here when I got back from fishing this morning. I've spent the last two hours looking for her."

"Hang on a second."

I heard him give orders to someone to bring around the patrol car before he came back on the line. "Okay, Mrs. F. Let's start from the beginning."

I explained finding the cabin empty and Maureen gone. I noted that she'd taken a book with her and her sunscreen, and probably some food, but that she'd forgotten to take her cell phone and hadn't left me a note as to where she was going or when she'd be back. I reviewed my efforts to find her, as limited as they were, and concluded with, "I'm so sorry, Mort. I'm sure she's fine. It's just that she's not here. I thought maybe she got engrossed in the book and lost track of time. But she certainly must realize that I'd be waiting for her by now, so I can't understand why she hasn't returned, unless she got disoriented walking in the woods and took the wrong path."

"And she bragged to me about earning her adventurer patch," Mort said. "Some Girl Scout! Can't even find her way to the cabin she's staying in. She probably made a trail of bread crumbs with the food she took."

"Mort, I don't think the situation is funny."

"I'm not laughing, Mrs. F. I'm in the middle of a major man-hunt for an escaped murderer, who's already killed another man, and, I've got to drop everything to run up there to hunt for my wandering wife."

"Do you want to give her a little more time to see if she finds her way back?"

"No, I don't want to give her more time. I knew this derby business was a mistake. She goes off half-cocked on this idea of learning to fish so we'd have a *hobby* together. I tell you, Mrs. F., I do not have time for hobbies, and when I see Maureen, I plan to tell her, too. I'll see you in an hour. Don't leave!"

If he'd been talking on an old-fashioned phone, he probably would have slammed down the receiver. As it was, he hung up before I had a chance to respond.

I looked at my watch. Hank Thompson was due back in less than a half hour to take us out fishing, but now my plans had changed. Instead of accompanying him back to the nearest office of the Department of Inland Fisheries and Wildlife and reporting Maureen's disappearance to the game wardens, I would have to stay put for Mort's arrival.

I sat at the end of the dock waiting for Hank, checking over my shoulder several times for any sign of Maureen. At three o'clock, I spotted the bow of Hank's boat rounding a promontory and sighed in relief. I got to my feet and waved.

"Well, I see you're eager to go out again," Hank said, as he used an oar to pull in closer, "but where's your friend? Is she feeling okay?"

"No. She's not okay. She's missing. And I'm waiting for her husband to get here."

"How long's she been gone?" he asked as he tied the boat to a cleat on the dock and climbed up beside me.

"She spoke with her husband after we took off this morning, but she wasn't here when I came in from fishing."

"Have you tried looking for her?"

I nodded and repeated the same tale I'd told Mort.

"You talked to Newt and Pete, huh?" He shook his head. "Bet you dollars to donuts they don't have a fishing license between the two of 'em."

"But they know which cabins on the lake belong to Mayor Shevlin, so they can guide Maureen if they happened to see her."

"She usually a responsible lady?"

"Of course."

"Do you think she would call out to someone if she wasn't sure of the direction? You know, sometimes people don't like to admit they're lost. They think it's embarrassing. I know the dangedest story about one guy—"

"Maureen has a lot of self-confidence, it's true," I said, interrupting him, "but she's not foolish. Yes, I think she would ask for help if she needed it."

"Seems to me it's a little early to call in the dogs for a search, unless you disagree," Hank said, watching for my reaction. "But the game wardens have an incident management team. We could go ahead and alert them."

"I can't go ahead and do anything," I said. "I want to be here if Maureen shows up. In any case, I promised her husband I'd wait for him to arrive."

"I'm sure she'll be fine. There's lots of people around the lake what with the derby on and it being summer, but just to be on

the safe side and ease your mind, let me get the process started."
He unwound the rope he'd just looped around the cleat and
climbed down into the boat, setting our two fishing rods on the
dock. "I'll tell the wardens to be on the lookout for her. Might
be they can divert some of those helicopters and dogs looking
for the escaped killer and put them to use finding your friend."
He chuckled and waved as he pushed off. "Nice meeting you."

I picked up the rods and walked back to the cabin to wait
for Mort, irritated at Hank for not taking Maureen's disappearance more seriously and curious as to why I found myself so
frazzled by it. After all, it hadn't been that many hours. Maureen
was a grown-up, a former Girl Scout, a strong, competent woman
as I'd repeatedly reassured her. Maybe she took her picnic up a
mountain and fell asleep after lunch. Maybe she was lying on the
grass finishing reading her novel. Maybe she was taking advantage
of a beautiful day while I was fretting that she hadn't bothered to
keep me informed. Was I overreacting? Was I sounding an alarm
too soon?

I hung up our fishing rods on pegs, sat on the picnic table
bench, and sighed, trying to let go of the tension that had built
up. Something about this situation nagged at me. It was more
than simply Maureen's lack of consideration if, indeed, I could
chalk it up to that. I took a deep breath and let it out. The *eau
de bear* I'd detected earlier had dissipated. I unzipped the canvas bag I'd packed to take on my search and emptied its contents, debating whether to store the extra sandwich in the ice
chest, which was no longer cool inside. It didn't matter; the
sandwich wouldn't spoil. Funny that I'd had to use a spoon to
spread the peanut butter and jelly. I gasped. That was it! The

knife. Where was it? I'd hung it on the magnetic rack last night but it was not there now. Not on the shelf. Not in the sink, nor in the cabinet underneath.

Feelings of unease washed over me again.

Could Maureen have taken such a big knife with her?

And if so, why?

Chapter Eleven

There was still some time before Mort was due, and I was impatient to do something, anything to speed along the search for Maureen. I knew that the longer you waited when someone was missing, the harder it was to find them, especially a novice hiker.

Our local trails are identified with painted blazes on the trees, although in some cases the paint has flaked off over the years, or the trees have grown or been felled by a lightning strike. The blazes are not always easy to see even if you know where to look.

I tried to remember what I knew of tracing someone who was lost in the woods. I should look for freshly broken branches, human tracks in the sand or where rainwater pooled before continuing downhill to the lake, compacted gravel where a heel dug in going uphill. If she'd climbed on a mossy log, there would be marks from her shoes where pressure had been put on the delicate greenery. What other signs would indicate a recent hiker?

Of course the first place to look for footprints would be in the cabin. Maureen's rubber clogs were not in our bunk room. She was probably wearing them. I sat on the picnic bench and looked down at the cabin floor to see if her shoes had left a mark. There were several prints I recognized as mine. I'd left them when I'd come up from the lake after fishing. My shoes had been wet from the water in the bottom of the boat, and they'd picked up some sand and dirt before I entered the cabin. There were other faint marks that could have come from Maureen's clogs, and a larger heel print near the sink that didn't belong to either of us.

That's odd.

I thought back to Hank Thompson's arrival that morning. He'd never come into the cabin. Careful not to alarm us since we didn't know him, he'd simply called out a greeting, staying outside the screen door and holding up his identification for us to see. But I had invited Brian in the day before. Would his rubber-soled shoes have made a mark like that? I didn't think so. Besides, he hadn't been standing anywhere near the sink.

Maureen had taken pictures with her cell phone the previous day. I pulled her phone from my pocket and looked for them. She'd been so excited about the bear prints on the shore of the lake that she'd photographed them to show to Mort. I tapped on one photo to enlarge it. There were shoe prints in the sand as well. I remembered Maureen saying she wanted to take a picture of the paw prints of the mama bear and her cub before people walked all over them. I enlarged the photo again. The bigger I made it, the blurrier it became, but I could make out a mark that resembled the heel print near the sink.

I tried not to step on the prints on the floor as I left the cabin. It was unlikely the bears' prints were still on the shore. The lapping lake water would have washed them away, and I'd probably tromped all over them that morning. But it was worth a look.

New prints had covered the old ones. These were mine and those possibly Maureen's, but none of them were as clear as the bear prints she'd photographed. I looked across the lake and sighed. Maureen had said she might go swimming. I hoped not. Sometimes the bottom of a lake drops off precipitously, surprising anyone swimming. Had she decided to don her waders and fish close to the shore? If so, I hoped that she'd worn a belt to prevent her waders from filling with water. But Maureen's waders were still hanging in the bunk room; it was her clogs that were missing.

I decided to use the few minutes before Mort's expected arrival to examine the foot path to Jim Shevlin's second cabin. If I didn't go far I would be able to hear the engine of Mort's cruiser coming up the dirt road. If he didn't see me, he'd honk the horn or set off the siren. I'd certainly hear that.

The trail was too rough for a bike and too narrow for an all-terrain vehicle. There were tree roots bulging out of the soil and loose stones where the earth rose up before plunging back down into a gully. I knew that it was not uncommon to come across a fallen tree blocking the path. In that case, I'd have to climb over it or find an alternate way through the brush.

I started on the trail with my eyes focused on the ground, looking for any indication Maureen had passed this way. Some thoughtless person had tossed a wrapper from a granola bar. Maureen never would have done that. I picked it up and stuffed it in my pocket. I pushed up a branch from a sapling that reached across the path and ducked under it. The sound of tires on gravel caught my attention. That must be Mort. I turned quickly and was slapped in the face by the low-hanging branch.

"Oh, for heaven's sake," I said as I rubbed my cheek and held the branch out in front of me. There, caught on a twig, was a strand of red hair. *Maureen! You did come this way.* I pinched the curl and gently tugged on it till the strands sprang free from the stem.

"Mort!" I called, hurrying back up the trail. I emerged from the woods to see our sheriff standing by his cruiser, fists on his hips, frown on his face.

I waved. "Here I am. Look! Look, I found some hairs. I think they may be Maureen's."

"Sheesh! You mean she hasn't gotten back yet?"

"No, but I think I know which way she went, at least when she first took off."

"Now you're really making me nervous, Mrs. F. I hope when we find her she has a good explanation for this."

"If she's lost, Mort, it's not exactly something she did on purpose," I said, coming up to where he stood. "She couldn't help it."

"Maybe so, but it would help if you didn't go zipping off to the countryside to throw a hook in the water while I'm trying to calm down the citizenry and keep them from marching on Town Hall because I haven't found a convicted murderer who may be lurking somewhere, threatening who knows what mayhem. It's worse than trying to corral the goats some bright do-gooder brought in to eat poison ivy in Central Park. You try catching goats on Fifth Avenue at rush hour. And it's always rush hour on Fifth Avenue."

"I know you're busy, Mort, but—"

"Busy! Yes, I'm busy. I left a crew combing the outskirts of Cabot Cove for the escaped convict. The governor wants to know what we're doing to find this punk. Troopers are stopping cars on every road out of town and making them open their trunks. I should be there. Instead, I'm up in the boondocks looking for a lost wife."

"I asked Hank Thompson to alert the game wardens that Maureen is missing."

"Who's Hank Thompson?"

"He was our fishing guide for this morning. Our guide from yesterday couldn't make it today." As I said it, Mort looked askance at me, and I had an uncomfortable feeling that he knew why Brian hadn't shown up.

"By any chance was Kinney your other guide?"

I pulled my shoulders back, ready for an argument. "He was."

"He's being detained."

"You arrested him? On what charge?"

"I didn't say I arrested him, Mrs. F. I said he's being detained. I asked him not to leave his house."

"For what reason?"

"He's a material witness."

"To what? The prison break? He wasn't anywhere near the prison when Jepson broke out. He's been working as a guide all season."

"They may have been in contact. Jepson doesn't have any family in Cabot Cove to my knowledge, but he does have friends—the boys who were in on the robbery at the mini-mart the day the grocer was killed. I don't know for sure who the other guys were, but I know that Kinney was one of his buddies."

"Mort, Brian can account for his time during the robbery. He was with Alice, his girlfriend at the time. A fellow training to become a guide attested to that. Brian was exonerated and released from prison."

"I know the whole story, Mrs. F., but he knows more than he was willing to reveal, and that puts a black mark next to his name in my book. I told him that I was asking him to stay put for his own safety, and he said he understood." He put his hand up to silence me when I started to say something. "I don't want to talk about Jepson or Kinney right now. I want to find Maureen and make sure she's safe. Now, where do you think she went, Mrs. F.?"

"I think she took the trail down by the lake. It leads over to Jim Shevlin's other cabin." I held up the strands of hair I'd found. "I'm assuming her hair caught on a branch while she was walking through the woods."

"Show me where you found it."

"There's something strange, though."

"What is it?"

As we walked downhill to the lake, I told him about the missing knife and the open ice chest.

"Why would she need a knife?"

"Perhaps for any food she was carrying," I said, "but I don't know why she needed to empty the cooler."

We took the path that followed the lake's perimeter. I showed Mort the branch where I'd found Maureen's hair.

"How long do you figure a couple of hairs would last on this branch?" he asked.

"Not long if there's a wind, or if some birds building a nest found them first."

"Okay. Let's keep going."

We walked in silence, keeping watch for anything else that might indicate whether Maureen had trod this path. There were a few branches and limbs that were split, but I wasn't sure how recently they'd been broken, and I found some green leaves on the ground that hadn't had time to dry out.

We eventually reached a clearing. Up ahead was the mayor's other cabin. Mort trotted up the steps to the front door.

"I was here this afternoon," I said. "The cabin is locked and all the windows are shuttered."

"The place was locked, huh?" Mort said, turning the knob and putting his shoulder to the door. It swung open with a squeal.

"It was locked," I said, joining him on the porch. "I know it was."

Mort pulled out his service revolver and motioned for me to be quiet. He stepped across the threshold. "Maureen, honey? It's me. Are you here?" He disappeared inside, reemerging moments later, his gun back in its holster. "No one's here, but there's a rancid smell, like spoiled food or maybe something died under the floor."

"May I see?" I asked.

The cabin was a duplicate of the one Maureen and I were staying in. I immediately sensed the same odor that Mort had mentioned. It was the same smell as the one I'd detected before. *No, it's not a bear*, I thought.

While Mort examined the main room, I checked the bunk room and bathroom.

"Someone was here recently," he called out. "There's water in the sink."

The cots were not made up. Sheets and blankets were folded at the foot. I was about to turn away when I spotted something beneath the cot. I bent over, placed my hand on the object, and slid it toward me. I gasped. It was one of the books I'd encouraged Maureen to read.

Mort heard me and came to the bunk room door. "What is it, Mrs. F.?"

"She was here," I said, holding up the book. "I lent this to her this morning."

"Why would she leave it here?"

"Maybe she forgot about it. Or—"

"What?"

"Maybe she *wanted* us to find it," I said, wincing at the sudden knot in my stomach.

Mort and I looked at each other with alarm.

"Yeah, maybe, but all she had to do was leave a note or—"

"Maybe she wasn't *able* to write a note," I mused, "and if that's the case, she might be—"

Mort didn't stay in the cabin to hear the rest of what I was conjuring about Maureen's sudden and frightening disappearance. He stepped out on to the small porch and barked into the radio that he wore on his shoulder, "This is the sheriff. Get a couple of deputies up to Mayor Shevlin's cabin on Moon Lake. Yes, that one, and make it fast. We've got a problem here."

Mort leaned against the porch railing, removed his Stetson hat, and wiped his brow with a handkerchief. Concern was written all over his square, rugged face.

I forced a smile, although it didn't reflect what I was thinking and feeling at that moment.

"I wouldn't be surprised to see Maureen suddenly emerge from the woods," I offered, my words also not representing what I was really thinking.

"Well, if she does," he said, descending the steps, "she'd return to the cabin where you're staying, so let's get back there."

"Maybe she's there right now," I said, following him to the path along the lake.

Mort stopped. "That'd be nice, Mrs. F., really nice, but don't count on it. Let me ask you something. Was Maureen—well, did she seem all right mentally?"

"Mentally? Yes. She'd suffered a bad sunburn. That's why she decided to take the morning off from fishing."

"Yeah, she told me about that," he said as he resumed walking. "But I'm thinking sometimes too much sun can—well, you know, it can affect your mind."

"I know that," I said, "but she made perfect sense this morning before I left with the guide. I'd have noticed if she wasn't thinking clearly. She did talk about her uncle Basil. I'd never heard her mention him before."

Mort smiled in spite of his worry. "She always trots out Uncle Basil when she feels the need for someone to back up her arguments. I never met the guy, but according to Maureen he's an expert on everything." The smile faded from his lips and he fell silent.

"Have you made any headway in the search for the escaped convict, Darryl Jepson?" I asked, changing the subject.

"What?" he asked.

"Jepson," I said. "Have you—?"

"You're thinking the same thing that I am?" he said.

I'd hesitated raising the possibility that Jepson, who was now known to be in the Cabot Cove area, might be involved in some way with Maureen's disappearance. But I had a hunch that Mort was already rolling that possibility over in his mind.

"I'm afraid that I am," I said.

"It never occurred to me when Maureen was set to leave on this fishing trip that she'd have to be on the lookout for an escaped murderer. Bears? Sure. An angry moose? You bet. But if Jepson has done anything to her, I'll—"

He turned away but not before I saw that his eyes had filled.

"Let's think positively, Mort," I said, my heart going out to him. "Maureen is fine. There's got to be a reasonable explanation for why she wandered off."

He nodded, inhaled deeply, replaced his Stetson on his head, and walked down the trail, and I knew that my feeble attempt to ratchet down the anguish he felt had done little to mitigate it.

It certainly hadn't for me.

Chapter Twelve

It wasn't long before Jim Shevlin's cabin on Moon Lake that Maureen and I had shared and its environs were crawling with members of law enforcement. Mort Metzger's call for deputies had resulted in two of them arriving. Minutes later the Maine state police were represented by three troopers. Two game wardens from the law enforcement division of the Department of Inland Fisheries and Wildlife showed up as well.

After photographing the cabin and the prints I'd pointed out on the floor and dusting for fingerprints, one of the wardens, Brandon Peabody, questioned me.

"You say you went out fishing with your guide, Hank Thompson, and left your friend alone?" he asked, taking notes on a pad.

"Yes, but it was only for three hours," I said.

"How long before you reported her missing?"

"I waited a while at the cabin hoping she'd return. When she didn't, I went looking for her. Hank Thompson came back several hours later—"

"When was that?"

"I'd say that it was around three o'clock, although I'm not certain of the time. I requested that if he saw you or one of your colleagues, he let you know that Maureen may have lost her way."

"Which he did."

"I understand that Sheriff Metzger called in the report to your office as well."

"But now you think that Mrs. Metzger isn't simply lost," Peabody said, rolling his pencil between his fingers. "You suggest that she might have been taken hostage by the escaped prisoner?"

"I don't like to think that's possible, Warden Peabody, but it can't be ruled out until we find her. The sheriff considers it a possibility, too."

"Do you have any evidence to support that suspicion?"

"I don't have any direct evidence," I said, shooting a glance at Mort, who was outside the cabin talking with one of his deputies and a state police officer. "I noticed that a large knife was missing from the cabin and that our ice chest had been emptied of food. There was a heel print on the floor I couldn't connect with anyone we knew. Later, Sheriff Metzger and I found a book that I'd lent to Maureen beneath a cot at another cabin owned by Mayor Shevlin and—"

"How do those things convince you that Jepson abducted Mrs. Metzger?"

"They don't convince me that *Darryl Jepson* has kidnapped Maureen, but I'm pretty certain someone has. Right now we're taking into account every possible reason for her absence, and

Jepson being loose in the area can't be ruled out. I think that both Sheriff Metzger and I started considering that possibility when we searched Mayor Shevlin's second cabin and found the book. I had been there earlier in the day and there is no doubt in my mind that the cabin had been locked. I had tried to push the door open and rapped loudly with my knuckles. If Maureen had been inside alone, she would have responded. But she didn't. If, however, someone was in the cabin with her and possibly threatening her, it's understandable why she wouldn't have been able to reply. In retrospect, I now believe that she left us a message the only way she was able to—by leaving the book."

While Peabody jotted notes on his pad, I added, "There's also the smell."

"What smell?"

"The sheriff and I both detected a smell in the cabin, the same odor I had noticed in this cabin yesterday when we returned from fishing."

"Couldn't it be from your fishing clothes?" the warden offered. "The aroma of fish is pretty powerful."

"But this smell was different," I said. "Sheriff Metzger told me that Jepson had a condition that results in acute body odor."

"A condition?"

"A medical condition. You'll have to ask him to get the medical name of it. I hadn't known that about Jepson, but I do recall hearing a former friend of his refer to him as 'Stinky.' I just chalked it up to a nickname boys give each other to tease."

We were joined by a member of the state police contingent who'd heard part of our conversation.

"And who would that friend be?" the state trooper asked.

"Brian Kinney," I replied. I was reluctant to give him Brian's name, but when asked a direct question by law enforcement, I give direct answers.

The warden pushed up the bill of his green cap and wiped beads of perspiration from his forehead. "Okay, Mrs. Fletcher, we may need to talk with you again. Please keep yourself available."

"I was planning to stay here all week," I said.

The state trooper shook his head. "Sorry, but that's not possible. We're going to have a lot of search personnel out, and we don't want to have to worry about civilians. We're asking all local campers to stay home while we conduct the search. We don't want to give Jepson—if that's who's behind your friend's disappearance—the opportunity to take other hostages."

"The derby is over, so most of the fishermen will have left anyway," Peabody said. "We'll let you know when it's safe to come back. Sheriff Metzger said he would have someone drive you into town."

The warden and state trooper joined Mort and other men outside while I packed my duffel bag. I would let our sheriff decide what to do with his wife's belongings. I didn't know when, if at all, I would be able to return, so I gathered everything I'd brought with me except canned food and bottled drinks, which I left for the next guest. I hoped whatever car would take me back could accommodate my bicycle. It's my main form of transportation; leaving it behind would make my life at home more difficult.

I sat on my cot and looked around. Maureen's fishing vest still hung on the wall. I sighed. Should I have refused her demand to stay here by herself? She would have been upset but would have gotten over it. Would the prospect of trying to take two women as prisoners have discouraged Jepson, *if* he was involved? If I hadn't agreed to let her to keep me company for the weekend fishing derby, she would be safe at home. Seth Hazlitt had predicted dire circumstances—he often does that— but even he couldn't have envisioned Maureen getting lost or being kidnapped as one of the dangers of camping.

Had she been kidnapped? It was beginning to look that way.

When I stepped out onto the porch, Mort and other men were poring over a topographic map of the area around Moon Lake. They had circled the two cabins and were establishing grids for search crews to use in their hunt for Maureen.

A lineup of vehicles filled the grassy driveway. A four-wheel-drive Jeep was parked next to Mort's cruiser and to the one that had delivered his deputies. An all-terrain vehicle had been left near the entrance to the trail that connected both cabins. A pair of state police cars had pulled around to the side of the cabin, their lights still flashing.

The sound of a helicopter overhead caused everyone to look up.

"Darn it!" Mort growled. "That engine noise will alert Maureen's kidnapper. The faster we get that thing out of here, the better I'll feel."

Mort took off his Stetson, waved at the pilot, and pointed to the dirt road. He trotted downhill, still waving as the air turbulence churned up by the chopper's rotors flattened the tall grasses on either side of the lane.

The helicopter teetered from side to side before settling on the ground. The pilot left the engine on, the rotors spinning, and opened the door on the side. A woman in the same uniform as the game warden who'd interviewed me hopped out. She ducked beneath the still-spinning blades and ran forward, leading a black-and-tan dog wearing a red collar with a badge attached, as well as an orange vest that appeared to be padded, or probably bulletproof.

As the helicopter took off again, Mort and the new officer walked up the hill to the cabin. She was a stocky woman with her straight black hair in a single braid pulled over her shoulder.

"This is Warden Gabrielle Ong," Mort said, introducing the dog handler.

She nodded to me and the others.

"And this is Tigger," Ong said, stroking the dog's head.

Tigger leaned forward and gave me a sniff.

"He's a Belgian Malinois."

"Kind of looks like a small German shepherd to me," Mort said.

"They probably share a common ancestor," Ong said. "We use both breeds, and sometimes a Labrador retriever as well. The Malinois is a high-energy dog. They're known for their intensity, endurance, and intelligence. This pup here is an excellent tracker."

"Our K-9 unit has earned a boatload of citations," Warden Peabody added. "We were among those helping out in New Orleans after Hurricane Katrina. Gabby was there with a different dog. Nice to see you again, Gabby."

"Same here, Brandon."

"We'll be looking for the sheriff's wife," Peabody told her, nodding toward Mort.

Ong's brows registered her surprise, but she didn't say anything.

"Okay, so how do we go about this?" Mort asked.

"Let's start with how many hours your wife has been missing," Ong said. "That way we can figure about how far away she could've gotten in that time frame. We know pretty well how fast someone can walk through the woods. If they're lost and maybe retracing their steps, and stop for a while, we can determine a rough search area. Was your wife an experienced hiker, Sheriff?"

Mort swallowed. "No. I couldn't say that she was—I mean, is."

"Well, who saw her last?"

"That would be you, Mrs. F."

All eyes turned to me.

"I went out fishing with our guide this morning. I'd say we left sometime between seven thirty and eight. But you talked with her after I left, Sheriff. What time was that?"

Mort took a deep breath. "Yeah, I did. She . . . she called me. What time was it? I think it was around eight, maybe a little later. I'd just gotten to my office and was briefing my deputies, right, Evan?" Mort's eyes scanned the group. "Where's Evan?" he asked.

"Right here, Sheriff." Mort's deputy raised his hand from the back of the crowd.

"What time was the briefing?" Mort asked.

"Eight to eight thirty, Sheriff," Evan replied.

Mort looked at Gabby Ong. "Okay, so I spoke with her right after, at eight thirty."

"And did she sound okay? Was her voice calm? Any indication that someone else might be there with her, threatening her?"

"No! She was happy. Oh, she said she got a bad sunburn, so she was going to take it easy this morning: nap, read, and maybe go out again this afternoon. She'd caught a trout and wanted a chance to get a bigger one."

"Okay, so we have her here at eight thirty. When was she reported missing, and who reported her?"

"That would be me, Warden Ong," I said. "I returned around eleven, and she wasn't here."

"Did she indicate to you where she planned to go when you talked with her this morning?"

"No. I gave her a book to read and expected she was going to stay in the cabin, or at least nearby while I was gone. She wasn't here when I got back. She didn't leave any notes, but the sheriff and I found the book in another cabin on the other side of the lake."

"So you gotta figure she's been gone eight hours, at the most," Mort said. "If it turns out she was in that other cabin when Mrs. F. checked it out, then she's only been gone maybe four or five hours. Can we get this going now?" He glanced at his watch. "We're going to lose daylight soon. The longer Maureen's missing, the more . . ." He trailed off. "Let's just give Warden Ong something of Maureen's so she can get started. Any suggestions, Mrs. F.? You know what she wore recently."

Warden Ong handed Tigger's leash to her colleague, and she and Mort and I entered the bunk room. "We probably shouldn't touch whatever it is you're using, right?" Mort asked.

"Just point it out to me," she said. "And if you have a new plastic bag, that would be helpful."

"Maureen wore the fishing vest hanging up over there," I said.

"Okay," Ong said, lifting it off the peg. "We don't need what's in the pockets. That'll just distract the dog." She rummaged through Maureen's vest, removing her lipstick, a packet of tissues, and other items, dropping them on her cot.

"Wait, what's that?" Mort said, plucking out Maureen's wedding ring from the pile the warden left on the bed.

"We were afraid her fingers would swell from the sunburn," I said. "I told her to take off her ring."

Mort schooled his expression, but I could tell it was an effort for him not to break down. He tried to slide Maureen's ring onto his ring finger, but it wouldn't go past his first knuckle. He put it on his pinkie and closed his fist over it.

Outside again, Gabby Ong conferred with her colleagues from the Warden Service. She listened quietly while they briefed her on the details of the reports Mort and I had given separately. She took the leash and checked her own belt to secure the dog's water bottle, but before giving Maureen's vest to Tigger to let the dog smell the scent he was to pursue, she talked with us again.

"Our search-and-rescue dogs are trained to give two kinds of alerts: an aggressive alert—that's barking and pawing at wherever he thinks his subject is—and a passive alert. Tigger is trained to give a passive alert. That means when he finds something, he won't bark or make a noise that might frighten the person we're searching for or warn a kidnapper if that happens to be the case. Is your wife afraid of dogs, Sheriff?"

"No. She loves animals."

"That's good. Once I give Tigger your wife's vest to smell, he's going to take off. You may see his nose go up and sniff the air. A dog's nose is ten thousand times more powerful than our own. He's not going to be smelling the ground like you see a bloodhound do in the movies."

"What exactly is he smelling?" Mort asked.

"All of us humans shed skin cells," Ong replied. "They float in the air for a period of time and leave a distinctive aroma the dogs can distinguish. Every time your wife touched a branch or the bark of a tree, she'd be adding even more cells to the air."

"How do you keep up with the dog?" I asked.

"We keep him on a thirty- to fifty-foot lead, but in the woods we may shorten that so we don't get tangled up. Once he starts, we don't touch him. We don't want to distract him from his mission."

"I understand," Mort said. "Can I go with you?"

Warden Ong hesitated. "I know how much you want to be here," she said. "That's only natural. But you're a law enforcement officer; you understand that we have a job to do. Just let us do what we do best. If your wife is in the vicinity, Tigger will find her."

"If you don't find her, what does that mean?"

"It means we have to look harder. Maybe bring in more dogs. Keep in mind, however, that if Jepson or some other kidnapper has her, he may have access to a vehicle. In that case, we may find out where they've been, but not necessarily where they are."

"No one has mentioned a vehicle before," Mort said. "Jepson's picture has been plastered all over the media. It's not as if he could show up somewhere and not be recognized."

"You and I know what he looks like," Ong said, "but I'm sure you won't be surprised if I remind you how many people don't read a newspaper or watch television. And those who get their information online are more likely to click on a funny cat video than a news story about an escaped con. Do you think your wife would recognize Jepson as the guy every cop is out looking for?"

Mort sighed. "I don't know. I kind of try to shield her from that kind of stuff. Maybe I shouldn't."

"We all want to protect our families from the ugly parts of life," Ong said.

Mort nodded and put on his Stetson. "I'll let you get to work. I gave everyone my contact information. Please keep me informed."

"We will. I promise."

Mort and I watched as Warden Ong and Tigger walked down to the lake. She took Maureen's vest out of the plastic bag I'd given her and held it under Tigger's nose. The dog snuffled the fabric, raised his nose in the air with his nostrils quivering, then sniffed along the shore where we'd seen the bear prints. He followed in a circle for a few seconds, then went straight to the path leading to the other cabin. In a moment, he and Ong and the other officers disappeared down the trail.

"They'll stop at the other cabin," I said to Mort.

"I know, but where they go from there will be the key." He sighed as he signaled to his deputies. "I'm going to drive Mrs. Fletcher home. Evan, get back to headquarters and man the phones. Any messages that come in, you call me immediately. Chip, get out to all the roadblocks and take notes. I'll see you at nineteen hundred hours for a full report." He turned to me. "Ready to go, Mrs. F.?"

"Whenever you are, Mort."

He looked around the campsite as the deputies backed down the driveway. "I don't want to leave," he said. "My wife is out there somewhere, maybe with a coldblooded killer."

"They'll find her, Mort. I'm sure they will."

"I wish I could be that confident, Mrs. F."

I wished that I could be that confident, too.

Chapter Thirteen

Mort decided to leave Maureen's belongings where they were for the time being. "There'll be plenty of time to collect them," he said. "And if somehow she manages to find her way back to the cabin, I want her to find her things. I don't want it to look like we didn't expect her to return."

"If you think that's a possibility, then shouldn't someone stay here?" I asked.

"I'm coming back tonight," he said. "I'll drop you home, check in with my men at headquarters, and drive back up. Those guys can only keep the dog going while they can see. It's too bad we got such a late start."

"I'm sorry—"

"I'm not blaming you, Mrs. F. Maureen could easily have gotten lost—she doesn't have the greatest sense of direction—and if she'd found her way back, we'd all look like idiots, panicking before it was necessary."

"That might still be the situation," I said.

"I pray it is but I'm not taking any chances, not with a killer on the loose."

The trunk of Mort's squad car was crammed with assorted material—accident and crime scene investigation equipment, flares and roadside emergency signs, rain gear and medical apparatus. There was no room for my bike. Instead we managed to squeeze it in the backseat on an angle. I climbed into the front passenger seat, after Mort swept a pile of papers and books that had occupied that space onto the floor. I held my duffel bag on my lap. Rather than chance damaging my fishing rod by fitting it in the backseat with the bike, we decided to leave it in the cabin to be retrieved later.

Mort turned the car around and slowly drove down the grassy slope to the dirt road and headed toward town. He was quiet for a long time, steeped in his thoughts, while I kept my eyes on the woods bordering the road, hoping I would spot a movement or a color indicating someone was walking there.

"You know what really scares me?" he asked after a while.

"What?"

"He already broke into one cabin. What keeps him from breaking into others? And there are hunters up here who keep their rifles in their camps." He shook his head. "I can't even think about what happens if he gets his hands on a gun." He fell silent again.

We passed a fisherman tying his kayak to the roof of his car. Where the road paralleled the water, I counted at least a dozen rowboats, bottom side up, that had been pulled on shore by their owners. I knew that the owners had taken the oars with them to discourage others from "borrowing" their craft, but I wondered if any careless person had left a paddle with his boat, making it easier for a thief to steal. What if Jepson put Maureen in a boat and rowed away? Would the dogs be able to find them?

Would anyone?

Jepson, as Brian Kinney had, grew up in the woods surrounding Cabot Cove. Like Brian he'd probably camped out frequently, fishing in the lakes and hiking the trails. I imagined that he still possessed familiarity with the terrain. Those days of tramping through the forest with his friends would be good recollections, imprinted on his memory.

"Assuming they don't find her tonight," Mort said, interrupting my thoughts, "I want to get the search started as soon as it gets light."

I remembered Maureen being horrified at having to get up at first light and how we'd decided to start our fishing day later so she could sleep in. Would Jepson want to be on the move as early as four thirty or five?

"I can coordinate the search from up here," Mort mumbled. His voice was low, as if he were talking more to himself than to me. "This car has a high-gain antenna, which means I'll always be able to find a wireless network. Your phone may not be able to make a connection, but my cruiser will."

"That's reassuring," I said.

He cocked his head at me. "Just how big was the knife he stole?"

The question startled me; we'd been discussing communications, but I recognized that Mort's mind was jumping from one topic to another, trying to cover all the pertinent facts and be prepared for anything.

"The knife that was hanging on the magnetic rack was a

bread knife, about ten inches long with a serrated edge," I said. "It wasn't terribly sharp."

"But sharp enough to threaten someone."

"Yes. That's true."

"And Jepson, by virtue of who he is and what he did, would be an intimidating figure. He might not even have to hold the knife up to her throat to keep her in line."

"I think Maureen would treat him just as she would a bear."

"A bear? How does that compute?"

"We discussed what to do if she came upon wildlife near the cabin. We saw paw prints of a mama bear and her cub, so we knew that was not out of the realm of possibility. I'd recommended that if Maureen encountered the bear, she should try to look as tall as possible and speak softly and back away. It's a bad idea to challenge wild animals."

Mort snorted. "Jepson's a wild animal all right, right down to his wild animal smell. He's a skunk *and* a rat."

"Your wife is smart," I said, hoping to distract Mort and keep him from raging against Jepson. "I think Maureen will do what she needs to do to cooperate and keep herself safe. Jepson has no reason to hurt her. She's more valuable to him as an unharmed hostage than she would be if he injured her. An injured hostage would just slow him down."

"You're right, Mrs. F. That's good thinking. She's a sharp cookie, all right, my wife. A lot like you, in a way."

"I take that as a compliment," I said.

It was close to dark when Mort pulled up in front of my house. I had left a few lights on timers as I usually do when I'm away, so I was grateful to come through the back door and see a lamp on in the living room.

Mort managed to extract my bicycle from the backseat with only a modicum of profanity, which I pretended not to hear. He wheeled it onto the back porch and took his leave.

"I may give you a call tomorrow, Mrs. F."

"I hope you will," I said. "And if you need my help with anything, you only have to ask."

"I'll keep that in mind. Good night."

I took my duffel bag upstairs and unpacked, separating the fishing clothes from those I hadn't worn. The action reminded me of Maureen laying out all her purchases on the cot so we could choose her outfit for fishing the next day. I remembered her saying that she wouldn't need so many clothes the next time and how I'd rolled my eyes, hoping that she didn't assume we would have an annual date for the Cabot Cove fishing derby. I sighed, chastising myself for such a selfish thought. If Maureen was found safe and sound, I would be happy to enjoy an annual fishing date with her.

I gathered all my clothing and dropped everything into a laundry basket. Even the things I hadn't worn had taken on the smell of fish. It would all need to be washed.

I sat on the bed and wondered what Maureen was doing. Was she frightened? Hungry? Fighting for her life? I shook my head. No! I wouldn't think that way. Better to learn everything I could about Darryl Jepson and what might motivate him and where he might go. The officers weren't letting me search the woods along with them, but there were still things I could do.

I carried the laundry basket downstairs and picked up the phone.

"Seth? I hope I'm not calling too late for you."

"Wondered when I might heah from you."

Part Two

Chapter Fourteen

"It could be one of two things," Seth said in answer to my questions about a medical condition that could produce a powerful body odor, such as the one that Darryl Jepson had. "There's hyperhidrosis, which is excessive sweating. If it's being produced by the apocrine glands, there's the possibility of strong reaction with bacteria on the body."

"Can anything be done?"

"Ayuh, there are a lot of treatments for that condition—antibacterial soap, diet changes, and medications depending on the exact diagnosis. Interestingly, people who perspire a great deal often don't produce any odor because the moisture, if it's produced by the other sweat gland, the ecrine glands, simply washes away the bacteria and moisture from the apocrine glands."

"But that's not the circumstances here. I was able to detect this odor after the man had left the cabin."

"Well, in that case, it's more likely to be trimethylaminuria."

"Can you spell that?" I asked, taking notes on our conversation and trying to keep up with his use of medical jargon.

"It's more commonly known as 'fish-odor syndrome' or by the initials of its components, TMAU."

"Not so easy to treat?" I asked.

"Much more difficult," he replied. "First off, it's very rare, so you might find a doctor who's either never heard of it or—if the doctor doesn't smell anything, which is possible in a surprising number of cases—thinks it's a case of body dysmorphia."

"And that is?"

"A preoccupation with an imaginary physical flaw. A lot of people with TMAU have gone undiagnosed because their physicians thought they had a psychological problem."

"But this odor wasn't imaginary."

"Poor fellow. It's a terrible condition to live with, and it has nothing to do with not being clean or bathing enough. Many people who have it don't even know they do. All they experience is people avoiding them or passing nasty comments."

"How awful. You never saw him for it, did you?"

"Jepson? No, he was never my patient. I can ask around at the hospital if you want me to."

"Would you, Seth? That would be helpful."

"Not sure how helpful it will be if someone objects to a possible breach of patient confidentiality, but I'll ask all the same." He paused. "Now that I've helped you, I want something in return."

"What's that?"

"You keep me up to date on the search for Maureen. I want to know as soon as she's safe. I feel responsible for tricking you into taking her along. If I hadn't done that, she'd be home with her husband right now."

"You didn't trick me, Seth. I knew exactly what you were doing."

"You're sure Jepson's got her? Couldn't just be that she got lost and the search-and-rescue people will find her?"

"I wish it were that simple. But if we go by odor alone, we know Jepson was inside our cabin twice, and again at the other cabin where we found the book."

"Course, if she hadn't been along, it mighta been you that Jepson took hostage."

"Are you going to find a way to make yourself responsible for my welfare as well?"

He harrumphed. "Nope! Too late for that. Gave up on you a long time ago. You're completely indifferent to taking chances, don't even recognize when you're doin' it. I just close my eyes and cross my fingers."

"I didn't mean to be unsympathetic, Seth. I thought the same as you did—wondered if I hadn't invited her to join me for the derby, would she be safe at home now? But it's too late for recriminations. All we can do is pray that Maureen is all right."

After we disconnected, I put up a load of laundry and sat at my kitchen table with a pen and pad. What did I need to know? Jepson had been in prison for a dozen years. Would he still be in touch with anyone in his hometown, someone who could provide insight into his character? I could have asked his lawyer, but someone had killed Wes Caruthers. Why? Was it Jepson, in retaliation for not getting him off in the grocer's murder? Or was it someone else who wanted to shut him up for another reason?

I went to the bookcase in my study and pulled out a Cabot Cove telephone directory. I know you can find this information online, but somehow it's never as easy as simply running your finger down a column of names. I flipped through the pages for the letter *J* and looked for the name Jepson. There were no listings. Yet I knew that Darryl Jepson had grown up here. I needed a telephone directory from a dozen years ago to see if there had been a listing for Jepson back then. That meant a trip to the library.

I might have been able to ferret out the information if I had access to his arrest record or the transcript of his trial, but I didn't want to upset Mort with such a request. He had enough on his mind and might see my interest in poking through old records as a waste of time and energy. I could imagine his irritation without ever testing my theory. No, there had to be a simpler way.

Where did Jepson live growing up in Cabot Cove, and with whom? Of course, any relative of his might have moved away. It wouldn't surprise me. It's difficult to stay in a small town when someone related to you is convicted of a serious crime. People talk—or worse, stop talking when such a person walks into a room. The mother of a criminal may be shunned, may lose her friends, may even be turned away when she tries to get service in a store. As wonderful and caring as small towns can be when people rally around someone who is ill or suffering, they can be equally cold and unfeeling to anyone connected with a criminal. And who was more criminal than a murderer?

Brian Kinney would know who Jepson had lived with, but would he tell me? He hadn't given Mort the names of his friends who were part of the plan to steal food from the mini-mart, and I doubted whether he would simply satisfy my curiosity without asking for a lot more information than I was ready to supply.

But maybe Brian's wife, Alice, would.

Alice must have known who his friends were, even though he had tried to keep her away from them. Brian had lived two different lives as a young man, one as part of a gang of juvenile offenders, the other as the straight-arrow suitor of Alice Pelletier. Like Alice's father, Brian had wanted to shield her from his more unsavory activities. But men sometimes underestimate the strength and resilience of women. Alice might be able to tell me a lot, if she was willing. I'd have to hope she was.

First, however, I had a question for my neighbor Tina Treyz. I would call her in the morning.

Chapter Fifteen

It was good to get to bed, but I can't say that I slept soundly. My mind kept churning. Maureen's face appeared in my dreams like an out-of-control slide show. Her exuberance about accompanying me on the fishing trip had been contagious, the way her fearless forays into her kitchen in search of a culinary breakthrough always were. She could be trying at times, but she was aware of it and quick to apologize. I thought about the curt answers that came to mind when she'd made a silly comment or asked a foolish question while we were together at the lake. Fortunately, I'd held my tongue, but I wished I'd been more understanding. It was her first experience fishing, and I'd had to work to keep my impatience from surfacing.

I was in bed that Monday morning trying to muster the energy to get up when the ringing phone snapped me fully awake. My hand knocked the receiver off its base and I fumbled to retrieve it.

"Hello?" I said.

"Jessica Fletcher?" a man said.

"Yes."

"My name is Special Agent Ian Perle, Federal Bureau of Investigation. I'm affiliated with the Bangor office."

"Yes, Mr. Perle—*Agent* Perle." I sat up quickly, my heart rate accelerating.

"Sorry to bother you, ma'am, but I need to speak with you about the disappearance of Maureen Metzger."

"Has she been found?" I held my breath.

"I'm afraid not, ma'am."

"Oh." I could feel all the adrenaline that had rushed through me drain away.

"I'm part of the task force that's been sent here to Cabot Cove to help in finding her."

I ran a shaky hand through my hair. "I'm pleased that you're here."

"Hopefully we'll be able to help. Sheriff Metzger informs me that you were the last person to see his wife before she went missing."

"Yes, that's true. Maureen is a good friend. We were on a fishing trip together when it happened. I'll be pleased to speak with you. Can you conduct the interview by phone?"

"Unfortunately not, since I'll need a signature on your statement."

"Where would you like me to come?"

"No need for you to travel anywhere, Mrs. Fletcher. I'll be happy to come to your home, if that's acceptable to you."

"Of course."

I gave him my address, although that obviously wasn't necessary. We arranged for him to come within the hour.

Showered and dressed forty-five minutes later, I tidied up the house before Special Agent Perle's arrival. Not that it would have mattered to him if things were askew, but my pride in my home automatically kicked in. I'd just finished running a dust cloth over some furniture when he rang my bell.

Special Agent Ian Perle was a handsome man by any standard, tall and lean, and with a face that exuded friendliness. After he showed me his identification and gave me his business card, I invited him in. He declined my offer of coffee or tea, or a slice of crumb cake in the kitchen, and we settled in my living room, a more formal setting. He flipped open a lined notebook and, after asking permission to record, set a small tape recorder on the table in front of my sofa.

"What can you tell me about Mrs. Metzger?" he asked.

I wasn't prepared for such an open-ended question and had to think for a few moments before answering.

"Maureen is a close friend," I said, "and her husband and I are friends, too. She's a sweet, honest person who wears her heart on her sleeve, if you don't mind that cliché."

He smiled. "She sounds like a very nice woman," he said. "The sheriff tells me that . . . well, he indicates that she can be a little—how shall I put it?—a little flighty at times."

It was my turn to smile. He was being careful with his words so as to not unfairly characterize Maureen. At the same time I had a hunch where he was going with the comment. Could Maureen's "flightiness" have contributed in some way to her sudden disappearance? Could she have simply decided to get lost for a while, maybe because of personal problems she was having that I wouldn't have been aware of?

"I don't know that I would use the word 'flighty,'" I said. "You know we writers are fussy about the words we choose."

"Choose any word you like."

"I don't like the word 'flighty.' That makes Maureen sound irresponsible, which I don't for a minute believe she is. Let me put it this way," I said. "Maureen Metzger can be somewhat unconventional at times. That's a better word. She embraces new experiences with enthusiasm, perhaps is a bit naive, but behind that is a bright, grounded woman. If you're thinking her disappearance is self-imposed, I'd have to strongly disagree. I understand that the possibility has to be probed, but Maureen is too considerate a person to leave me or Mort worrying about her, which I'm sure she knows we are. She walked out of our cabin without leaving me a note, yet she left behind a book I'd lent her in another cabin. That tells me that she was trying to think of a way to communicate and was very much opposed to what was happening to her."

He nodded that he understood.

"Did the sheriff speak with you about the possibility that the escaped convict, Darryl Jepson, might have been involved in her disappearance?" I asked.

"Yes, of course. That's what we're focusing on. I sympathize with your sheriff. It's hard enough spearheading a search for an escaped killer without having your wife missing, too."

"And possibly abducted by that same killer," I added.

He paused while considering his next question. "What about Sheriff Metzger, Mrs. Fletcher?"

"What about him?"

"You've met your share of law enforcement officers in your

career. Do you think Sheriff Metzger is up to the task he's been handed?"

My initial reaction was to be offended by the question on Mort's behalf. But I also realized that as a member of the assembled task force, Special Agent Perle had to cover all the bases. I hadn't spoken with Mort since he'd dropped me off at home the previous evening. I could only imagine the agony he was going through.

"To give you the short answer, Agent Perle, I'm confident that Sheriff Metzger is up to any challenges he faces. Mort Metzger is a cool-headed, dedicated lawman, someone equipped mentally and physically to handle adversity, even when that adversity involves his beloved wife."

"I appreciate your point of view, Mrs. Fletcher, but having Sheriff Metzger working the case is a little like having a doctor treat a member of his or her own family. Officially it's frowned on. There are just too many complications."

"Surely you can't believe Mort had anything to do with his wife's disappearance?"

"Most likely not, but as a responsible law enforcement officer, I can't ignore the possibility. Perhaps you can talk him into taking a step back and assigning one of his deputies to be the point person for the sheriff's office."

"Have you suggested that yourself?"

"We have."

"Is that why you wanted to interview me, to get me to ask Mort to withdraw from the case?"

"Among other reasons. Just talk with Metzger. He may view us as impinging on his territory; he's much more likely to listen to your logic."

I could feel myself getting hot. "I doubt Mort views you as competition. In fact, I'm fairly certain he's grateful to have all of you helping to find his wife."

"The sheriff is fortunate to have a loyal friend like you."

I took a deep breath. The FBI agent was right. It wasn't appropriate for Mort to spearhead the search for his wife, much as all his instincts told him to do just that. "I'll see if I can get him to come for dinner. I'm sure that with Maureen gone, and the pressure he's under, he hasn't been eating the way he should."

"That's a perfect excuse."

"It isn't an excuse," I said, tamping down my annoyance. "That's the way people are here in Cabot Cove. We take care of each other. I can only pray that Maureen will show up safe and sound."

"That's why the FBI is here. Is there anything you can offer about Jepson? We initially received reports that he was somewhere up north, on the Canadian border, and then we heard that he might be here in Cabot Cove."

"I just want him apprehended," I said.

"You and me both, Mrs. Fletcher."

"With Maureen's disappearance and Jepson's escape from prison, the murder of the attorney Wes Caruthers seems to get lost in the mix."

"We haven't forgotten about him," Perle said.

"You do know, of course, that Mr. Caruthers was assigned to defend Jepson."

"Jepson doesn't think he did a very good job of it, from what I hear. His cellmates told prison authorities that Jepson had it out for two men, Caruthers and Metzger. Another reason, perhaps, to see the sheriff step away, and let others manage the case."

His comment fed into something that I'd been thinking all along. Had Jepson known Maureen would be up at Moon Lake with me? There had been a small mention in the Cabot Cove *Gazette*, but would he have seen the paper? Had he been hiding out somewhere in town before Caruthers was killed, before Maureen and I had gone up to Moon Lake, and before Maureen had been abducted?

After Perle left, I set my mind on what I intended to do that day. I'd already resolved to visit Alice in hopes she could help me identify some of the other members of Jepson's gang, other than Brian, of course. In the haze of events, it was easy to forget about Brian and his connection with the escaped killer. Agent Perle had mentioned two men Jepson was eager to get revenge on, but could there be more? Was Brian on Jepson's list of enemies? After all, he had escaped the harshest penalty and been exonerated and released while Darryl Jepson languished in prison. Was Jepson angry about that? Apparently Brian had thought he would be or he wouldn't have left his wife and child in Alice's girlhood home with a father who had no love for Brian, much less respect. Yes, I would start with Alice and see where the day took me from there.

John Pelletier owned the car dealership downtown and lived in the white colonial in which he had raised his daughter following the death of his wife. An older woman answered my ring. Her black hair, shot through with white strands, was pulled back in a loose ponytail. She wore baggy jeans and a blue-and-green-striped button-down shirt over which was a neatly pressed orange apron.

"Who is it, Helen?" I heard a woman call out.

"Don't know yet," the housekeeper replied.

"Hello. My name is Jessica Fletcher. I'm a friend of Brian's. Well, not exactly a friend, but he was my guide for the recent derby up at Moon Lake. I was hoping to speak with Alice. Is she available?"

"Lady says she knows Brian," Helen called over her shoulder.

"Well, invite her in." Alice said, coming to the door. "Oh, Mrs. Fletcher, how kind of you to stop by. Please come in. Can we offer you a cup of coffee or tea?"

"Please don't fuss on my account," I said, stepping across the threshold.

"It's no fuss," Helen said with little grace. "Water's already hot."

"Then a cup of tea would be lovely," I said.

"I'll have the same, if you don't mind, Helen."

"Already said it's no fuss."

"Thank you."

Alice led me to a breakfast room off the kitchen. On the way, she picked up a naked fashion doll with half its hair colored blue and tossed it in a toy bin next to the window seat.

"I'm sorry to barge in unannounced," I said, "but I just learned yesterday that Brian had been asked to stay home while the search for Darryl Jepson is under way."

"Yes. The sheriff said it was for his own protection, but frankly I don't believe it." She glanced at Helen, who placed three empty mugs on a tray along with a saucer of tea bags and a sugar bowl and creamer.

"Brian must have thought something like that might happen when he urged you to stay here with your daughter. How is Emma, by the way?"

"She's fine, a handful but a delightful one. I just put her down for her morning nap. Hopefully, she'll give us twenty minutes or so."

I heard Helen grunt. "Won't listen to nobody, that naughty baby," she said, but there was fondness in her voice.

"Have they found Mrs. Metzger yet?" Alice asked.

"Oh, I didn't know if you knew about that," I said.

"Hard not to know. It's all over town this morning. I've had a call already."

I nodded. My phone had been ringing all morning as well. It was what motivated me to get out of the house as soon as Agent Perle had left.

Helen brought the tea to the table. "You want crackers?" she asked Alice.

The younger woman shook her head. "Just black tea right now, thanks." She looked at me. "My stomach is a little queasy these days."

"So Brian told me."

"It should go away in another month and I'll be fine."

"I'm sure you will, but until then, I brought something for you," I said, setting my bag in my lap and groping around inside it. I pulled out a plastic box and set it on the table next to Alice. "My neighbor Tina Treyz said she used to rely on these during her pregnancies."

Helen peered over the box and pushed it with her index finger as if it contained something alive. "What are they?"

"They're acupressure wrist bands," I replied. "Most people use them for seasickness, but Tina said they were a big help to her."

"I've heard of them, but I've never tried them," Alice said, opening the box and taking out the instructions. She slid one of the elastic bands over her hand and positioned the round bead it held on the inside of her wrist. "It's a little snug."

"Put on the other one," Helen said. "If you're going to test-drive them, do it right."

Alice giggled and did as instructed.

"Nice of you to bring those," Helen said to me as she passed around the mugs of hot water and sank into the chair next to Alice.

"I have to admit it's not the only reason I came by. I'm hoping you can help me track down who Darryl Jepson lived with when he was a teenager in Cabot Cove."

Alice's eyes opened wide. "Gee, I don't have the faintest idea. I'd heard his name, of course. Brian used to call him Stinky. I told him that wasn't very nice, but he said that's what all the guys called Darryl. But they were a couple of grades ahead of me and I never knew where any of them lived. Brian kept me away from them. Even now, I don't think he keeps in touch with any of them."

"He was afraid one of those bad boys would try to lure you away from him, that's what it was," Helen said, chuckling. "He wasn't taking any chances. My thinking."

"Did you know the other boys?" I asked Helen.

"Only by reputation. Not to talk to. You know Harvey Richardson that runs the local Gas-and-Go? He hired Jepson and one of his pals to help change tires and run errands and the like."

"Is that Jed Richardson's brother?" I asked. Jed was a former commercial airline pilot who now ran a charter operation from our local airport; he'd been my flying instructor when I was earning my pilot's license.

"That's him. That family always was mechanical. Gas station, airport. I think there's another brother works for the school bus company."

"Do you know the names of any of Jepson's other friends?"

Helen shook her head. "Me? No. Alice, Brian ever mentioned any other names to you?"

"Honestly, I don't remember. I might have heard him talk about a Steve once, but I don't recall if he was one of the gang or someone they were giving a hard time to. Brian used to try to keep the others from preying on the nerdy ones—you know, the smart kids—but he wasn't always successful."

Helen raised an eyebrow at Alice. "You're thinking your husband wouldn't want you to identify who his friends were, aren't you?"

"No. No. Really. I just never knew their names."

Helen looked at me. "Likely story."

"I think I hear Emma," Alice said, pushing back her chair and hurrying from the room.

"She didn't hear nothin'," Helen said, sipping her tea. "I know that child like the back of my hand. Been raising her since she was seven. She knows those names. If I come to remember any of 'em—or get her to tell me—where do you want me to call you? I don't believe in protecting lawbreakers, and those boys saw every law as a challenge. Only his love for Alice straightened Brian out. That and trying to prove Mr. Pelletier wrong. He's still working on that one."

Chapter Sixteen

Harvey Richardson's Gas-and-Go was on the road leading out to the airport. I had passed it many times but never had occasion to stop in there. The station was self-serve when it came to pumping gas, but it had a full-service mechanic on duty, around the side of the building where the garage bays were open and country music poured out loud enough to muffle most car engines.

I parked my bike near the front door, which another customer held open for me as he left. A young man sat behind the cash register inside a small office that also sold windshield wiper blades, hanging air fresheners, and other automotive accessories. Several soda and candy machines lined one wall for those too busy to stop in town for a snack.

"Hi, Josh," I said, reading the young man's name tag. "Is Harvey Richardson in today?"

He shook his head but didn't look up from the smartphone he was typing into with his thumbs.

"When do you expect him back?"

"Didn't tell me."

"Does he usually come in every day?"

"Sometimes."

He was too young to remember when Brian and Darryl and friends were getting in trouble, but I figured it wouldn't hurt to ask questions. "I'm trying to find someone who used to work here about a dozen or so years ago. Would you know the names of the people who worked here before you came?"

He shook his head again.

"Do you think your mechanic might know?"

"Dunno. You could ask."

"What's his name?"

"Jeff Grusen."

"Has he worked here for a long time?"

"Not long."

"More than a year?"

"Probably."

That didn't look promising. "Then, may I leave a note for Mr. Richardson for when he does get back?"

A shrug.

I scribbled a note on the pad of paper I always carry, folded it, and held it out to the clerk, whose head was still buried in the phone. I cleared my voice, and finally he looked up. "Will you remember to give it to him?" I asked.

"I guess."

"I'm asking, Josh, because it's important that I speak with him. I'm relying on you to be responsible. Mr. Richardson must think you are a responsible person or he would never leave you in charge of his business."

Josh straightened in his seat and put down his phone. "I guess."

"I'm sure. Now, here's the note. I've left my phone number. I know that you'll make sure that Harvey Richardson gets this."

"Okay, Mrs. . . . ?"

"Fletcher, J. B. Fletcher."

"Okay, Mrs. Fletcher, I'll make sure old Harvey gets this."

I felt myself sigh. Trying to capture the attention of young people on their cellular phones was not an easy task. "Thank you very much, Josh."

I walked my bicycle around the side of the building to the air pump and put down the kickstand. I glanced over to the garage. A portion of the garage floor had been excavated to accommodate the installation of a lift. There was a car up on the lift, and the mechanic was standing in the pit peering up into its interior parts using a flashlight. I hoped he would be more helpful than the clerk. After all, he couldn't read text messages on his phone and work on a car engine at the same time, could he? There was only one way to find out.

I unscrewed the valve on the tire, dropped it in my pocket, and pressed my fingernail down on the stem until I heard the hiss of air as it escaped. The mechanic was still craning his neck to look up into the engine. I pinched the tire of my bike to be sure I'd taken enough air out, walked into the open bay, and leaned down to see the back of the mechanic's head.

"Excuse me," I shouted over the music.

The mechanic, whose age was almost impossible to gauge thanks to a cap covering his hair, didn't answer.

I walked to the front of the car, squatted down, and waved. I would have done a little dance if I thought it would catch his eye. I debated jumping down into the space where the mechanic stood, but I didn't want to alarm him. Eventually, he looked up, raised gray brows, then frowned at me. I couldn't tell if he was growing a beard or if the shadow on his face was a result of grease marks.

"Can I help you?" he shouted.

"I hope so," I shouted back. "Are you Jeff?"

"Wait a minute." He put down the flashlight, climbed up out of the pit, grabbed a paper rag from a dispenser box, wiped his hands, and turned down the radio.

I shook my head. I would be deaf in no time if I listened to music at that volume all day. I gave the mechanic a quivery smile.

He was taller than I'd realized, and younger. His brows were blond, not gray. He looked to be Brian's age and my heart sped up at my luck, but quickly subsided. According to Josh, the mechanic hadn't been here long, so maybe he was new to town.

"What can I do for you? Where's your car?"

"I don't have a car. It's my bike," I said, waving toward where it stood by the air pump. "I think I have a flat."

"You need a gauge?" he asked, pulling one from his breast pocket and offering it to me.

"A what?"

"An air pressure gauge to measure the air pressure in your tires?"

"Is that what I'm supposed to use?"

"Oh, for Jupiter's sake." He threw his dirtied rag into a can and stalked to where my bike gently listed near the air hose.

"Thank you so much," I said, jogging after him. "You must

think me a silly old woman, but I've never had to do this before. You see, my husband, my late husband, used to take care of all these mechanical details for me, so I never needed to learn them myself."

"It's not hard. I'll show you just what to do, so next time you can put the air in yourself." He kneeled down by my bike. "See? Here's your problem. Your valve cap is missing."

"My what?"

"Your valve cap. The thing you screw into this stem that keeps the air from escaping. You might have a slow leak in the valve."

"It's so nice to meet someone so helpful. Have you worked here a long time? I don't remember seeing you before."

"You come here often?" he muttered, smiling to himself. He checked the air pressure using his gauge. "Your air's definitely low."

"How can you tell?"

"There's a number on the side of your tire tells you what the pressure should be. Then you check it with the gauge, like this, and if you need more air, you push the top of this hose on the stem until it starts inflating the tire. Want to try it?"

"You do it. You're better at it than I am. By the way, I used to teach in the high school, but you don't look familiar. Did you grow up in Cabot Cove?"

He shook his head, laughing. "I grew up here all right, but I spent most of my school days in juvie. Am I shocking you?"

"Juvenile detention." I made a tsking noise. "Thank goodness you've outgrown it."

"I'm glad you think so. There's others in this town . . . never mind." He stood and put the gauge back in his pocket. "I probably have another one of those caps I can contribute to the cause," he said, walking toward the garage. "Otherwise you'll be back here before you know it. Just give me five minutes to find one in the drawer."

"Thank you," I said, following him. "You've been so helpful. I don't know what I would've done if you hadn't been here. How much do I owe you?"

"Owe me? Nothing. It was nothing. Just wait while I find you another cap. We always have a dozen of them around."

"At least let me buy you a soda. It's Jeff, right? I wouldn't forgive myself if I couldn't do something nice for you, Jeff."

"Yeah, it's Jeff." He stopped, exasperation clear on his face. Finally, he sighed. "Okay, while I'm looking for your cap, you can get me a can of Moxie. They have them in the machine in the office."

I returned moments later with two cans of soda. I handed him one and opened the other for myself, settling on a battered leather desk chair next to the tool case he was pawing through in search of a valve cap.

He winced. "That's not the cleanest, just so you know."

I shrugged. "Too late now." I smiled at him. "Tell me, Jeff. Did you happen to know Stinky Jepson when you were in juvie?"

"Stinky! How the heck did you know Stinky?" His face lit up, then sobered. "Oh, I know."

"He's been in the news a lot lately, hasn't he?"

"Yeah. The sucker."

"Did you know him then?"

"Sure. We were in a rough gang together."

"Really?"

"We used to call ourselves 'the five musketeers' after an old movie we saw on TV. We'd camp and cook out down near the railroad tracks. Stinky would whittle swords out of branches and try to interest us in fencing and knife throwing. Guess that didn't turn out so good for him."

"Do you still keep in touch with the other guys? Brian Kinney? Who else?"

He counted on his fingers. "Stinky, me, Brian, Hank, and Cory." He let out a whoosh of air and returned his attention to the drawer. "Brings back memories."

"You're too young to be so nostalgic. Don't you still get together with some of these guys?"

"Nah. Cory joined the army. Last I heard he was in Afghanistan. Brian and Hank must live somewhere in town, probably. We don't keep up. We're pretty much scattered to the wind."

"Too bad. Do you know if Stinky's parents are still in Cabot Cove?"

"Ah! Got one." He held up a valve cap, identical to the one in my pocket.

I put out my hand and he dropped it in my palm.

"Want me to put that on for you?"

"I think I can manage that much," I said.

"I'm sorry. What did you ask?"

"I was asking if Stinky's parents still lived in town."

"I don't remember his having parents. His aunt Darcy lived up in the trailer park. He stayed with her a lot."

"I don't think I ever met her. Darcy Jepson, you say?"

"She was his aunt but must've been on his mother's side. I don't remember her last name."

"That's okay. I'll find her."

"Why are you looking for Stinky's aunt?"

"I'm not. I'm looking for Stinky."

"You and every cop in Maine. Hey, are you a cop or something?" He eyed me warily.

I laughed. "No such thing."

"Rumor has it he's holding the sheriff's wife. My girlfriend heard it at the post office."

"I heard that, too."

"So why are you looking for Stinky's aunt Darcy?"

"The sheriff's wife is a friend of mine. I'd like to see her get back home safely."

"And you think Aunt Darcy can help?"

"I won't know until I find her." I stood, brushing off the seat of my pants, and dropped my soda can in the recycle bin. "Thank you, Jeff. You've helped me a great deal today." I held up the valve cap.

"Yeah. Don't lose that. And thanks for the soda."

"An even exchange," I said, walking to my bike, where I screwed the cap Jeff had given me into its proper place. By the time I climbed on my bike, he had turned up the radio to deafening levels and I was grateful to pedal away.

Special to the *Cabot Cove Gazette*

SHERIFF'S WIFE MISSING!

AUTHORITIES FEAR SHE MAY HAVE BEEN TAKEN HOSTAGE

MANHUNT FOR ESCAPED KILLER CLOSES IN ON CABOT COVE

Maureen Metzger, wife of Sheriff Mort Metzger, disappeared on a camping trip to Moon Lake, where she was participating in the Cabot Cove Derby Days. Mrs. Metzger, who was staying in a cabin owned by Mayor James Shevlin, was a guest of mystery writer Jessica Fletcher, who reported her missing Sunday afternoon to the Warden Service division of the state's Department of Inland Fisheries and Wildlife. This newspaper has learned that efforts by the K-9 unit have been unsuccessful so far in locating Mrs. Metzger, who authorities now fear may have been kidnapped by Darryl Jepson, the convicted murderer who escaped from the penitentiary in Warren earlier this month. Jepson is also suspected in the killing of attorney Wesley Caruthers, whose body was discovered after the convict's escape.

Mayor Shevlin announced that the governor has called in additional state police to assist in the search, and noted that agents from the Federal Bureau of Investigation are also on the case. Helicopter teams have been combing the camping areas around Moon Lake, and roads leading into Cabot Cove are being patrolled by various policing authorities. Residents are advised to expect delays at the checkpoints, where all vehicles are subject to search.

"This is a difficult time for our community," Shevlin said. "We're asking residents to please be on the alert and to report any suspicious activity to the police."

Annabelle Lodge, president of the board of education, said there are no plans to date to postpone the start of the school year, which is two weeks away, despite calls from worried parents. However, summer school classes were dismissed early and the extra-credit wilderness course that had been due to start next Monday has been canceled until further notice.

Regarding local travel restrictions, downtown merchants have expressed dismay at the damper they're putting on back-to-school sales, but the Chamber of Commerce is promising extended retail hours once the situation is resolved. When that will take place, however, is still up in the air.

Both Sheriff Metzger and Mayor Shevlin promised an update at their next daily press briefing. Efforts to reach Mrs. Fletcher for a comment were unavailing.

Chapter Seventeen

Back in my kitchen by noon, I put the newspaper aside and took up my hastily scribbled notes on the names of Jeff Grusen's "five musketeers" and the little, if anything, I knew about each. The gas station mechanic had been free with information about his boyhood friends, which not only endeared him to me, it made me deduce that he had a clear conscience about his own activities during those days. I hoped I was right. I had first names, but not all the last names: Darryl Jepson, Brian Kinney, and Jeff Grusen. But who were Hank and Cory? Cory was a veteran. He shouldn't be too hard to look up. Maybe Harvey Richardson knew Hank.

I could give the list to Mort, but I didn't know if it would mean anything all these years after the grocer's death and Darryl Jepson's murder conviction. But one or more of these men—boys at the time—had agreed to meet up with Jepson at the mini-mart and may or may not have been his accomplices in the crime. Was the information pertinent now? More important, would it help to find Maureen?

The timer went off and I got up to check the pot roast I had in my slow cooker. Mort Metzger had appeared on the television news looking haggard. I knew he hadn't been eating well since Maureen joined me up at Moon Lake, and now that he was struggling with fears about her disappearance it looked as if he wasn't eating at all. I'd left a message at the sheriff's office for him to come for dinner, or if he was too busy, I'd pack a sandwich for him to take with him. I hadn't heard back, but when I told Seth of my plans, he said he'd stop by as well to see how Mort was doing, and bring a blueberry pie from Sassi's Bakery.

I'd left a note on my front door saying I was not available for comment, and let the answering machine pick up my calls so I could screen them. Nevertheless, someone had rung the doorbell several times. I knew it wasn't one of my neighbors, who would more likely simply come in through the back porch without a by-your-leave. It was probably one of the reporters camped out on my lawn who'd kept me a virtual prisoner in my house since I'd returned from the Gas-and-Go. If I was tempted to report them to the sheriff's office, I reminded myself that Mort had a lot more to worry about than someone invading my privacy. I did pick up one telephone call that I had been expecting— or at least hoping would come in.

"Jessica? Harvey Richardson here," a voice said into my machine. "I see you left me a message at the station today."

I grabbed the phone. "Hello? Harvey? Are you still there?"

"I'm here."

"Thank you so much for returning my call."

"No problem. What can I do for you?"

"I'm trying to track down the boys who were friends with Darryl Jepson when he was growing up in Cabot Cove. I understand you employed some of them back then."

"Got one working in my garage right now. Did you meet Jeff Grusen?"

"I did."

"Good man. He spent a couple of years in Windham, but he's settled down now."

"What was he in for?" I asked.

"Assault, I believe. They had him in some kind of woodshop program there. I'm trying to teach him auto mechanics now. These new cars are all computer controlled. He has trouble with those, but he's learning. Of course, he's better with the older cars, but there's fewer and fewer of them these days. Always tried to put those boys on the straight and narrow. Some take to it—like Jeff; some don't—like Darryl." He laughed. "You're looking into all the old gang members, huh?"

"Any others?"

"Brian Kinney and Hank Thompson work as guides. I guess you know that. Tough road for Kinney, all those years in prison, but he seems to have gotten over it. You know John Pelletier, owns the dealership downtown?"

"Yes, Alice's father."

"Right. He keeps me up to speed on Brian. John doesn't like him, but he's getting over it. His little granddaughter is a nice compensation."

"What about Cory?"

"Caruthers? He started as a helper on the lobster boats. When his buddies were convicted, he quit and joined the army, but I hear he came home last week."

"Cory Caruthers?"

"Yeah, that's who you were asking about, right?"

"Harvey, was he related to Wes Caruthers?"

"His son, I believe, although they never got along. That's why Cory went into the armed services, I'm sure. Wanted to get as far away from Cabot Cove and his father as he could."

I thanked Harvey for the information. After we hung up I added carrots to the pot roast, reset the timer, and checked my watch. I had a few hours before Mort would arrive, if he came at all, and I debated how best to use them.

The FBI's supposed interest notwithstanding, the Wes Caruthers murder case had taken a backseat to the search for Darryl Jepson, although Mort would likely say they were one and the same. It seemed to me that the timing was awfully close for Jepson to have escaped prison, made it down to Cabot Cove, known where to find Wes Caruthers in order to kill him, and run back up to the woods around Moon Lake to kidnap Maureen. But stranger things have happened. It would mean that earlier sightings of Jepson in Calais and elsewhere around the Canadian border were mistaken. It would also mean that Jepson had spent a lot of time planning his moves before the escape.

I called Dimitri's Taxi Service and arranged to meet the driver around the corner from my neighbor Tina Treyz's house, in order to avoid the prying eyes of the press. I walked into Tina's backyard, stealing a look over my shoulder at my front walkway, where a reporter and two of his colleagues were engaged in watching something on their phones.

The cab pulled up on the side street and a minute later we were on our way into town with no one the wiser. I had intended my first stop to be Town Hall, where I knew a press conference was scheduled for later in the day. But when we passed a pair of television trucks with their antennas reaching into the sky, I changed my mind. With everyone crowded into Town Hall for the daily update, it would be easier to move about unnoticed.

It was tempting to drop into Mara's Luncheonette to hear the latest scuttlebutt, but if the last time Cabot Cove had been inundated with press was any indication, Mara's would have become press central for visiting members of the fourth estate. Instead, I walked over to Charles Department Store, a less well known, if reliable, gathering place for information and news about goings-on in town. I was startled to see a placard in the window with Maureen's photograph and the offer of a reward for her safe return.

Several people looked up briefly when I came through the door, then went back to their shopping. I greeted Dave, one of the owners, who was behind the counter changing the paper roll used for printing the cash register receipts. He wore a yellow ribbon pinned to his shoulder. "Any news?" he whispered to me.

"I was hoping you would have some," I replied.

His mouth was a grim line. "I heard they put a third team of dogs on the search. You know the region around Moon Lake is a pretty big area, and all the little rivulets and streams cutting through make it hard to get from one section of woods to the other. Easier if you're in a boat than if you're on land. One of the guides involved in the search was here this morning buying bug repellent. He said all the hatches are making it harder. No fun tromping through a cloud of insects. Kind of takes away your attention to the task when you get a mouthful of bugs."

David's assistant joined us at the counter. She wore a yellow ribbon as well. "I heard they're doing a shoulder-to-shoulder search in the fields north of Moon Lake," she said.

"Shoulder-to-shoulder?" David said, his eyes wide. "Don't they only do those when they're searching for a body?"

"They had the dive team out, too," she said. "Maybe they think Mrs. Metzger drowned when she tried to escape from her kidnapper."

"I'm sure the authorities are being thorough and responsible," I said, shivering at the possibilities raised. "But it makes much more sense for Jepson to keep Maureen safe. A live hostage is valuable; a dead one is not. She's an important negotiating card for him. Besides, if the authorities really thought they were looking for a body, the dogs would be much more helpful."

"There have to be hundreds of camps up in those woods," David said. "Jepson could be hopping from one cabin to the next going north. There would be nothing stopping him for miles."

Dave's brother, Jim, slid a carton of yellow ribbons onto the counter. "Here you go, Dave, another two hundred. I'll have to order more of the yellow grosgrain. I'm all out." The ribbons were stapled into a loop like the pink ribbons used to commemorate breast cancer victims.

"Did you find the safety pins, too?" Dave asked.

"I did," Jim replied, pulling out a plastic container. "Here you go, Jessica. You're just in time. We ran out of the first batch. They're going like Mara's pancakes." He handed me a yellow loop of ribbon and a safety pin. "They're for Maureen Metzger, in hopes we get her back soon."

I pinned a yellow ribbon on my shoulder, feeling slightly sick to my stomach. Maureen's disappearance was now part of the media event surrounding the search for escaped convict Darryl Jepson.

"We've got flyers all over town, too," Dave said.

"Is that what's in your front window?" I asked.

"Yes. The local print shop stayed open all night to print them."

"Who's offering the reward?"

"The Cabot Cove Chamber of Commerce. We want our sheriff to know the community is standing behind him, so we canvassed the membership as soon as we learned his wife was taken. The reward is twenty-five hundred dollars for information leading to Maureen's safe return."

"I'm sure the sheriff will appreciate the support."

My cell phone rang and I looked down at my screen to see Mort's name. "Please excuse me," I said, taking the phone to the front door and out onto the street. "Hello, Mort, is everything all right?"

"Everything is about the same, Mrs. F. No news yet," Mort replied.

"Did you get the message I left for you at headquarters?"

"I did, and thank you. I'll try to get there by six but I don't know how long I can stay."

"Seth is bringing a pie. He said he'd like to see you if you can wait around."

"I have to play that by ear. Right now I've got a press conference."

"We understand. Take whatever time you can spare."

I left Charles Department Store intending to slip into the press briefing at Town Hall, but when I saw our local editor pausing on the steps and surveying the crowd, I changed my mind. Evelyn Phillips would spot me in an instant and I would be bombarded by questions I'd rather not answer. This would be a good time to visit Mara's Luncheonette instead with all the reporters gone from there.

Maureen's face looked back at me from the flyer in the luncheonette window as well. Mara was carrying a stack of dirty dishes to the kitchen when I opened the door. "Don't let the air-conditioning out," she yelled over her shoulder.

I slid onto a stool at the counter and accepted a glass of water from a college-student waitress Mara had hired for the summer. Barnaby Longshoot was two stools down, paging through the latest edition of the *Cabot Cove Gazette*.

"Mrs. Phillips says here efforts to reach you 'were unavailing,'" Barnaby said, pointing at the last line of an article. "What's that mean?"

"It means she wanted to ask me a question but I wasn't available," I said.

"So unavailing means unavailable?"

"Not exactly," I said.

"It means leave her alone, Barnaby," Mara said. "That's what it means. Want some iced tea, Jessica? I'm mixing up a new batch."

"Yes, thank you."

"I'll have one, too," Barnaby called after her.

"Barnaby, do you mind if I ask you a question?" I said.

"Me?" he said, closing the newspaper and straightening on his stool. "Sure. What would you like to know?"

"Do you know Cory Caruthers?"

Barnaby thought about it a minute. "Big guy? Army fatigues? Works lobsterin', sometimes? Doesn't talk much? That the one?"

"I don't know; I haven't met him. Who does he work for, do you know?"

"Last I heard he was on Levi Carver's boat or maybe it was

Linc Williams." He shrugged. "One of them anyway. Why d'ya want to know?"

"That's not your business, Barnaby. Here's your tea, Jessica," Mara said, placing a tall plastic glass in front of me with a straw sticking out of the cover. She crossed her arms on the counter and lowered her voice. "Are you working on Mrs. Metzger's case?"

"Trying to," I said. "Any chance you would happen to know a lady named Darcy? I don't know her last name but she used to live up in the trailer park. I don't know if she's still there."

Mara shook her head. "Name's not familiar. Want me to ask in the kitchen? Cook has a double-wide up there."

"If you wouldn't mind," I said, realizing that I could have asked David and Jim at Charles Department Store the same question, but I didn't want to set off a round of rumor, and I hoped I wasn't doing it now.

"I don't know any ladies named Darcy," Barnaby chimed in, "but give me another name. Maybe I'll know someone else."

"Okay. How about Jeff Grusen or Hank Thompson? Do you know them?"

Barnaby frowned. "Are they lobstermen, too?"

"I don't know," I said.

"I don't think they are," he said. "I would know their names if they're lobstermen."

"That's helpful, Barnaby. Thank you."

"Sure. Any time, Mrs. Fletcher. I like to help."

Mara came back from the kitchen with a piece of paper that she handed me. "Cook says he doesn't know any Darcy, but there's a Mrs. Luce has the last trailer up the hill. She's been there a long time. She might know who you're looking for."

I pulled out my wallet, but Mara waved my money away. "On the house."

"How did you know I'd want it in a take-out container?"

"Just figured Nudd's was your next stop," she said, winking.

"Do I get one on the house, too?" Barnaby asked.

"Do I ask you to vacate that stool that you occupy all day, keeping paying customers from having a seat?"

"No, ma'am."

"Then there's your answer," Mara said.

I thanked Barnaby for the information and Mara for the tea and walked along the docks until I reached Nudd's Bait & Tackle, a gathering place for lobstermen, although they were more likely to be there at four in the morning than two in the afternoon. The flyer for Maureen had been tacked up on the front door. Inside, Tim Nudd was stapling pictures of fish to one of the wooden posts in his shop.

"You got a good-size rainbow there, Mrs. Fletcher," he said, tapping the picture of my catch that I'd e-mailed in.

I smiled. "You should have seen the one that got away. It was even bigger."

"The ones that get away are always bigger," he said with a grunt. "But you need the proof to win a prize."

"Are all the derby entries in now?" I asked.

"I'll give 'em another day or two to e-mail in the pictures. With all the hoo-ha in town, some of 'em probably forgot to send 'em."

I scanned all the photos of rainbows, brown trout, brook trout, and lake trout, looking for Maureen's fish, and there it was. I remembered how proud she was to catch that trout and what a terrible price she paid with a bad sunburn that led to her skipping the second morning of the contest and getting lost or kidnapped in the bargain. It was frustrating not to be among the searchers in the fields around Moon Lake, and I imagined it must be a lot worse for Mort, who had to juggle the visiting press while coordinating his responsibilities with the various law enforcement agencies on the scene.

"Do you know Cory Caruthers?" I asked Tim Nudd.

"What do you want with that miserable lumper? I gotta watch my register every time he steps in here."

"Does he step in here often?"

"Not really. Levi Carver's the only one'll give him work. Soft-hearted, Levi is. But only when Caruthers is off the juice; otherwise, he'd tumble overboard hauling in the first lobster pots. Takes after his father. As they say, 'The apple doesn't fall far from the tree.'"

"Has he been in here lately?"

"Let me think on it. He weren't here this mornin', nor this weekend past. Now I remember he said he was fishin' in the derby. Bragged he was gonna win the big money prize." Nudd stepped back and looked up and down at all the fish pictures he'd hung up. "But he ain't sent in one picture. Not gonna win that way."

Chapter Eighteen

I'd stationed myself just inside my front door and peered out though a small window in anticipation of Mort Metzger and Seth Hazlitt arriving. I'd stopped answering my doorbell because a small contingent of press camped across the street regularly sent one of its flock to ring my bell or knock despite the note I'd posted on the door informing them that I had no comment.

Mort was the first to arrive. He pulled his cruiser up to the curb in front of my house at five thirty, exciting the reporters and prompting them into action, surrounding him as he exited his vehicle and flinging questions at him.

Mort waved them away. "I already gave you everything I know at the press conference," he shouted loud enough for me to hear through my closed door. "This is private property. Make sure you stay off the lawn."

He was joined a minute later by Seth Hazlitt, who parked

behind the police car. He carried a white box, which became the subject of more questions from the reporters.

"What are you bringing to Mrs. Fletcher's house?" a woman asked.

"Will she be giving us a statement?" asked another.

"Any progress in finding your wife, Sheriff?" queried another.

I waited until Mort and Seth had reached my door before opening it.

"Maybe we should have come in through the back porch," Seth said.

"No, this is fine," I said, quickly closing the door behind them.

"Vultures," Seth muttered.

"They're just doing their job," I said.

"They won't leave me alone," Mort said. "I'm tired of having to avoid them."

The tension of the past day's events was written all over our sheriff's broad face. His usually bright eyes were lifeless, his complexion gray, and deep lines bracketed his mouth, adding to his sad expression. My heart went out to him, and I renewed my pledge to myself that I would do what I could to lift his spirits over a decent meal and lighter conversation. Was that possible? Probably not, but it seemed the right thing to aim for.

I had already set the kitchen table for three, guessing that Mort would prefer to eat and run than sit down to a more formal meal in the dining room.

"Smells good in here," Seth said, setting the box on the kitchen counter and cutting the red-and-white twine with a pocketknife.

"What do you have there?" Mort asked, hanging his Stetson on a hook and peering over Seth's shoulder.

"Low bush blueberry pie. Charlene Sassi said her brother

dropped off a sack this morning. Right out of the oven. Can't get berries any fresher than these."

"They're kind of small, aren't they?" Mort said.

"Wild blueberries are usually small," I said, taking down a plate to put the pie on.

"Highly concentrated antioxidants," Seth said. "It's healthier, and by the looks of you right now, Sheriff, I'd say you need all the antioxidants you can get."

"You're prescribing blueberry pie for me, Doc?"

"Yes! After Jessica's pot roast. You need some nutrition if you're going to keep the hours you've been working. We don't want Maureen coming home to find you a shadow of your former self."

"I don't need any antioxidants," Mort said. "What I need is for Maureen to come home." He swallowed a lump in his throat and sighed. "I still can't believe this is happening. I see her face all over town everywhere I look. I know they're only trying to help, but it feels like I'm in a bad movie. I keep trying to leave the theater but I'm always pulled back into my seat. I just can't accept it."

"You're in denial," Seth said, "which is natural. Any promising news?"

Mort shook his head and sat at the table, his head bowed. "I'm in constant touch with the wardens and with the state police liaison up at Moon Lake. The dive team came up negative, thank God. They've had three teams searching with dogs. They're doing the best they can, but there's still no trace of Maureen—or that rat Jepson. If he's harmed her—" He brought his large fist down on the table, causing the utensils to bounce.

I looked at Seth before saying in as soothing a voice as I could muster, "Not eating won't solve anything. You need a good, hot meal, Mort. I know it's a cliché but you have to keep up your strength."

"Thanks. I have to admit I am hungry."

"Then you've come to the right place," I said, placing several slices of pot roast on a plate along with potatoes and carrots, and setting a small pitcher of gravy on the table next to the salad bowl. I filled two more plates for Seth and me, and the three of us sat down to dinner.

"Would you like anything to drink?" I asked.

"Just water," Mort replied. "I don't want to lose my edge."

"You're edgy enough as it is," Seth said. "At least let Jessica make you a cup of tea."

Without waiting for Mort's reply, I put up water and we ate quietly until Seth asked, "Anything new come up at your press conference today?"

Mort shrugged. "Nothing new on the search, just more of the same. Every time they *don't* find something I heave a sigh of relief." He took a bite of pot roast and waited to swallow before continuing. "The Caruthers funeral is tomorrow. That promises to be another media circus, and I have to find guys to cover it. My staff is getting spread real thin."

"Why does the funeral need police coverage?" Seth asked.

"Traffic, if nothing else."

"Do you think there will be that many people at Wes Caruthers's funeral?" I asked, pouring hot water over a tea bag and putting the mug next to Mort.

"You never know. There'll be lots of press, though. We'll be needed to handle them, keep them from intruding on Caruthers's family and others mourning his death. It's like feeding the lions at the Central Park Zoo. If you don't give them fresh meat, they howl. Murder is always newsworthy. These guys have nothing else new to write about, so they go wherever Mrs. Phillips goes—and I'm sure she'll be there. A funeral makes great copy, huh? They sure won't have much to see, just an empty hole in the ground."

"Empty?" Seth asked.

"Caruthers has already been cremated," Mort said. "Those were the instructions he left with his secretary. We had no reason to hold the body after the autopsy—no question about how he died—so we released it to the funeral home. They'll be burying his ashes. The FBI will probably have an agent or two there checking the faces in the crowd for Jepson, probably a couple of guys from the state police, too." He shook his head. "They're wasting their time looking for him there." He paused to take another bite of his food. "Jepson may be a foul ball, but he's not stupid enough to come out of the woods to attend the funeral, not when his face has been plastered all over the media and the immediate world is looking for him."

"That *would* be stupid," I said.

Mort looked at his watch. "Maureen's been missing more than twenty-four hours now. I don't know which is worse, thinking that Jepson's got her or that she's lost somewhere in the woods with no food or shelter and maybe being attacked by wild animals. I have nightmares about both. At least if Jepson is holding her hostage, she won't be starving. I figure he knows how to break into a cabin, but then again—" He trailed off and put down his fork.

"I was at Nudd's Bait and Tackle today," I said brightly. "Tim Nudd was hanging all the pictures of the derby entrants. I think Maureen may have caught the biggest rainbow trout. Won't she be pleased when she gets back?"

"You think she'll ever want to fish again?" Mort asked, irony in his voice.

"I'm betting she will," I said.

"Absolutely the best thing," Seth added. "Climb back on the horse after you've fallen off. Get her to teach you how, Mort. That's what you should do. Be nice for you and Maureen to share a hobby like fishing."

I had to hand it to Seth. He'd been against me entering the derby and spending time alone in the cabin on Moon Lake, and had manipulated me into agreeing to have Maureen come along. I knew he felt guilty about that. But he was rising to the occasion and trying to put a positive spin on what was anything but a positive experience for our sheriff.

Mort shook his head slowly. "I know what you guys are trying to do and I thank you," he said, "but the longer Maureen is missing, the smaller our chances are of finding her alive and safe. That's reality. You know they finally found that missing lady who was hiking the Appalachian Trail. Two years went by with no trace and hundreds of people searching for her. *Hundreds!* Her body was found only a half mile off the trail. She was an experienced hiker with knowledge and the appropriate equipment. Maureen is not experienced, and as far as we know, she's only wearing shorts and a T-shirt and rubber clogs. Not much protection against the elements."

"Yes, but remember that it's summertime, Mort," I said. "It's still warm at night. Besides, Maureen told us that she knows how to build a wickiup."

"A what?"

"A wickiup, a rough shelter made from brush."

"Like the Indians used to build," Seth put in.

"Yeah, my wife, the scout," Mort said grimly. Then he sighed. "Thanks for dinner, but I gotta go," he said. "The mayor has been pressuring me to assign someone else to supervise the case and I don't want to give him any reason to criticize me."

"Why would he do that?" Seth asked while I sliced a piece of pie and wrapped it in aluminum foil for Mort to take with him, along with some of the leftover pot roast in a plastic container.

"'Conflict of interest,' he keeps throwing at me. I know the Feds are annoyed I'm still around, but what do they expect me to do, sit on my porch and twiddle my thumbs while the world is out looking for my wife and an escaped murderer? No way! I want to know everything as it happens, and the only way that will take place is if I keep my ear to the radio and monitor daily reports."

"Can't you still do that if you're *not* supervising the case?" I asked.

"Don't you start on me, Mrs. F.," he said. "I gotta do what I gotta do."

"Of course," I said, sorry that I'd questioned his decision.

I tucked a napkin and a plastic knife and fork into the paper bag with the food. "Just make sure you take the time to get enough to eat," I said, handing him the bag.

"And if you think you need something to help you sleep, come see me," Seth said.

Mort's eyes went from mine to Seth's. "I appreciate all you're doing for me. I know Maureen would thank you if she were here."

Seth cleared his throat. "You'll have to get your wife to cook us up a special dinner when she gets back."

"Yeah, I'm sure she'd like that," Mort said, grabbing his Stetson off the hook on my wall. "Thanks for the food—and the friendship." His eyes clouded over with tears and he quickly left, shouting at the reporters to find something better to do as he got behind the wheel and sped away.

"Delicious dinner, but I'm not sure he tasted any of his food," Seth said as I cleared our plates.

"The idea was to feed him, and we did. Would you like a piece of your pie for dessert?"

"Don't mind if I do."

I cut two more wedges of blueberry pie, took a quart of vanilla ice cream from the freezer, and put a dollop on each plate.

"Ayuh, Mrs. Fletcher, you certainly know the right way to serve blueberry pie."

"Seth, I want to ask you something," I said as I set his plate in front of him.

"I'm listening."

"I've been looking into the group of boys who were Darryl Jepson's friends at the time of the robbery and killing at the mini-mart."

"Humph. Didn't think you'd be standing idly by."

"I don't know if learning about them will help find Maureen, but it's given me something to pursue. Like Mort, I don't want to sit on my porch and twiddle my thumbs."

He scooped up a spoonful of pie and ice cream and looked me in the eye. "I suppose you'll be wanting to attend the service for Wes Caruthers."

I feigned surprise. "Why would you think that?"

"We've been friends for a very long time, Jessica. I know the way the mind of J. B. Fletcher works."

"Am I that transparent?" I asked.

"Not a matter of transparency, Jessica. It's just that I've never known you to sit back when there are questions to be answered. Now, I'm still waiting for you to tell me what it is you wanted to ask me."

"Nothing important," I said. "I just wondered whether you'd give me a ride to the funeral tomorrow."

His smile was self-serving. "Happy to," he said. "By the way, is that your phone ringing?"

"My what? Oh, good heavens."

I'd left my cell phone in my shoulder bag across the room, but by the time I found it my caller had hung up.

"Anyone important?" Seth asked.

"It was Mort, but I took too long to answer and his call went to voice mail."

"You're going to listen to his message, aren't you?"

"Of course," I said. "I hope it's good news."

I pressed the button for voice mail and turned on my phone's speaker so we could both hear Mort's message.

"Mrs. F., don't say I didn't tell you, but your buddy has taken off."

There was a lot of noise in the background and I tried to raise the volume even higher.

"What's he mean?" Seth asked.

"I'm not sure," I whispered.

"Did you hear that, Mrs. F.? Your buddy Brian Kinney has flown the coop. He agreed to house arrest. Just in case, I had an ankle bracelet on him with a GPS. I thought he was a late sleeper. The GPS indicated that he hadn't moved for hours. But he must've figured out how to get the bracelet off. I'm on my way there to

pick it up. He's probably gone to meet up with his old buddy Jepson. Another one out in the woods. Wish I'd locked him up." Click.

"Oh, dear," I said, looking at Seth. "This is getting worse and worse."

Chapter Nineteen

ort's prediction about attendance at the graveside service for Wes Caruthers proved accurate, but he wasn't there. In addition to two of Mort's deputies, I spotted Evelyn Phillips, editor of the *Cabot Cove Gazette*, and a gaggle of other reporters who followed her around like goslings.

We gathered with the other mourners around a newly excavated square grave, in the center of which sat a marble box with an engraved pewter plaque affixed to its side. In the crowd of about thirty people was a young man dressed in army camouflage whom I presumed was Cory Caruthers, son of the man whose passing we were marking and who Harvey Richardson said had arrived in town days before his father's murder. I'd never met Cory Caruthers, but how many young men in uniform would be attending the funeral? Besides, he looked like his father, a younger version of course, but with Wes's prominent jaw and high cheekbones.

While the face of the young man in camouflage was familiar only because of his genes, the face of the man standing next to him was one I'd recently come in contact with. It was Hank Thompson, our second-day guide in the fishing derby.

So some of the "five musketeers" Jeff Grusen had spoken of did still keep in touch with each other, was my thought.

"Is that Sharon Bacon over there?" I asked Seth, pointing to the opposite side of the gravesite.

"Believe it is. Didn't she work for the attorney Cyrus O'Connor Sr.?"

"She did, at least until he died. She then worked for Cy's son until he left for greener legal pastures in New York."

"Caruthers had a secretary, didn't he?"

"Several, I believe, although he was known as a loner. The scuttlebutt around town is that he was impossible to work with, irascible, inconsistent—"

"Might as well say it," Seth said. "The man had a reputation in legal circles as a heavy drinker."

"Where did you hear that?"

"Jessica Fletcher is not the only one in town who asks questions."

I raised one brow at my friend and gave him my best skeptical look.

"All right, I'll tell you, but keep it to yourself."

"Of course."

"Judge Jacob Borden is a patient of mine—never mind what for. Anyway, Judge Borden said Caruthers gave the legal profession a black eye with his poor performance, showing up in court unprepared and on too many occasions less than sober."

"That kind of behavior must have lost him a lot of secretaries," I said, "not to mention clients."

"Might've made him some enemies, too," Seth said.

"Maybe Sharon would know," I said, keeping an eye on my old acquaintance. But before I could abandon Seth to make my way to her, the minister opened his Bible and began the service. While he said a prayer for the deceased, I scanned the crowd looking for other faces I might know. Standing on the other side of Cory was a middle-aged woman dressed in a black suit and wearing a hat with a veil covering half her face. I didn't know her, but I did recognize a number of people I'd seen about town but whom I hadn't had occasion to meet formally. Then my eyes settled on a man I could name: John Pelletier, father of Brian Kinney's wife, Alice.

I found it interesting that Pelletier would attend the funeral of the man who'd done such a poor job defending Brian from a murder charge, and I wondered if Alice had objected to her father's presence, or even known about it. His stern face reflected his reputation as a my-way-or-the-highway sort of man. I wanted to speak with him, too, but that would have to wait for the service to end.

The minister read through several pages of *The Book of Common Prayer*, after which the young man I was sure was Cory Caruthers stepped forward, scowled, and threw a rose on the marble box as if trying to knock it over. Without saying a word, he turned his back on the grave and walked away. The woman wearing the hat with the veil touched his shoulder as he pushed through the crowd. She murmured something to him. He shook his head, stormed off without responding, vaulted onto a motorcycle, and was gone.

The minister waited until the growl of the engine faded, then scooped up a shovelful of dirt, tossed it on the casket, and invited others in the crowd to do the same. "Earth to earth, ashes to ashes, dust to dust . . ."

As some mourners came forward, Seth and I stepped back. He glanced down at his watch. "I've got patients coming in less than an hour, Jessica. If you want a ride back with me, we'll have to leave soon."

"Can you give me ten minutes?" I asked.

Seth tapped the face of his watch. "Ten minutes it is."

I threaded my way through the mourners and waved down Sharon Bacon.

"My goodness, Jessica Fletcher," she said, giving me a fast hug, "I haven't seen you since Hector was a pup, as my mother used to say. What brings you to this event? Don't tell me Wes ever did any legal work for you. If he did, you have my condolences."

"I never had occasion to use Wes Caruthers as a lawyer, Sharon, but I am interested in how he died."

"Of course. Silly me. Fodder for the next book, huh?"

"Not really," I replied, although I'd learned early in my writing career that everything I experienced in real life ended up, one way or the other, in my novels. "Do you have some time to talk with me?" I asked.

"Not at the moment. I'm helping Peggy Abelin set up the postfuneral luncheon. We didn't think we'd get a crowd—there was barely anyone at the wake. If all these people show up, it'll put a dent in the budget."

"Peggy Abelin was Wes Caruthers's secretary, wasn't she?"

"Yes, one of many, as it happens. The ones before her didn't last long. Wes was—how can I put it delicately?"

"No need to explain," I said, "but why are *you* involved with Peggy and the funeral?"

"When Wes was found dead, Peggy called and asked me to come out of retirement to help her make sense out of his office."

"It was that bad?"

She raised her eyebrows. "It was a mess, Jessica. The man was such a slob. When I saw his office, I thought it would take years to bring some order to it, but we needn't have worried. The police arrived shortly after and cleaned the place out in no time. After they photographed everything, they walked off with all Wes's files, plus his and Peggy's computers. There was nothing left to sort out except the furniture. The authorities really worked fast, which is to be expected I suppose. After all, they're saying now that Wes Caruthers didn't just drown; he was a murder victim."

"Did the police find anything that might indicate who or what killed him?"

"If they have, I'm not aware of it. All his papers are being stored at the district attorney's office, and I assume that what's on the computers is being examined by the state police's tech experts." She shook her head. "How the DA will get through all of those files without Peggy's help I can't imagine. Anyway, Peggy asked if I'd mind helping out with the postfuneral plans."

"Did Wes leave a will?"

"He should have. He was a lawyer. Not that that means he did anything, right? Do you want me to give you a lift to the luncheon? I have to get there to see how many people walk through the door."

"Thanks. I'd appreciate that."

I saw Seth scowling in my direction. I waved good-bye, pointed at Sharon who waved at him, too, and made a motion as though I were steering a car. Seth nodded that he understood and walked toward where he'd parked. I followed Sharon to her car.

"I thought I was having fun being retired," Sharon said, snapping her seat belt over her ample stomach. "My garden has never looked so good."

I put on my belt as well. "And now that you've been dragged back into business?"

"I love it!" She chuckled. "I suppose I shouldn't say that. The circumstances are far from ideal. Wes was murdered, after all, but I was really looking forward to examining his papers and using my years of experience to pick up on all the legal errors I know he must have made."

"You might want to offer your services to the district attorney's office as a disinterested legal expert."

"Now, there's a plan. I'll get hold of them after I help Peggy empty the office. There's a veterans' group that takes used furniture."

"What about where Wes lived?"

"His apartment? His son, Cory, is staying there. He was at the funeral."

"Yes, I saw him. He seemed to be—well, he seemed more angry than grieving."

"I suppose that having Wes Caruthers as a father might make *any* son angry," she said. "And as they say, the acorn doesn't fall far from the tree."

"What do you mean?"

"Wes was always itching for a fight. Rumor has it that Cory also has a combative personality. He received a less-than-honorable discharge, I'm told, something about getting into brawls on the base where he was stationed."

"I'd heard he'd served in Afghanistan," I said, thinking of what Jeff Grusen had passed along. Was this a case of the Cabot Cove rumor mill making up an excuse for Cory's bad behavior? "He's out of the service?"

"Evidently, but who knows what the truth is? In any case, I don't know how long he'll be able to stay where he is."

"You mean in Wes's apartment?"

Sharon nodded. "It wouldn't surprise me if Wes was far behind in his rent when he died. Peggy said he seemed to let everything slide in the last year or so. Bit of an alcohol problem, you know. She got tired of taking the dunning phone calls and kept threatening to quit, but he prevailed on her to stay. I think she felt sorry for him despite how problematic he could be." She laughed. "He asked her to keep copies of his keys, including to his apartment in case he ever lost them. He was forever losing his keys, according to her."

"So was she the one who let the police into his office and apartment after he was killed?"

"The office, yes, but I think Cory must've opened his apartment for them."

Sharon pulled into the parking lot next to Peppino's, a popular downtown Italian restaurant, and we went inside, where the proprietor's son, Joe, directed us to a private room in which several people milled about waiting for the buffet to be set up.

While Sharon went to take care of details, I found a seat at an empty table set for four. I kept my attention on the doorway in the hope that Cory Caruthers or John Pelletier would arrive, but they weren't among the people who came through. I took out a notebook with the intention of jotting down a few questions to ask when I was joined by FBI Special Agent Ian Perle.

"Mind if I sit with you for a few minutes?" he asked.

"Not at all."

"Funny to find you here," he said, pulling out the chair opposite mine and sitting.

"Why would you find that humorous? I live here. Wes Caruthers was an attorney in town and—"

"A friend of yours?" he asked, interrupting me.

"No, I wouldn't say that he was a friend exactly."

"But he represented friends of yours."

"Yes, he did, but only a few times. Why are *you* here?" I asked.

"I told you we haven't forgotten about Caruthers. With Jepson still on the loose, and with the sheriff's wife missing, we wanted to see who would show up this morning."

"And who did?"

"You would know more about the people who were at the funeral than I would. I was hoping you might share that information with me."

"I didn't see *you* there," I said.

"I stayed in the car. What about the people who were at the grave site? Anyone you found particularly interesting?"

I cocked my head. "Are you by any chance asking for my help, Agent Perle?"

He sat back as though I'd startled him. "Would that be so unusual?"

"I don't know. Does the Bureau allow ordinary citizens to become involved in its cases?"

"All the time. Besides, according to what I've been told you've given assistance to the Bureau before. A former buddy of mine, retired now, said you helped him solve a case where an old and ineffective antimalarial drug was being passed off as new and shipped to Africa."

I smiled. "How is Rick Allcott?"

"Living on his boat and happy as a clam at high tide."

"You're beginning to sound like a real Downeaster."

"Maybe I've been here too long. So, is it a deal? Can I count on you to pass along any pertinent information you uncover?"

"If I can figure out what's pertinent, I'll be happy to," I said.

He smiled. "I'll take that as a yes."

He stood and tossed his business card on the table. "In case you didn't keep the last one," he said.

Sharon arrived just as Perle was leaving.

"Who was that handsome man?" she asked, dropping into the seat Perle had vacated.

"His name is Ian Perle," I said, sliding his card into my bag. "He's with the FBI, part of the team the Bureau has sent."

"I hope he and his team get to the bottom of things." Her shudder was exaggerated. "Can you believe what's happening in sleepy Cabot Cove, Jessica? Bad enough there's an escaped killer on the loose, but poor Maureen Metzger has gone missing. I feel so sorry for her husband. The man must be beside himself." She raised her eyes to the ceiling and shook her head.

"I'm sure this is a difficult time for him," I said, reluctant to talk about Mort. To change the subject, I asked how preparations were going at the restaurant.

"They're a joy to work with," she said, brightening. "They promise to double the pasta dishes if a bigger crowd materializes. Peggy is at the door greeting the 'mourners.' I say that facetiously. I don't know where Cory went. He should be here. After all, he was the deceased's only flesh and blood that we know of. Did you check out the food? Do you think it's enough?" She patted her red Shirley Temple curls. "It won't be good for my waistline if I have to take half of this home."

"You can always send some over to the sheriff's office," I said. "Those guys are working round the clock and don't get much time for a dinner break."

"What a good idea!"

"What's a good idea?" *Gazette* editor Evelyn Phillips asked, pulling out a chair and joining us. She set down her plate of penne alla vodka and draped a napkin over her knees.

"Jessica suggested we send the leftover food to the sheriff's office since they're working extra shifts," Sharon said.

"Nice gesture. Do you mind if I write it up? I can say that Wes Caruthers always worked well with law enforcement and would have appreciated knowing that he'd done something nice for the officers."

"Let me check with Peggy. She's the one running this show," Sharon said, getting up. "Back in a moment."

"Do you think there's really vodka in this?" Evelyn asked.

"Supposed to be," I said, "but they probably cook all the alcohol out of it."

Evelyn scooped up a forkful and savored it. "It's delicious! How are you, Jessica? You've been dodging my calls."

"I'm fine, Evelyn. Thanks for asking."

She grunted as she took another taste of the pasta. "You're not denying that you've been avoiding me, are you?"

"I've said 'No comment' to all press inquiries," I replied, "but I still have reporters hanging out across the street from my house."

"Why so closemouthed? Did you have a fight with Maureen before she took off?"

I looked at her incredulously. "A fight with Maureen? Of course not. Why would you even think such a thing? In fact, I wanted to stay behind and keep her company Sunday morning, but she insisted I go out fishing with the guide."

"Bet you're sorry now."

"Very."

"Why didn't you stay with her?"

"Why should I have? Maureen reminded me that she was a strong, capable woman, which she is, and was perfectly content staying alone for a few hours."

"But then she was gone when you got back."

"Unfortunately."

"How did that make you feel?"

"How would you feel, Evelyn, if a friend staying with you went missing?"

"I would be worried that she was captured by a convicted murderer."

"Then you don't need to ask me that question."

"Don't get your back up, Jessica. It's not my fault Maureen is missing, nor is it my fault an escaped killer is roaming the woods around Cabot Cove. It *would* be my fault, however, if I ignored the biggest story that ever landed in my lap. The *Gazette*'s readers deserve to learn everything that's going on. Do you know that there are some people in town cowering in their homes, afraid to go out to buy a quart of milk in case they run into Jepson?"

"Don't you think that reaction is a little extreme?"

"*I* think it's nuts, but what I think is irrelevant. I'm just reporting on what's happening around me. The state is stopping every car on the roads out of town and making them pop open their trunks. Some people who have been inconvenienced have said that's nuts, but the troopers are acting out of an abundance of caution. If they happen to open a trunk in which Maureen Metzger is tied up and with duct tape over her mouth, I'll be the first in line to cheer them."

"So will I," I said, wincing at the image.

"Did Agent Perle ask you to assist the FBI with their investigation?"

I'd been uneasy that Evelyn might have seen Perle talking with me.

"He was just passing along greetings from a mutual friend," I said, stretching the truth.

"Uh-huh." She ran the side of her fork around the plate to catch every bit of the pasta sauce, closed her eyes as she finished the dish, and hummed her approval. "I wish I could cook like that, but my mother was more the type to make macaroni and cheese from a box, a far cry from this."

"You could learn," I said.

"I'll leave that to Maureen. Maybe I can convince her to give me some cooking lessons when she gets home."

"I'm sure she'll be happy to."

"Oh, by the way, did you see that John Pelletier was at the funeral today? I asked him if he was a friend of Caruthers's, but he brushed me off."

"I understand he's a gruff individual," I said.

"Not if you're buying a Mercedes," Evelyn said. "Then he turns into Mr. Charm. Not that I'd know this firsthand, of course, but it's nice to know he has that ability."

Sharon rejoined us and said Peggy Abelin was delighted to have Evelyn write about the family of Wes Caruthers donating food to the sheriff's office. "She said Wes could use all the positive publicity he could get. Not that he'll know, poor soul. Peggy asked if you'd give Cory credit even though he's not here to confirm the donation."

"No problem," Evelyn said. "I think I'll talk with Peggy now. It's nice to have someone welcome my questions." She leaned over and patted my arm. "Chin up. We'll get her back."

I felt my eyes well up but managed a nod.

"What was that all about?" Sharon asked.

"Maureen Metzger," I said, clearing the lump from my throat. "Evelyn's been asking me for a statement and I've been ducking her calls."

"Oh, I'm sorry. I wouldn't have left you alone at the table with her had I known."

"No apologies necessary," I said. "Evelyn is a friend of long standing, and we understand each other. We're both worried about Maureen and looking to learn as much as we can. We just address it in different ways."

"Different missions, huh?"

"Exactly," I said, managing a smile. "I'll have to remember to use that phrase the next time Evelyn pressures me for information."

Sharon beamed. "Cy Senior used to say I had a way of getting to the heart of a controversy. What a wonderful man he was, and as honest a lawyer as you'll ever meet. I hope you'll let me know if I can help."

"You *can* help," I said, lowering my voice. "May I talk with you privately later?"

She looked at her watch. "You really need to talk with Peggy, and she could use a break around now. Let me introduce you."

Peggy Abelin sagged against the side door of Peppino's, the strain of the day's events showing in her face.

"Do we still have enough food?" she asked Sharon when the two of us approached.

"We'll be eating penne alla vodka till the cows come home," her friend replied. "Have you met Jessica Fletcher? She was a good friend of my late boss, Cy O'Connor."

"I certainly know your name," Peggy said, extending her hand. She was a neatly dressed small lady with a cap of brown curls, wearing a navy blue suit and no-nonsense black lace-up shoes. She reminded me in both looks and demeanor of a very strict math teacher I once knew who brooked no misconduct in her classroom. I had both admired and feared her, and I wondered if Peggy Abelin had the same effect on Wes Caruthers's clients.

"Jessica has some questions for you and I thought you wouldn't mind taking a break from staffing the door to talk," Sharon said to her.

"Not only don't I mind, Sharon, I'm desperate to sit down. I'm starving. Didn't have time for my oatmeal and blueberries this morning and I'm fading fast."

"Why don't I get you both a nice big portion of the penne

before we give the rest of it away? There's a little table by the kitchen door where no one will disturb you, and I won't tell anyone you're there."

Peggy and I did as instructed, happy to put Sharon in charge of our lunch. I was also grateful to be away from Evelyn's prying eyes, not to mention the curiosity of Agent Perle.

"So, did you know my poor boss?" Peggy asked as we slid into the seats of the table Sharon had pointed out.

"Perhaps more by reputation than personally," I said.

She chuckled. "Oh, dear, that couldn't be good."

"How long did you work for Wes?" I asked.

"On and off for twenty years."

I sat back surprised. "I didn't realize you were his secretary for that long."

"Don't let me mislead you," she said, as Sharon placed two bowls of pasta at our places with a cheery *"Buon appetito."*

We waited for Sharon to leave before Peggy resumed her story.

"You were saying you didn't want to mislead me," I reminded her.

"I worked for him for twenty years, but it wasn't twenty years of continuous work. He must have fired me a dozen times."

"But he kept hiring you back?"

"I was the one he always came crawling to when he offended yet another secretary who quit over his disorganization, foul language, or irresponsibility, or found it embarrassing to have to bail him out of jail after a drunken brawl."

"That's quite a list of offenses," I said.

"You would think a lawyer would know how to talk himself

out of a tricky situation, but when Wes was in his cups, he lost whatever skills he ever had, if he ever had them."

"And you were willing to put up with his bad behavior?"

"I thought of myself like the guy who cleans up after the elephant in the circus parade."

"That sounds horrible."

"Someone has to do it. And don't you worry, Jessica. I charged him for it. When he couldn't get anyone else to come in, he always returned to me."

"And you never turned him down."

"Not at those prices. I'm sorry if I'm coming off as grasping, but I could make more money rescuing Wes than at any other job in town. He was willing to pay my salary until he sobered up enough to realize he could get another secretary for a lot less. Then he would fire me with great flourish and we'd start the process all over again. It hasn't been a bad way to make a living, if a little uncertain."

"What exactly did you do for him as a secretary?"

"Mostly damage control, plus the usual office duties: backing up the files, keeping the books, the calendar, renewing his license, paying the bills when there was any money."

"How did he earn any money if he couldn't stay sober?"

"He had periods of sobriety, especially when he was broke. Most of the other lawyers in town try to get out of assigned cases, but Wes welcomed them and a few of the judges would throw cases his way for old times' sake."

"Had you backed up his files last Friday?" I asked.

"It's automatic. All his peripherals are synced."

"Does that mean you could gain access to what was in his files, if you needed to?"

"I suppose I could. Not the hard copies, of course. The police took those."

"Could you find out for me who his last phone calls were to or from?"

"Sure, but it will take a little while."

"Do you happen to remember if he had any appointments scheduled for the day he died?"

Peggy shook her head. "He didn't. He'd gotten in a few checks and decided to take the morning off to celebrate his good luck by fishing. He'd even signed up for the derby the next day."

"And where were you at the time?"

"At the bank depositing the money. I told Sheriff Metzger this."

"I'm sure you have," I said.

She chuckled again. "I wanted to make sure the funds cleared so I could write a check to myself and get Wes to sign it. Ironic, huh? And now I'm arranging all this for no pay."

"Do you think Wes could have been drunk the morning he was killed?"

"If he wasn't, he was probably planning to correct that situation later in the day."

"Do you happen to recall who paid Wes, whose checks you were depositing?"

"Oh, sure. That would have been Pelletier Motors. They sent in a check every month."

"Had Wes bought a car from them?"

"Not that I know of."

"Did he do legal work for the company?"

"Not to my knowledge."

"How do you explain the payments, then?"

"I figured Pelletier must have been paying Wes for some past service that happened when I wasn't his secretary. I never really knew what. But now that Wes is dead, I suppose it doesn't really matter anymore."

But it mattered to me.

Chapter Twenty

After lunch with Peggy, I lingered among the guests at the postfuneral luncheon hoping to see Hank Thompson, or the lady who had spoken to Cory Caruthers, or the son himself, but most of the faces were unfamiliar. At least I had an idea why John Pelletier had been at the funeral. He'd had some kind of relationship with Wes, the exact nature of which it would be interesting to know. With not a lot else to show for my time, I called Dimitri's Taxi Service and waited outside Peppino's to be picked up.

"Home, Mrs. Fletcher?" my driver asked.

"Not at the moment," I replied. "You know that trailer park on the way out of town?"

"You mean the one calling itself Ocean Heights Mobile Homes?"

"That sounds right," I said. "Please take me there."

"Do you have an address? There's gotta be fifty or sixty trailer homes up there."

"Is there a management or rental office?"

"There should be."

"Let's start with that."

A sign at the entrance to Ocean Heights Mobile Homes indicated there was no vacancy. Looking for anyone who might guide us to a manager's office, we drove up and down the winding lanes of neatly kept ranch-style trailers, most of them painted white and each with its small garden and narrow porch leading up to the side entrance. The park wasn't as attractive as other neighborhoods in Cabot Cove, nor was it the vision of squalor that Brian had painted when he'd told me the story of his father sending him for a bottle of gin. The roads were nicely paved and there was a little stream that ran along one side of the property, bordered by willow trees and the occasional park bench. Here and there residents had put up wind chimes or birdhouses or garden gnomes to personalize a space identical to the one next door except for the house address painted in large black numbers on the wall of the short end.

As we approached a section of wider homes, I remembered that Mara's cook lived here. He had said to look for the last trailer up the hill owned by Mrs. Luce, who was a longtime resident.

I had the driver let me out at a bus stop next to an empty lot—apparent not only by its lack of a home but by its unmown state—and arranged for him to meet me at the same spot when I called to be picked up.

The day was warm and still, and I was grateful to have an opportunity to walk after the funeral and sitting at the luncheon.

The trailer park was arranged so that each home had a driveway long enough for one car in front. There were cars in many of the driveways, and strains of music or sounds from television shows were audible. I ambled by but no one was outside working in their garden or sitting in a rocker on the porch, and I hesitated to knock at a stranger's door.

The wider homes were on slightly larger lots and were located uphill from their narrower neighbors. I wondered if this was a less-than-subtle ranking of the residents. The road through this section doubled back on itself as it climbed the hill, and I was grateful when it ended in a circular cul-de-sac where I could catch my breath. Another bus stop was located at the turnaround, and I happily sank down on the bench and drew a bottle of water from my bag. I also checked my cell phone, but there was no update to the message Mort had left me the day before.

There were three houses that could qualify as the "last one up the hill," two of them painted white, the third a soft blue. As I stood making up my mind which to approach first, a car pulled into one of the driveways, and an elderly lady got out, leaning on a cane. She was dressed all in black and I wondered if she might have been at the funeral that morning.

I hurried over, calling out "Excuse me" and waving.

She looked up from her bag, in which she had been rummaging for her keys, and waited, keys in hand, until I reached her.

"Yes? Can I help you?" she asked.

"I hope you can," I said. "I'm Jessica Fletcher and I'm looking for Mrs. Luce. Would you happen to be she?"

She gave a bark of a laugh. "'Would you happen to be *she*,'" she mimicked. "You sound like an English teacher. Bet you were one, right?"

"As a matter of fact, I *was* an English teacher at one time."

"I can always tell. Yessiree."

I persevered. "And are you Mrs. Luce?" I repeated.

She laughed again. "Clear as day you've never met her or you wouldn't ask. What do you want her for?"

"Someone suggested I speak with her since she's lived here a while and might know of others who lived here years ago."

"Well, I certainly can't help you there. I only moved in six months ago. Nice enough place. Better than an old-age home. The neighbors keep to themselves. I'd prefer if they were a little friendlier but that's the way it always is with newcomers, isn't it? You want a cup of coffee while you wait for her?"

"Which house is hers?"

"The blue one, of course."

"Why 'of course'?"

"Because it's one of the original ones. She was grandfathered in under the old rules when the new owners decreed every house be painted white. Stubborn thing she is. I like her."

"How do you know she's not home now?" I asked as I followed the lady who had yet to give me her name up the walkway to her porch.

"Ain't it obvious? No car in the driveway. Boy, you'd make a terrible detective, Jessica."

"I guess I would," I replied, hiding a smile. "May I ask your name?"

"Didn't I give it to you?"

"Not yet."

"I'm Harriet Bliss," she said, putting her key in the lock and pushing open the door. "Call me Harriet. Mr. Bliss passed on some years ago, but it's not so bad. I can do what I want now. Put your bag over there," she said pointing at a bench with an embroidered cushion of flowers and butterflies. "Made that cushion myself, from a kit, of course. Took me forever, but I'm very proud that I finished it."

"It's lovely," I said, glancing out her window to the driveway of the blue house.

"Don't fret now. I'll leave a message on her machine to come collect you when she gets in."

"Thank you," I said, following her to a tiny kitchen with a built-in booth opposite the sink and stove.

She waved me into the booth. "Coffee or tea?" she asked putting up a kettle of water.

"Tea, please."

"Glad you said that. I only have instant coffee. Dreadful stuff, but my nephew must have his coffee when he comes to visit." She picked up a wall phone and dialed a number. "Dee? I've got a friend of yours over here. Step in when you get back."

"I'm not really a friend of hers," I said when she'd hung up.

"Oh, I know that, but she's hardly likely to come over if I say, 'There's a stranger here to see you.' Sounds like someone from the police. You're not from the police, are you?"

"No, I'm not," I said, smiling.

"Didn't think so. Pegged you as an English teacher right away, didn't I?"

"You did. Is 'Dee' Mrs. Luce's first name?"

"Yup! Short for Dorothy. I don't have a nickname. Never did."

"Have you lived in Cabot Cove for a long time, Harriet?" I asked.

"Told you I only moved in six months ago. Are you having problems with your memory?"

"I remember what you said, but you could have lived elsewhere in town before relocating here."

"Could've, but didn't. We lived inland. Ran a little bed-and-breakfast over in Bridgeton. Good three-season place. Got the hunters and fishermen in the summer, the leaf peepers in the fall, and the skiers and dogsledders in the winter. Only time I got to rest was the spring, mud season. Course I got lots of time to rest now."

"Are you looking for things to do?" I asked. "Because our senior center offers lots of activities and courses."

"Do I look that old to you?" she asked indignantly.

"They have a gym and a pool," I said, wondering what topic of conversation was not going to set her off. "I take some of their classes."

Thankfully, the whistle of the kettle interrupted us, and I stole a glance out the window while Harriet fussed with the tea bags and mugs.

"So where do you live, Jessica?" Harriet said, putting the mugs on the table. "You take lemon? If you do, you're out of luck. I don't have any."

"This is fine as it is," I said, wondering how soon I could politely take my leave.

"Did you hear me? Where do *you* live?"

"I have a house on Candlewood Lane, not too far from downtown."

"'Not too far from downtown,'" she echoed. "Is that important?"

"It is for me. I don't drive, so—"

"You don't drive?" She let out a cackle. "I'm ninety-two and I drive. What's wrong with you?"

"It's a long story why I never learned to drive, but I do fly a plane, so in a sense, it makes up for it."

"Well, aren't you a surprise."

There was a knock at the door and I heaved a sigh of relief as Harriet went to answer it. I slipped out of the booth, took a sip of my tea, and rinsed my mug in her sink.

"Was that you who left me a message, Harriet?" a voice at the door said.

"Course it was me. Who'd you think it was?"

I lifted my shoulder bag from the bench, came up behind Harriet, and gave Mrs. Luce a big smile. "Your neighbor has been so hospitable," I said to her. Turning to my hostess, I added, "I'm very grateful, Harriet. Thanks so much." I squeezed around her to step out on the porch. "I left the mug in your sink. I hope that's okay."

"Of course, it's okay. Where else would it go?"

I followed Mrs. Luce down the steps and across the lawn toward her house, pausing only to look back and wave good-bye to Harriet, who was watching us closely.

"And just who are you?" Mrs. Luce asked under her breath.

"My name is Jessica Fletcher. I was hoping to speak with you for a few minutes. I won't keep you long."

"I trust you don't mind if we sit at my picnic table in the backyard. I've heard your name but I don't really know you and, unlike my neighbor, would prefer not to invite a stranger into my house."

"I understand," I said. "I'll go anywhere convenient for you."

We settled at a round metal table at the rear of her property overlooking the stream.

"You look familiar," she said, cocking her head. "Why?"

"Perhaps because we were both at Wes Caruthers's funeral this morning."

She shrugged. "That must be it."

Dorothy Luce was a much younger woman than I had anticipated, in her early fifties at the most. She was still dressed in the black suit she'd worn to the graveside services but was no longer wearing the hat with the veil.

"I saw you talk—or try to talk," I amended, "to Cory Caruthers. Is he related to you?"

"No. I've just known him a long time, that's all."

"And do you know his other friends as well?"

"Such as?"

"Such as Hank Thompson, Brian Kinney, Darryl Jepson." I let the last name linger in the air.

"I'm not sure I want to answer your questions, Mrs. Fletcher. What is your interest in this matter? Are you a private investigator?"

"I'm a private citizen and a good friend of Maureen Metzger. She was my guest at Moon Lake this past weekend. Maureen is Sheriff Metzger's wife. She disappeared and I think Darryl Jepson may be holding her hostage. I'm simply trying to find people with a connection to him so I can get him a message."

"And you think I have a connection?"

"I don't know; do you?"

Her eyes dropped to her fingers, where she twisted a ring that she wore. "What message did you want to pass along?"

"I want him to know that I'm willing to negotiate a settlement, that I'll serve as a messenger—a go-between, if you will—between him and the authorities. I don't want him to get hurt, nor do I want my friend Maureen to be hurt. I'll gladly trade places with her. He can hold me hostage while we're trying to settle this peacefully."

"Why come to me?"

"I know that Darryl spent a lot of time with his aunt Darcy, who lived in this trailer park."

"Who told you that?"

"Jeff Grusen."

She gave a soft laugh. "You should have been a detective, Mrs. Fletcher."

"Please call me Jessica."

"All right, Jessica. You're looking for Darryl's aunt Darcy. What else did Jeff tell you?"

"I know the names of all the five musketeers and have been trying to find one who knows where Darryl may have gone to hide out."

She shook head vehemently. "I don't know where he's hiding out."

"So you are Darryl's aunt Darcy?"

She sighed. "I go by Dee now."

"But you are his aunt?"

"We haven't seen each other in years. Once he got sent away, he cut all ties."

"Even so, he would recognize your name and hopefully still holds some affection for you."

She gave a soft snort. "I wouldn't count on that. What did you think I could do to help you?"

"I hoped you could give me a message that I could pass along to him so he would trust me enough to allow me to see for myself that Maureen is safe. She was badly sunburned the last time I saw her and not feeling well. If he's been keeping her on the run, she must be worn out, exhausted, sick, in danger of collapsing."

"If she collapsed, he'd have to let her go."

"Assuming he didn't kill her."

She winced at my words.

"Weak, left alone in the forest, lost. That would not be an improvement in Maureen's condition," I said. "She's not familiar with the woods around Moon Lake, hasn't been exploring them since she was a child as he has, doesn't know how to break into a cabin if she could even find one. She could die of exposure or from an animal bite or starve to death. Do you want her death on your conscience? I don't want it on mine."

"What do you want me to do?"

"Just give me a message to pass along and something of yours he would recognize to prove it came from you."

She sighed heavily. "The police have already asked me questions about Darryl, where he might have gone, things like that."

"I wasn't aware of that," I said.

"I told them the same thing I'm telling you. I haven't seen Darryl since he was sent to prison. I have no idea where he might be. I was shocked when I heard about his escape. It was foolish of him to do that, but he was always prone to do foolish things."

As she reflected, her expression changed. This was not easy for her.

"You have to understand, Jessica, Darryl was basically a good kid. Oh, he and his buddies all got into trouble, but nothing terrible. Then he hit puberty and this dreadful thing happened to him." She began to cry. "He couldn't stand it. He would shower three times a day, try covering up the odor with cologne, which only made it worse. None of the doctors could help him.

One of them actually told him he was imagining it. But at school, all the kids teased him, called him Stinky, even his best friends, but at least they didn't abandon him, until . . ."

"The mini-mart."

"They all promised to be there and only one of them showed up," she said, shaking her head. "They never came to the trial to support him either."

"They were planning to steal food for a picnic," I reminded her, "so it wasn't as if they were innocently shopping."

"That's what the police said. I'm not sure. Darryl had enough money to pay."

"The security tape showed him putting items in his pocket, Dee."

"I know. But even so, I certainly don't think he planned to kill for them. Olberman, the grocer, had been vicious in his name-calling. Don't ever let anyone tell you that names don't hurt. Sometimes they're worse than a beating. He threatened to shoot Darryl if he didn't leave, said he was 'stinkin' up the joint,' told him his money was no good there, that he didn't even want to touch a bill that Darryl had held in his fingers."

"You said he threatened to shoot him. Was the grocer armed?"

"I know that he had a gun, only I couldn't say if he pointed it at Darryl."

"It's important information if your nephew thought he was being threatened."

"Well, it's too late now. It was Darryl's knife that killed him. There wasn't ever any doubt of that. Darryl told me later he threw it hoping to disarm him. Instead, he wounded him badly and Olberman died later from loss of blood. Darryl and his stupid knives. He loved those knives, thought he was a pirate in some movie, like Errol Flynn, somebody like that. Just a kid's imagination running wild."

"It's a tragic story," I said.

She nodded sadly, dabbing her eyes with a tissue. Then she looked around warily. "Come inside. I don't want to give the neighbors anything more to gossip about."

Too late, I thought. I could imagine Harriet Bliss embroidering whatever she'd heard, much as she had embroidered the cushion on her bench.

Dee's mobile home was painted inside with the same soft blue color that had been used on her outside walls. On one side of the main room she had a yellow linen sofa across from a faux fireplace with framed photos and knickknacks on the mantel. Those were the only feminine touches. Everywhere else sports equipment hung on or leaned against the walls: snowshoes, skis, fishing rods, nets. It looked to me as if she was hoping her nephew would return.

After retrieving a box of stationery, she sat at her kitchen table, a round one rather than a booth like Harriet's, and asked me what she should write. "You're a famous writer," she said. "I remember now seeing your picture and hearing stories about you."

"I don't think you need my help to write a note to your nephew. Write whatever's in your heart."

I listened as her pen scratched on the paper.

When she was finished, she folded the sheet, tucked it in an envelope, and sealed it. "It's private. Is that okay?"

"I don't have to know what's in it, I just need something to prove to him that it's from you."

She handed me the envelope, walked to the fireplace, and took something from the mantel. "This is his lucky rock."

She placed a piece of smoky quartz in my palm.

"Please don't lose it. It means a lot to him. He picked it up on the last good day he spent with his father."

"Do you mind telling me what happened to his parents?"

"I'm ashamed to say his mother, my sister, left when Darryl was a baby. His father died from colon cancer when he was ten. That was before Darryl contracted that terrible smelly condition. My brother-in-law was a good guy, but a real macho type. I don't know how he would have reacted to Darryl's disease. I'm almost happy he died before Darryl was diagnosed. I did the best I could, but it was a lot to bear for a boy. Thank goodness he had his friends. I think they saved his life more than once, even if they deserted him in the end."

I zipped up Dee's letter and Darryl's rock in a side compartment of my bag, and thanked her. When I got outside, I realized my phone was vibrating. I'd forgotten to turn up the volume.

Alice had called a half hour earlier, probably when I'd been sipping tea with Harriet Bliss. She hadn't left a message. I returned the call.

"Thank goodness, it's you," Helen said when she answered my call. "That child is driving me and herself crazy, and the baby has been whining all afternoon. You know children pick up on their parents' moods, and Alice has been beside herself all day."

"What's wrong?" I asked.

"You tell me. It's another bit of craziness messing up my well-ordered routine. She left home when she got married; now she's back, giving me orders, no regard for my schedule. I like taking care of the baby, but Alice, she can do for herself, pregnancy or no. I'm a housekeeper, not a lady's maid."

"You said another bit of craziness. What was the first one?"

"Thought we had a break-in here on Friday morning."

"What made you think that?"

"I come home from shopping and I hear someone in the laundry room. I'm holding the phone to dial nine-one-one, and when I push open the laundry room door, there he is in his unmentionables, feeding his clothes into the washer."

"Who?"

"Mr. Pelletier. I've been doing his laundry for twenty-two years. He never complained about my washing before. Now all of a sudden, he wants to do his own laundry."

"Did you ask why?"

"Said he spilled something on himself and didn't trust me to get it all out. Didn't trust me! He never told me that before. I told him I'd been doing his laundry for twenty-two years and he never had cause to complain before. He told me to mind my own business. If he wanted to do his own laundry, he would, and I had nothing to say about that. I was this close to telling him if he wanted to do his own laundry, he could do his everything else, too, but I didn't."

"That was probably wise," I said. "It's best not to make an important decision when you're angry."

"Well, I'm not sure if I made the right decision or not. The next night Alice moves back home with the baby. I thought maybe she and Brian are having problems, but no, she says Brian wants *me* to keep an eye on her while she was so sick to her stomach and trying to take care of a three-year-old at the same time. So I guess I have some value, after all."

"Of course you do, Helen."

"Except, I can't keep up with Alice's moods. Today, she is carrying on hysterically. Who knows what to expect next?"

"What is she upset about?"

"Who knows? I like it nice and quiet. I swear I'm going to retire if this keeps up. Excuse me while I go distract that little girl. Now where did that blue-face doll get to?" She raised her voice. "Alice! Pick up the phone. It's Mrs. Fletcher."

Alice came on the line. She was at the edge of hysteria. "Oh, Mrs. Fletcher. I can't thank you enough for calling me back. I know I was rude to you the other day. I'm so sorry. So sorry."

"I didn't think you were rude."

"And after you being so nice and bringing me the acupressure bands."

"Are they helping you?"

"Oh, yes, but that's not why I called. I really need your help. Brian needs your help. He's in such trouble. I'm afraid he's going to get shot."

"Shot! Why would he get shot?"

"The police are after him. He got that ridiculous ankle bracelet off. I don't know what he was thinking. He's going to get himself killed."

"Slow down," I said. "Let's take this one step at a time. Mort is not going to shoot Brian when he finds him."

"But he'll arrest him."

"Probably, but we can deal with that."

"Oh, no. They're already convinced he was guilty the first time, and they'll send him back to prison. And what will happen to Emma and our infant son with their father in prison? I don't want to be a widow. What will happen to me?"

"No one wants to be a widow, Alice, but you're exaggerating how things will turn out."

"I can't live with my father forever. Do you know what a horrible man he is?"

"Alice! Calm down."

"I'm trying. I'm trying. I'm okay now, I think."

"Good. This is what I want you to do."

Chapter Twenty-one

I remembered from Brian's story about the day of the mini-mart robbery that the trailer park known as Ocean View Mobile Homes—where he lived with his father—was not too far from the neighborhood where Alice grew up and where she was staying once again with her father. I hadn't realized there was still a difficult relationship between John Pelletier and his daughter, but it shouldn't have surprised me. He had tried to come between Alice and Brian before, and still didn't approve of their marriage, notwithstanding the beautiful granddaughter he'd gained and the soon-to-be-born grandson. If Alice was resentful, I could only imagine how irritated Brian was with a man who not only never trusted him but still lobbied against him.

After I assured myself that Alice was composed enough to drive, I gave her instructions on where to pick me up and called the taxi company informing them I wouldn't need a ride home.

I made my way downhill to the bus stop by the empty lot and waited only a few minutes before Alice arrived.

"Helen promised to take care of Emma. I think she was relieved to get me out of the house," Alice said when I climbed into the front seat next to her. "I'm sorry I was so hysterical when you called. It's just that—"

"I understand, but let's not go over that again." I didn't want her to work herself into another frenzy.

"When I spoke with Brian yesterday, I should have known that something was up. He was so guilty about Mrs. Metzger, blamed himself for her sunburn, took responsibility for her capture."

I snapped on my seat belt. "So he's convinced that Jepson has Maureen?"

"He said, if you were able to smell him, he had to have been there, and if he was there, that's probably how Mrs. Metzger disappeared. There was no point in simply stealing food. Darryl knows how to hunt and fish. They've been doing it since they were kids. But if he needed security, a way to ensure that they'd let him escape, having her as a hostage was going to be his bargaining chip. Brian was afraid Darryl wouldn't have enough patience with her, might have picked up some bad habits in prison. Brian was frustrated not being able to help. He kept saying, 'They're locking up their best searcher.'"

"If we want to find Brian before Mort or any of the other authorities do," I said, "we need to figure out where he might have gone."

"And you think he might have left a message for me at the house?"

"For you or for someone else."

"Someone else? Who else would he leave a message for?"

"I don't have the answer to that, but I suggest that we look around. Maybe you'll recognize something different or find some indication of where he intended to search. I can't go to your house by myself. I have no legitimate reason to be there. But you do."

The small home that Alice and Brian shared with their daughter, Emma, was a typical two-story backwoods camp with wood siding and a metal roof, not far from the district office of the Maine Department of Inland Fisheries and Wildlife. When Alice pulled up, there was still yellow crime scene tape strung across their driveway, but she drove right through it, her lips pressed together in anger.

I put my hand on her arm before she could release her seat belt. "You have to control your emotions if we're to get anything accomplished. No storming around the house, no shock at whatever condition the police may have left it in. Are we clear?"

Alice took in a deep breath and nodded.

"I wouldn't be surprised if there were remnants of finger-printing powder left on doorways and cabinet doors," I said. "They may have left drawers open or emptied closets. I don't know. Just don't be angry at anything you find. Beds can be remade. Everything can be cleaned up. What's important today is that you think like Brian. You know him better than anyone, so put yourself in his place. That's what you need to do."

Alice dashed away a tear from under her eye and said, "I'll be okay. I promise."

The house was not as bad as I'd anticipated. If Mort and his deputies had looked for Jepson's prints, it wasn't obvious. There were closet doors ajar, but again I didn't know if they'd been left open by Brian or by an investigating officer.

Alice skipped through the house, quickly checking each bedroom and the bathroom upstairs before joining me in the living room, her eyes roaming over the bookcase.

"It all looks all right," she said. "If they were looking for something, I don't know what it might be."

"Take a look in the kitchen cabinets," I suggested. "Have things been moved around?"

She did as instructed and clucked her tongue at the disarray on some of her shelves. "This could just as easily be Brian as someone else," she said. "He's not exactly the neatest when he's cooking." She rejoined me on the brown corduroy couch, which sat across from a small television perched on a table. "I don't know what I'm looking for, do you?"

"Not yet," I said, "but if Brian were to take off searching for Darryl Jepson, what would he be likely to take?"

"His cell phone? His compass. A few days' rations and water. An emergency kit. Maps."

"Can you look and see if any of those things are missing?"

Alice went to sit in the rolling chair next to the pine desk adjacent to the bookcase. She opened the drawers, one by one. Swiveling in the chair, her eyes went to the series of pegs by the back door, which held several light jackets. "His backpack is gone."

"Where does he keep the records for his business?" I asked.

"Right here," she replied, patting the top of the desk.

"Is everything where it should be?"

"I guess."

"Where would Brian keep maps?"

"Most of them are in the car, and there are two hanging in the baby's room."

"In Emma's room? That's unusual."

"We spent all our money on baby furniture and didn't have any left over for cute pictures, so Brian suggested we hang the maps. He loves the woods and he wanted Emma to love them, too. He points out all the roads and where the lakes are to her before she falls asleep. She's getting to be a good little map reader."

"May I see them?"

"Sure."

The bedrooms upstairs were small, but cheerful. In Alice and Brian's room there was just a bed with a colorful comforter, dresser, and empty cradle awaiting its next occupant. Emma's space, however, was filled with toys and books, and her own crayon drawings were tacked up on a bulletin board. On the wall over her dresser, which had been converted from a baby's changing table, was a colorful tourist map of Cabot Cove and the wilderness area surrounding our town.

I walked over to admire the map, tracing my finger over Moon Lake and Martha's Pond, where Maureen and I had fished with Brian's guidance. I skimmed my fingers over the map again, feeling a bump. "There's something tucked behind here," I said.

"What are you doing?" Alice asked as I pulled out a corner pushpin that affixed the map to the wall. "It took me forever to get that hanging straight."

"It will still hang straight," I said, sliding my hand behind the map and slowly pulling out a folded topographical map similar to the one I'd seen Mort and the wardens poring over when we began the search for Maureen. "Has this always been here?" I asked.

"I—I don't believe so."

"Let's go downstairs and take a look at it."

Alice and I unfolded the large map and spread it out over the coffee table in front of the sofa. Brian or someone else had circled areas several miles north of Mayor Shevlin's cabins. The circles made a crooked path going deeper and deeper into the wilderness areas.

"This could be where Brian is planning to search," I said, refolding the map.

"Maybe, but how would he get up there? Those places are more than ten miles from here and I have the car. We only have one."

"Could Brian have called someone to pick him up?"

"I guess, but I don't know who."

"Of course you do," I said, feeling myself begin to lose patience. "Brian is not without friends. This is not a time to cover up, Alice. If you truly believe Brian's life is in danger—and I do believe that Maureen's is, too—we need to act quickly. Please give me the names of everyone Brian might conceivably have called for assistance."

"I know you think I'm hiding information, but really, we live a very quiet life."

"You never share dinner with another couple? You don't know anyone with children Emma's age? I'm finding this hard to believe, Alice. You grew up here. Are you telling me you don't have any friends?"

She shook her head. "Not really. My father was always over-protective. Still is."

"You've never met Brian's colleagues in the guide business?"

Alice hung her head. "Well, I guess there's Hank. He's another one of the guides."

"Hank Thompson?"

She nodded; her expression was unhappy.

"What about Jeff Grusen? Is Brian ever in touch with him?"

She looked up, surprised. "Only when he goes to put gas in the car."

"Uh-huh. What about Cory Caruthers?"

Alice's voice was very soft when she said, "I thought he was away in the army." She began to chew on her lip.

I knew I was pressing her about the five musketeers, but she had denied knowing any of Brian's old friends and yet recognized each name as I raised it.

"Unless Brian plans to hitchhike north to the places on this map," I said, holding it up, "he was expecting someone to take him there or meet him along the way. There are dozens of wardens and troopers all over the woods searching for the same people we are, and now I'm sure that Sheriff Metzger has added Brian's name to the list of fugitives. Brian can't elude them for very long, Alice. We have to find Jepson before he does and gets himself in more trouble."

Part Three

Chapter Twenty-two

Alice offered to drive me home, an invitation I accepted. But as we drove downtown past all the media trucks and posters in store windows, and people wearing yellow ribbons on their shoulders, I said, "On second thought, would you mind dropping me at police headquarters?"

Her expression was quizzical.

"I think we'd better give this map we've found to Sheriff Metzger right away," I said.

"Why?" Alice asked. "Won't it get Brian in trouble?"

"Sheriff Metzger's priority is his wife and Darryl Jepson, in that order. If there's any chance that the locations Brian circled will help Mort and the other officers find wherever Jepson is hiding out, we need to make certain they have every bit of information available at their fingertips."

I didn't know where Mort Metzger was. Would he be at headquarters, or was he back at Moon Lake with the other searchers?

I couldn't ask Alice to drive me to the search area. She had to get back to her father's house and take care of her child.

Although I'd lived in Cabot Cove and had fished its myriad lakes and streams for years, I hadn't realized until Maureen went missing just how vast and dense the surrounding woods were. If Brian's map could be of aid in any small way, Mort had to have it—and have it fast.

As we turned into the parking lot of headquarters, my optimism level went up a few notches. Mort's official cruiser was parked in front of the main entrance; unless he'd been driven somewhere by a deputy, chances were he was in his office.

"You've been a big help, Alice," I said as I prepared to get out of her car.

"I just want to see Brian back home safe," she said. "Please tell Sheriff Metzger we know he was foolish to have done what he did."

"I'm sure Brian thought he had a good reason," I said, hoping to comfort her.

I was about to close the door behind me when Alice said, "And I hope Mrs. Metzger is okay. I didn't mean to leave her out."

I forced a smile. "We all hope that, Alice. Thanks for the ride."

A deputy on desk duty looked up when I approached. "Hello, Mrs. Fletcher," he said.

"Hello, Jerry. Is the sheriff in?"

He nodded. "But he doesn't want to be disturbed."

"I see. Well, maybe he'll allow me to have a few minutes with him, just a few."

I could see wheels spinning in Jerry's head and knew what he was thinking. If Mort had left instructions not to be disturbed, Jerry could be in for a tongue-lashing from our sheriff if he violated that order.

"Just tell him that Jessica Fletcher needs to speak with him and that she has something that might help in the search for his wife."

"Okay, Mrs. Fletcher, seeing that it's you." He got up and disappeared in the direction of Mort's office. After a few minutes passed, I wondered whether Mort would refuse to see me. But then Jerry returned. He was smiling, a good sign.

"Go on back, Mrs. Fletcher," he said.

Mort was standing at a large map of Cabot Cove and its surroundings into which a series of different colored pushpins had been inserted.

"Come on in, Mrs. F.," he said, not turning. He pushed a few new pins into the map, stepped back, surveyed the map, and turned to me.

"Have a seat," he said, taking his chair behind the desk. "Jerry says you have something important to show me."

I unfolded the map Alice and I had found behind the other map in Emma's room.

"What's this?" Mort asked as he put on half-glasses to read it.

"It's a map Alice and I discovered at their house," I explained. "Alice told me Brian was frustrated at not being allowed to help in the search."

Mort grunted. "And Alice was okay with you handing over this map?"

"She was. She worries about her husband putting himself in danger. You can understand that."

"And who would this helper you mentioned be?"

"It's just a guess on my part, but I think he could be another guide, named Hank Thompson."

"Okay, so Kinney has this map and maybe is with Thompson. You think these circled spots on the map are places they planned to meet up?"

"That's a reasonable assumption," I said. "But it could also indicate where Brian thinks he might find Darryl Jepson. If that's true, it could also mean that—"

"That it's where Maureen might be, too," he said, finishing my sentence.

He got up and carried the map I'd given him to the larger map on the wall. He used his index finger to indicate on the larger version the location of the marks that Brian had made on his smaller map.

"That's rugged terrain," Mort mumbled, more to himself than to me.

"Is it?"

"That section of the woods is pretty much all mountains, Mrs. F. The search teams haven't gotten to it yet."

"Because it's impassable?" I asked, realizing when I said it that if Jepson had chosen a difficult section of the woods, it hadn't been impassable for him—and hopefully not for Maureen.

Mort returned to his desk and sat in silence. It gave me a minute to scrutinize him. While he'd been gaunt, his eyes sunken, when he'd come to dinner at my house, he was even more so now.

"Why do you think Brian knows more than we do where Jepson might be holed up?"

"He and Jepson and their pals used to roam those woods as teenagers, Mort. It may be a shot in the dark, but I wouldn't rule out the possibility that Brian is on to something. Alice said he complained to her that the authorities were locking up their best searcher. Let's give him the benefit of the doubt."

"He broke the law, you know," Mort said grimly, "violating his house arrest."

"Yes, I know, Mort, but I believe he's trying to help you find Jepson and, of course, Maureen."

"I'll level with you, Mrs. F., every hour that passes means less chance of finding Maureen alive."

"Don't think that way, Mort. Maureen is no wilting flower. She'll make sure to stay strong so she can come home to you."

Whether I was as confident as my statement sounded didn't matter. I hated seeing my good friend fall into a pessimistic funk.

He seemed to realize that his sinking mood wasn't helping anything. He came forward in his chair and said, "Thanks for bringing this. I'll head up to Moon Lake and get together with the guys leading the search."

"I'd like to come with you," I said.

"No way, Mrs. F. If we do manage to find Jepson, the last thing I want to worry about is you."

"I'll stay out of the way, Mort. It's just that—"

"Forget it!" he said with finality. "I'll have one of my men drive you home."

"There's no need for that, Mort, but thanks anyway."

He grabbed his Stetson from a wall peg and we walked outside together.

"Looks like rain is coming," he said, squinting at the overcast sky. "Sure you don't want a ride home?"

"I'll be fine," I said, fully understanding Brian's frustration at not being able to help. But if I couldn't convince Mort to let me participate, I'd have to be patient and find another way.

He snugged down his hat. "Thanks for bringing the map, Mrs. F. I'll let you know if anything comes of it."

I watched him get in his squad car, shout into his radio, and drive away. Mort Metzger was a good and decent man, devoted to his job and the people he served. My heart went out to him in his moment of unbearable grief as he not only was charged with finding and apprehending an escaped murderer but faced the possibility that his wife was in that murderer's hands. I shuddered at the thought that Maureen Metzger might no longer be alive. But I also feared that Mort might take drastic action instead of giving Jepson a chance to negotiate his way out of the predicament he'd put himself into, a situation that could add threats to Maureen's life, assuming she was still alive.

I walked down to the docks, thinking to stop into Mara's Luncheonette to distract myself while I imagined the authorities combing Brian's map and deciding where to start.

On the street behind me, a police car, siren wailing, lights flashing, sped out of town, pursued by two media trucks trying to keep up.

"Sounds like something's happening," Mara said, as I entered and took a seat at the counter two stools down from Barnaby Longshoot.

At Mara's words, two reporters abandoned a table, throwing down cash and rushing out the door.

"Iced tea, Jessica?"

"Yes, thank you, Mara."

"What about you, Barnaby?"

"Sure thing, Mara."

While Mara poured my iced tea, the cook pushed through the door from the kitchen carrying a bin of freshly washed dishes to leave for the busboy to put away. He deposited the bin on the counter and nodded at me. "Ever have time to look up Mrs. Luce?" he asked me.

"Yes," I said. "Her neighbor, Mrs. Bliss, was very helpful. She let me wait until—" I could feel the blood drain from my face as I realized that Dee's note to Jepson and the piece of smoky quartz that was his lucky stone were still zipped into a side pocket in my shoulder bag. Mort had given me such short shrift when I'd delivered the map that I'd forgotten all about passing them along to our sheriff and the search party. My whole plan to switch places with Maureen depended on Jepson getting the note from his aunt and his "lucky stone" that proved it was from her.

"I'll pay you later, Mara," I called out, swinging off the stool at the counter and hurrying out the door.

"I'll start a tab for you."

Outside, more sirens filled the air. When I burst into police headquarters, the radio was blasting. "We think we have them cornered. Sheriff Metzger has called for backup from the wardens and state police. The whole area is cordoned off. The press are warned to stay out of the vicinity. Reports will be forthcoming. No one, repeat no one, will be allowed within a mile of the cabin. All roads are blocked off. Any unauthorized personnel found within the search zone will be summarily arrested."

A group of reporters surrounded the front desk, demanding more information and shouting into cell phones as they gleaned tidbits from the radio reports.

"Jerry, you have to call the sheriff. I forgot to give him something and it's vital that he have it."

"I can't call him, Mrs. Fletcher. We're in a siege right now."

I ran outside and dialed Mort's cell number, but of course he declined to answer my call. I left a detailed message hoping he would take the time to listen, and returned inside hoping I hadn't been overheard by anyone else.

Five minutes later Jerry beckoned to me and led me to the hallway off which the offices were located. "The sheriff just called. He said he wants me up there. Gladys will cover the desk. The sheriff said for you to give me the message for Jepson and I'll deliver it to him. He'll know what to do with it."

"Oh, no, he won't," I said, hoping I wouldn't get arrested for obstructing justice. "I go with the message or it doesn't go. You can tell Mort I said so." I took Jerry's arm and pushed him toward the back door, where, if there were any left, the police cruisers were parked.

"You're going to get me in trouble, Mrs. Fletcher."

"Trust me, Jerry. If anyone gets in trouble, it'll be me. Mort knows that I'm assertive when I have important evidence." I pushed him out the back door just as Gladys came inside. A civilian dispatcher, Gladys was always on call when all the uniformed deputies were on assignment.

"Hi, Jessica," she said, waving. "Had a hunch I might see you here."

"Hi, Gladys. Cross your fingers this will be over tonight."

Jerry rolled his eyes. "I hope you're right, Mrs. Fletcher," he said. "I'd like to keep my job."

"You'll be the hero of the day," I assured him, as we climbed into the last marked car in the lot.

The radio crackled and Mort's voice came over the line. "Metzger, here. Are you on the road, Jerry?"

"Yes, Sheriff."

"And you have Mrs. Fletcher with you?"

Jerry flashed me a worried look. "I do, Sheriff."

"I knew you wouldn't be able to keep her away."

"I didn't exactly hold him at gunpoint," I said. "But, Mort—"

"Did you do this on purpose, Mrs. F.? You were right there with me. You could have handed over the important message and let me do my job."

"I wish I could admit to being that conniving," I said, "but frankly I simply forgot I had the note and the stone."

"What stone?"

"It was Jepson's lucky stone, a piece of smoky quartz, a last memento. His aunt gave it to me so I could prove to him the message was truly from her."

"And what do you think this is all going to mean?"

"Is Maureen in the cabin with Jepson?" I asked.

"We think so, but we're waiting for a drone to get a look inside to confirm her presence without jeopardizing any personnel."

"I want to talk with him, to convince him to let me switch places with Maureen. That way we can get Maureen medical help, but Jepson will still have a hostage to hold for negotiations. I'm hoping he'll see the value in that."

"You're dreaming, Mrs. F. You'll just be giving him a bigger weapon—two hostages to threaten to kill. With that philosophy, we could hand over the whole town. At what point do we get him to surrender? Or do we have to kill him to stop his escape?"

Chapter Twenty-three

I've been in cars that were driven fast before, but never like the squad car driven that day by Mort Metzger's deputy, Jerry. He turned on the siren and flashing lights and pulled from the parking lot in front of headquarters, tires squealing. I struggled to put on my seat belt and saw that he hadn't bothered with his.

"Your seat belt," I shouted over the roar of the engine and the sound of air coming through my open window.

"What? Oh."

How he managed to buckle up without slowing down was a tribute to his dexterity.

There were many times during that wild ride that I considered asking him to slow down. Maybe my fear was exacerbated by not being a driver and wondering how he could control the car at the speed he was going. All I could think was that if we had an accident, the note and the meaningful stone I carried from Jessup's aunt Darcy would be worthless to Mort and his men. But I didn't say anything as he drove on the shoulder of some roads, swerved to avoid slower-moving cars, and at one point even drove on the wrong side of the road, causing oncoming traffic to pull over to give him clear passage. I pressed my fists against my stomach to stave off nausea from the car's sudden movements, abrupt stops when the way wasn't clear, and when he took curves on two wheels—well, maybe not literally but it felt that way.

I was terrified during the ride but tried to focus on what Mort had said, that they thought someone else was in the cabin with Jepson. Was it Maureen? It had to be, and I silently repeated a simple prayer over and over that it was. My mind went into overdrive. If Maureen was in the cabin with Jepson, what shape could she be in? Had he injured her? Had they had anything to eat?

I could only imagine what was going through Mort's mind at that moment. His mission, and that of the other police personnel, was to capture Jepson and return him to prison, a task complicated by the possibility that Mort's wife was being held hostage by the escaped murderer.

The deputy turned off the main road and started up a steep incline, a dirt road barely wide enough for the vehicle. We splashed through deep pools of water from the rain that had fallen the previous evening; at times he had to stop before slowly circumventing a fallen tree or a rock that had slid onto the road, which seemed to become even narrower, if that were possible. Trees and bushes on either side encroached on our progress, causing the deputy to swear under his breath.

"Are you sure this is the way?" I asked, hoping I wasn't offending him.

"Yes, ma'am. This is where the sheriff told me to come."

At one point the road leveled out but then began another ascent. The car's front wheel hit a large rock and I was sure that it would stop us. It didn't. The deputy forged ahead until . . . until we reached a plateau where dozens of official vehicles were parked haphazardly, doors open, flashing roof lights casting shafts of macabre light in every direction, radios on at top volume. We came to a stop. I looked at the deputy and managed a smile.

"Thank you," I said weakly, realizing that I'd dug my fingernails into the palms of my hands and that my legs were shaking. I wondered whether they would support me when I exited the car.

"No problem," the deputy said, returning my smile.

I got out, thinking that I was very glad that I didn't drive, that I had no desire to learn how to drive, and that I had just received a hundred-point lesson on why my usual modes of transportation were infinitely preferable to careening around behind the wheel of a vehicle that was every bit as dangerous as a lethal weapon.

I leaned against the car until I was confident that my legs would work and took in the scene before me. The cabin was located on a bluff, the area surrounding it seemingly empty. Yet I could see black helmeted police snipers perched in a half-dozen trees looking down on the roof. On the ground behind the cabin, technicians were setting up giant lights aimed at the windows. If the standoff lasted into darkness, the whole area would be illuminated to keep anyone from sneaking out without being seen.

I walked in the direction of Mort's sheriff's car with its distinctive markings. He intercepted me.

"Well, I see you managed to get here," he said.

"Yes," I said breathlessly, stifling the temptation to suggest that he had a deputy who belonged on a NASCAR track.

"Give it to me."

"What?"

"The note for Jepson from his aunt."

"Yes, of course, but I think that—"

"Maureen's in there with that madman," Mort said.

"*She is?* Definitely? She's all right?"

"I don't know how all right she is, but at least she's alive—and I want to keep her that way."

My reaction had been one of joy, but it quickly changed to match what I was sure were Mort's thoughts. His wife was still being held hostage by a convicted murderer. Jepson had sworn vengeance on our sheriff, according to Brian Kinney. Jepson still had time to take out his hatred of Mort on Maureen.

"Have you seen Brian Kinney?" I asked cautiously.

"That punk? Yeah, he's over there with the wardens unit. C'mon, Mrs. F., give me this all-important letter."

I unzipped the side pocket of my shoulder bag to retrieve the note from Jepson's aunt Darcy when a deputy approached and said, "Sheriff, the SWAT commander wants to talk with you." Mort took off, following the deputy, leaving me with the note and quartz stone in my hand.

I saw Brian standing with a group of young men, including Hank Thompson, and walked to where they stood in a circle of uniformed state police, some of whom had binoculars trained on the small cabin. He saw me approaching, waved, and broke away to join me.

"Mrs. Fletcher," he said. "Wow! I didn't think you'd be here."

I started to explain about having found his map and the note from Jepson's aunt Darcy, when a police helicopter swooped down from behind a ridge, its engine drowning my words. The blast from its rotors was strong; I instinctively reached for my hair as though to ensure that it hadn't been blown away.

"You found the map," he said once the chopper had passed.

"Yes, with Alice's help," I replied. "Why did you violate the sheriff's order and leave your house?"

"I couldn't just stay there knowing that Stinky was up here."

"Here? In this cabin? How did you know that?"

"I didn't know for sure, of course, but we used to come here when we were hanging out together. It was one of our secret places to meet up. He told me once that if he ever wanted a safe place to go underground he'd look for the highest cabin he could find. This one fits that description."

"Who owns the cabin?" I asked.

He shrugged. "I don't think anybody does anymore. It's been abandoned for years. Every time we came here it was empty, didn't have much in it."

"Food?"

"Maybe some canned goods, left by others who used the cabin. It's kind of camping courtesy to leave something for the next hikers who come along. There's usually a tin of something sealed up and some basic utensils, tin plates, stuff like that that the mice can't get to."

Mort beckoned to Brian, and I followed him to listen to their conversation. "Can you tell me what it looks like inside?" Mort asked.

"Pretty standard one-room cabin," Brian replied. "Central door, kitchen area to the left, bunk beds to the right, bathroom in back."

Mort, who was a few feet from us and stood behind a tree fifty feet from the cabin, held up a yellow electronic bullhorn.

"Darryl Jepson, this is Sheriff Metzger," he said into it, his finger on a trigger that activated its amplification. "We know you're in there and that you have a—that you have a hostage. Don't make things any worse than they already are for you. Release your hostage and come out with your hands in the air, and no one will get hurt."

All eyes were on the cabin door.

Please, I thought, *let Maureen come through that door.*

There was a deathly silence as we waited.

Nothing happened.

Brian said to me, "I suggested to the sheriff that he let me talk to Darryl through the bullhorn, but he brushed me off."

"That would seem worth a try," I said.

I turned to Mort. "Why not let Brian try to talk Jepson into releasing Maureen? They were buddies years ago."

Mort glared at me, a look that I'd become familiar with over the years of our friendship.

"It wouldn't hurt to try," I pressed gently.

Mort grunted and looked at the ground while considering what I'd said. Finally, he motioned for Brian to come to his side.

"Go ahead, Kinney," he said, handing the bullhorn to Brian. "Just don't say the wrong thing and make it worse."

Brian took the bullhorn and pondered what to say.

"Tread on your prior friendship," I said to Brian. "Tell him you don't want to see anything bad happen to him today."

Brian drew a deep breath and started talking into the bullhorn.

"Pull the trigger," Mort growled.

Brian did as instructed, and now his voice was amplified.

"Hey, Stinky, it's Brian, Brian Kinney. We got some of the old gang here to help you out. Hey, man, I know you're in a tight squeeze here, but nobody wants to see you or anybody else get hurt. Come on, man, let the lady go and come out. We'll do whatever we can to make it easier for you. I promise."

The answer came from the single window at the front of the cabin, which was cracked open. The barrel of a rifle suddenly appeared, pointed in our direction.

"Where'd that gun come from?" Mort shouted. He grabbed the bullhorn from Brian's hands and growled, "That's enough. He hears you and he starts firing. Everybody move back, get behind something."

We did as we were told. My legs, which had gained strength since leaving the deputy's car felt weak again, and my hands shook.

The officer in charge of the state police came to Mort. "We're not making any progress," he said. "We've got a new protocol in these situations. No more waiting it out like we used to. I say we go in and take him."

"With my wife in there?" Mort said. "Not on your life. I'm in charge of this operation, and I say we wait a little longer, give it time to resolve itself."

"But now we know he's got a gun."

"Yeah," Mort said, "but we don't know if it's loaded. He could just be waving it around as a threat."

Mort's response obviously didn't please the state police commander, who muttered under his breath and returned to where he'd been crouched with a half dozen of his officers.

I remembered the note I had.

"Mort," I said, "about that note that Jepson's aunt wrote to him. Here it is."

"What's it say?" he asked.

"I don't know. The envelope is sealed."

He started to say something, but I interrupted. "Mort," I said, "I have this feeling that Jepson might listen to me if I'm the one to tell him about the note."

"You? Why?"

"Because—well, because I was the one she entrusted the note to. Besides, Jepson has no reason to dislike or distrust me. With you he—"

"Yeah, I know, he's no fan of mine."

"He blames you for putting him behind bars when actually it was his lawyer, Wes Caruthers, who did such a terrible job that he was convicted of a higher charge. Look, Mort, the last thing I want to do is get in your way, but because Jepson's aunt wanted *me* to deliver the note to him, I think that I'm the one to do it."

"'Deliver the note to him'? Not a chance, Mrs. F. The man's a murderer. He won't hesitate to kill you, too."

"Then I won't suggest that I give it to him, but at least let me try to talk sense to him. As I said, he doesn't have any reason to distrust me."

Mort processed what I'd suggested. "All right, Mrs. F. You can talk to him through the bullhorn. But like I told Kinney, don't say or do anything to make things worse. Maureen is in there with him and—"

His voice cracked as he handed me the bullhorn. I wanted to wrap my arms around him, but this wasn't the time to be sentimental. I'd been handed the means to communicate with Jepson and knew that it would be my only chance.

I examined the bullhorn as though it were an alien device, some bit of electronics from another planet. I'd never used one before and hoped that my voice would remain steady as I spoke into it. I sensed that everyone who'd formed a perimeter around the cabin now looked at me.

Do it, Jess! Do it right!

My hands still shook as I raised the bullhorn to my mouth and pulled on the trigger. "Hello," I said, weakly; the bullhorn made it sound loud but tinny. "Hello," I repeated, a little stronger this time. "Darryl Jepson, can you hear me?"

I realized immediately how silly that question was. Of course he could hear me, and it was unlikely that I'd receive an answer.

"This is Jessica Fletcher, Darryl. I'm here with the police, but I'm not one of them. I'm here because a very dear friend of mine, Maureen, is with you, and I'm sure she'd like to walk away from the cabin a free woman." I glanced at Mort before continuing. "I know that you have a beef with Sheriff Metzger, but that's not a reason to take it out on his wife, who has done nothing to hurt you. Please, Darryl, let Maureen go."

No sound came from the cabin.

"What about the note?" Mort said to me.

"Right. The note," I said. I raised the bullhorn again and spoke into it. "Darryl. It's Jessica Fletcher again. I spent time with your aunt Darcy recently. She's such a nice lady and loves you very much. She told me that you'd had a rough bringing-up and that—"

My impromptu speech to Darryl Jepson was interrupted by the arrival of two state police officers from the hostage negotiating team and a third carrying a drone. I'd never seen one in person and was fascinated as they prepared to use it. I asked an officer standing behind me what it was intended to accomplish.

"They can fly it right up to the window and take a look inside," he said. "It's got a camera that'll transmit pictures back to the monitor they have."

My first thought—a worry actually—was that seeing the drone hovering just outside the cabin window would panic Jepson and cause him to do something foolish. But I put those thoughts aside as the officers launched the drone and directed it to the window using a handheld device of the sort that model plane lovers use to guide their small aircraft. I shifted my position enough to be able to look over the shoulders of the officer flying the drone and his colleague who peered at the handheld monitor.

The drone flew to a point above the window. Then, through a signal transmitted by its pilot, it slowly descended until its camera sent back a picture of the cabin's interior, at least the portion of it in the camera's field of vision. I gasped. Although the cabin's interior was dimly lighted, Maureen Metzger could be seen standing next to a bunk bed. I strained to better see. It appeared to me that she was tethered in some way to the bed. I craved to get a better view of her, but it wasn't going to happen. Jepson poked the muzzle of his shotgun out the window and batted the drone to the ground. The drone fluttered, then fell. The monitor screen went dead.

"He hit it out of the air," the officer who'd been controlling it snarled.

"She's alive," I said.

"What?"

"The sheriff's wife, Maureen Metzger. She's alive. I saw her."

"I saw her, too," Mort exclaimed enthusiastically.

I put the bullhorn back up to my lips and said, "Darryl, it's Jessica Fletcher again. I have a note for you that your aunt Darcy wrote. I don't know what's in it, but she wanted very much for you to have it. Can I—would it be all right if I give it to you?"

I didn't expect a reply. But then, to my surprise and I'm sure to the surprise of others on the scene, a man bellowed through the half-open window. "Darcy gave you a note?"

I looked to Mort, who indicated I should answer him.

"Yes," I said through the bullhorn. "It's a personal note to you. She wanted me to promise that you would receive it."

Everyone waited for a response from Jepson.

"How do I know you're telling me the truth?"

"She also gave me your lucky stone, the one you found with your father." I held up the stone but had no idea if he could see the smoky quartz in my hand.

"What's the note say?" Jepson yelled.

"I don't know," I replied. "It's in a sealed envelope. She wanted only you to see it."

"Bring it to me," Jepson commanded.

Mort shook his head.

I ignored him and said, "I'll be glad to bring it to you, Darryl, provided you allow Mrs. Metzger to go free."

"Bring it to me," he said, "and no tricks. You bring the note to me and keep the sheriff away. Got it?"

"What about letting Mrs. Metzger go?" I asked through the bullhorn.

"When you bring me the note."

"Can I trust you to keep your word?"

Behind me I could hear Mort grumbling. "You can't trust him to do anything."

A face appeared in the window: Darryl Jepson's face. "Come on," he said in a gravelly voice. "Bring it here."

I handed the bullhorn to Mort. "I'll do what he says," I said.

"No, you won't, Mrs. F. I don't want your death on my hands."

"He won't kill me, Mort," I said. "He has no reason to. If I can gain access to the cabin, it might help Maureen get free. Please. I know it's risky, but I'll be fine. At least let me try."

The state police commander who'd overheard our conversation said to Mort, "If she's willing to risk it, it's worth a try, Sheriff. We're not getting anywhere standing around like this."

As he walked away, I said, "Mort, the state police are getting impatient. I know that you have jurisdiction, but they can overrule you if they think the situation has deteriorated. If they decide to storm the cabin, Maureen will be in greater danger than she already is. Please. Let me try. I was with Maureen when she disappeared, and I want to be instrumental in helping free her."

"Go ahead, Mrs. F.," he said, "but don't push Jepson. Hand him the note and get out of there."

I agreed, drew a series of deep breaths, and started walking toward the cabin. There was stirring among the armed officers, but they were told to stand down.

I'd never realized before how aware one can be of steps being taken. Each one I took seemed meaningful, monumental, one foot in front of the other, my senses on high alert for any sounds coming from the cabin. I was halfway there when I wondered whether I should abandon the mission, turn around, and flee back to the safety of the dozens of armed men. But I knew that I couldn't stop now.

The cabin didn't have a porch; two slabs of rock led up to the door. I took them one at a time and reached out my free hand, the other carrying the note and piece of quartz. Should I try to open the door or knock? I knocked. I heard shuffling inside, was aware of someone breathing deeply on the other side of the door. The doorknob slowly turned. It swung in. I was face-to-face with Darryl Jepson, who held a rifle.

It was pointed directly at me.

Chapter Twenty-four

The sight of the rifle brought forth a gasp, and my hands automatically went to my chest in a defensive motion. I almost dropped the note and stone.

"Close the door," Jepson growled.

My instinct was to drop the note and stone and try to run back through the door to safety, but I looked past Jepson and saw Maureen Metzger. She was seated on the lower bunk, which contained no mattress, only the innerspring. It's amazing how much you can notice in only a second or two. Maureen's one arm was tied to the bunk bed's frame. She still wore what had once been a white T-shirt and tan shorts, but her pink clogs were gone. She was barefoot. I almost didn't recognize her face. It was thin and drawn, the skin peeling off in flakes. Her red hair hung in lank ringlets over the sides of her face.

Jepson was barefoot, too. He'd obviously been injured during his flight from the authorities. His feet were crusted with dried blood. I looked up at his face, which also bore proof of his having encountered solid objects and sharp vegetation. He'd obviously come across a change of clothes, probably in one of the many cabins in the area that were seldom used. He wore a torn blue denim shirt and a pair of chinos that were much too big for him. They were secured around his waist with a length of clothesline. His beard was matted, his eyes wildly darting back and forth between me and the open door.

"Close it, I said!" he snapped.

I reflexively reached back and closed the door.

"Go over there," he said, indicating with the rifle that I was to cross the small room to where Maureen was seated.

"Jessica," she said in a voice so small it could have belonged to a child.

"Hello, Maureen," I said. I didn't know whether Jepson wanted me to remain standing, but if he did, he was disappointed. I sat next to Maureen and placed my arm over her shoulders. "It'll be all right."

She started to weep, each shudder sending her shoulders into spasm. I tightened my grip and kept saying over and over, "It'll be all right. It'll be all right."

Jepson approached. "Gimme the note!" he said.

I held it out, and he snatched it from my hand.

"And the stone. Let me see the stone." He grabbed it from my hand, staring down at a piece of his past, his last connection with his father.

Maureen and I watched as he went to a far corner of the room, keeping the rifle aimed in our direction. He tore open the envelope and began to read. He was silent as he read. He finished the first of two pages and started on the second. That was when he started to cry, a few gulps at first, then more sustained, the rifle pointed at the floor.

I was moved by his unexpected reaction, as well as jolted into wondering whether it might provide a time for us to escape. I removed my arm from Maureen and twisted away from her to allow me to see the bonds that secured her to the bunk bed. It appeared to me that the rope he'd used was loosely knotted; Maureen's slender wrist could probably slip out of it with some encouragement. I surreptitiously used one hand to gently pull on the rope. I'd been right. Maureen, who sensed what I was trying to do, manipulated her hand and wrist until it was almost free. But as she completed the maneuver and pulled her hand loose, Jepson, who'd been in a sullen crouch across the room, stood and waved the rifle about.

I stood.

"Darryl," I said, "isn't it time for you to let Mrs. Metzger go, and turn yourself in to the authorities?"

His gaze was that of a bewildered, trapped animal. It was impossible to read what he was thinking or planning to do next.

"She hasn't done anything to hurt you," I said.

"Her husband, he's the one who did me in, him and that crackpot attorney."

I shook my head. "No," I said, "Sheriff Metzger was only doing his job. I agree with you about the attorney, Caruthers, but the sheriff—"

"Caruthers," Jepson mumbled scornfully.

"I know that he was a bad attorney, Darryl, and you have every right to be angry with him. But not the sheriff."

I was tempted to add, of course, that Jepson had been convicted of killing the mini-mart owner because, in fact, he'd been guilty of the crime, but I didn't want to engage him in that sort of debate, or any debate for that matter. Even if Caruthers had been a better, more conscientious attorney, the jury probably would have still found Jepson guilty. But if Caruthers had fought for his client, perhaps generated a modicum of sympathy for Jepson and the hardscrabble upbringing he'd experienced, the jury or the judge might have cut him some slack. From everything I'd heard about the trial, though, Caruthers hadn't even tried, and I had a feeling I knew why.

"Caruthers is dead," I said matter-of-factly.

"He is?" Jepson said.

"He was murdered."

His laugh came in a short burst. "Somebody did him in before I could get to him, huh?"

Then, as though coming up with an important realization, he added, "It wasn't me. I didn't kill him."

"I know that," I said. "Look, Darryl, there's nothing to be gained for you by keeping us here. Maureen needs medical help. So do you. Aren't you hungry, tired of running? Why don't you give me the rifle and we can all walk out of this cabin? I assure you that neither Sheriff Metzger nor anyone else wants to hurt you," praying that the words I was saying were the truth.

It appeared that Jepson was about to pass out. He put his hand to his head and swayed, then reached to steady himself against a wall.

"Please," I said. "Let's do the right thing."

I detected a slight smile on his craggy face, covered with a week's growth of gray beard. He said, "My aunt Darcy wrote me a nice note, a real nice note. She always loved me, more than I can say about anybody else in my family."

"I know," I said, approaching him, my hand outstretched. "Let's go, Darryl."

"I never wanted to hurt nobody, even when they called me Stinky."

"Your friends used that name affectionately," I said.

He sat on a low stool and fought to put his battered feet into a pair of boots. I winced as he groaned against the pain he was experiencing. Then he stood, closed the gap between us, and handed me the rifle. It happened so suddenly that I almost refused to accept it. But I did, hating the feel of the weapon in my hands. I've never owned a gun nor wanted to.

"Can you walk okay?" I asked Maureen, who'd witnessed what had transpired in silence, shivering against a cold that only she could feel in the stifling hot cabin.

"I think so."

Aware that Jepson was watching us, I led Maureen across the room and to the door, opened it, and stood to allow the dozens of police to see that it was us, hoping one of them didn't panic and pull the trigger. Confident that everyone understood, I guided Maureen through the door and onto one of the stone slabs that served as a step. I sensed that Jepson had followed and now stood directly behind us.

"It's Jessica Fletcher and Maureen Metzger," I shouted, feeling Maureen slipping from my grasp and tightening it to keep her erect.

We stepped down to the second slab and walked a few feet to where Mort and the others stood. Jepson came down the steps and stood at Maureen's side.

Mort didn't hesitate. He quickly started in our direction, his handgun drawn and ready to be used. As he neared, I looked in Jepson's direction. I couldn't believe what I saw. He'd pulled a knife from the waist of his pants, raised his arm, and threw it with force in Mort's direction. But before it found its intended mark, Brian Kinney, who'd stood only a few feet from the sheriff, flung himself between the two men and took the knife in his right shoulder. Simultaneously, a contingent of state police rushed at us and wrestled Jepson to the ground, pushing me out of the way and releasing my hold on Maureen, who'd slumped to her knees, letting out an eerie cry of pain and relief. Mort scooped her up while EMTs from two waiting ambulances immediately descended on Brian, who sat on the ground moaning, his hand pressed to his wounded shoulder.

"We need more medical help here," Mort shouted, gently settling Maureen on the ground. "*Stat!*"

An EMT broke away from Brian, as another team hurried up the hill and came to where Maureen sat, leaning against her husband, tears quietly sliding down her cheeks.

"It's okay, hon," Mort crooned to her while the tech took Maureen's blood pressure. "You're safe now. I'll get you home as soon as I can."

"Oh, Mort. I thought I'd never see you again."

I moved off to get out of the way of all the police and emergency personnel and to give the reunited couple some privacy.

"Mrs. F.?" Mort called out.

I turned around.

"Thanks." He shook his head as if searching for words. "Just, thanks!"

I smiled.

"You okay?" he asked.

"I am now."

Chapter Twenty-five

I watched as all the commotion evaporated as if it had never been there. Two ambulances left within minutes of each other, bound for Cabot Cove Hospital, one holding Brian Kinney, the other carrying Maureen Metzger, with her husband, Mort, aboard. Darryl Jepson was handcuffed and hustled into a state vehicle that would transport him back to prison, where he would receive medical attention, too. Above, the rotors of a helicopter stirred up the dust as the chopper lifted into the sky and flew back to home base. The huge emergency vehicles, topped by satellite dishes, departed one by one, the cacophony of their radio transmissions fading in the waning day.

"Ready to go, Mrs. Fletcher?" Mort's deputy asked.

"May I have a few moments, please, Jerry?"

"Sure. Take your time."

I waited while state crime scene personnel exited the cabin

after photographing the scene and taking away what little evidence remained inside.

"We're going to string some tape here so if you want to look you can, but please don't touch anything," one said to me.

"I'll be careful not to," I replied.

I climbed the stone stairs and entered the jail Jepson had used to hold Maureen. What I had once thought was *eau de bear* lingered in the air. *Funny,* I thought. *I had been so focused on my hopes for a prisoner exchange and a peaceful ending to the hostage-taking, I hadn't even noticed the odor my first time inside.*

I turned in a circle, impressing the vision of the cabin on my memory so that I would never forget this day, especially the relief and gratitude I felt for Maureen's rescue and for the recapture of Jepson.

"Ready, ma'am?"

"Yes. Thank you for letting me look inside."

As Jerry walked downhill toward the few remaining vehicles parked in the scrubby grass, I gave the cabin one last look and noticed something resting among the pebbles of the path. I leaned down and picked it up. It was Jepson's lucky stone. It must have fallen from his pocket when the state troopers tackled him before escorting him to the police van. I hoped he still had the note from his aunt Darcy that had incited such an emotional reaction in him. Chances were that it was among the items the crime scene techs had saved in plastic bags. At least he'd had a chance to read it, and it had given him some comfort.

It was difficult not to feel sorry for Darryl Jepson, for his dreadful condition and the teasing he had endured at such a vulnerable time in his life. But as even his aunt Darcy had admitted, he'd made terrible choices and had acted rashly, striking out as he had this afternoon when the prudent course of action would have been to submit quietly. Now, he faced a whole new raft of charges that would lengthen his time in prison—and his misery.

I was certain that Mort Metzger would charge Jepson in Wes Caruthers's death. I was also certain, however, that Jepson's fingerprints would never be found on the attorney's boat because— well, because I didn't believe that he'd killed him, and I thought I knew who did.

"Would you like me to turn off the radio, Mrs. Fletcher?" Jerry asked as we started out.

"That's not necessary, Jerry, but I would appreciate a slower ride into town than the hair-raising one you gave me earlier."

Jerry grinned, and our return to town took twice as long as the trip up to Moon Lake, if not longer. I let the recaps of the day's activities coming over Jerry's radio lull me, and I felt my eyes beginning to close as each law enforcement unit thanked the others for their service and signed off.

Jerry dropped me at my house. I'm always grateful to arrive home after being away on a trip. Of course, this had hardly been a trip—only one day—but the feeling of relief and welcome I enjoyed as I opened my front door was palpable. I was also delighted to see that the little contingent of press that had haunted the area across the way was gone.

One of the cruiser's radio transmissions had mentioned a joint press conference at Town Hall to be held the next day, with all the participating law enforcement services present. I made a mental note of the time and place, but decided that I could use my time more profitably.

I nibbled on leftover pot roast and vegetables, sorted through the mail that had been gathering in both my mailbox and my e-mail box, and listened to my voice mail messages—returning only a few that I felt were important.

Evelyn Phillips called begging for a statement. I told her I would think it over and get back to her.

Peggy Abelin called to say she had the information I requested and left me the name.

And Seth Hazlitt called to say he'd admitted Maureen to the hospital and that he would pick me up in the morning on his way to check up on her. No "would you like to join me," just an assumption that I would. He was right.

But first sleep, deep, wonderful sleep. I hadn't closed my eyes peacefully since Maureen's disappearance and was looking forward to a restful night, and I imagined that Mort felt the same.

"I trust you slept well," Seth said in greeting as I opened the passenger door of his sedan early the next morning.

"Very well," I said. "I'm glad I set the alarm clock, though, or you would have been out here throwing pebbles at my window."

"Lucky you I didn't. My aim with pebbles is not the most accurate."

"Have you spoken with Maureen this morning?"

"Not yet, but the shift nurse reported that she had a quiet night, only waking in a nightmare once. They soothed her with a cup of chamomile tea and she fell right back to sleep."

Seth parked in the doctors' parking lot and I accompanied him into the building.

"Best I see her alone at first, Jessica," he said when we entered the lobby.

"Why?" I asked.

"Maureen is a strong woman," he replied, "but she's been through a terrible ordeal. I want to make sure she's emotionally strong before seeing anyone who shared that ordeal with her. After all, you were instrumental in her release from that madman, Jepson."

"Whatever you say, Seth."

"I shouldn't be long. I'll call you when it's time for you to see her."

I passed the time waiting to hear from him by reading that day's special edition of the *Cabot Cove Gazette*. Evelyn Philips had done a fine job of summing up the tumultuous events of the past few days; her interviews with Mort Metzger, Brian Kinney, FBI Special Agent Perle, and members of the state police imbued the long article with a sense of immediacy and provided readers with a clear understanding of what had happened and why. Naturally, Evelyn was eager for an interview with me because of the role I'd played, but I'd given her a simple statement instead, expressing my relief and gratitude to all the federal, state, and local organizations who had contributed to the search efforts. As far as I was concerned, the only thing that mattered was that Maureen was no longer a captive.

I didn't mention that I hoped Maureen had emerged unscathed, at least physically, if not mentally. Maybe it was because I harbored some guilt over having agreed to take her on the fishing trip to Moon Lake. Maybe it was because the thought of reliving that tense scene with Jepson was anathema to me. The days since her disappearance, and her eventual release, had taken an emotional toll on me, too, although it was nothing when compared to what that poor woman had endured. I was just glad that it was over, and wanted it locked in the dustbin of my past. Evelyn eventually said that she understood and stopped pestering me for more, for which I was grateful.

I'd just finished the article when a candy striper at the desk said, "Mrs. Fletcher, Dr. Hazlitt is on the phone for you."

"Seth?" I said. "How is Maureen?"

"A little thinner and a few scratches, but she'll be fine. All the tests have come back negative. She's looking forward to seeing you. Room three-twelve."

"I'll be right up."

Maureen was sitting up in bed having her vitals checked by a nurse when I walked into the room. The minute she saw me she put out her arms and started crying. I went to her and wrapped her in a hug. "Hey," I said, "cry all you want, but it's over."

"Because of you," she managed through her tears. "And just in time."

"What do you mean?"

"He swore he was going to make me his mountain wife and that I'd never see Mort again. I pleaded with him but he just ignored me. Told me he'd never had a wife and promised we'd have a sunset ceremony. I was terrified."

"Well, enough of that, then," Seth interrupted. "He's a sick man. You're safe now. It didn't happen. Will never happen. I'll be discharging you first thing tomorrow. What you need today is to enjoy a full day of gourmet hospital food, together with all the spa treatments Cabot Cove Hospital is famous for."

Maureen and I both chuckled at his facetious statement.

"That's a sure way to dry the tears," said the nurse as she wrapped her stethoscope around her neck. "What spa treatment did you have in mind, Dr. Hazlitt? The facial where we smear petroleum jelly on your face, or physical therapy where we make you circle around the unit with the hospital gown hanging open at the back? We can ask the cook to come up with his specialty, soft scrambled eggs and Jell-O. That the kind of spa day you had in mind?"

"Well, I'll admit the food is a tad less than gourmet," Seth said, "but at least someone else will be cooking for her."

Maureen brought herself under control and dabbed at her eyes with a tissue. "Poor Mort," she said. "He looked awful when he visited me. He's skin and bones."

Seth laughed. "I'd hardly say he's *that*, Maureen, but I'm sure he'll appreciate some of your home cooking when you're up to it. I trust he heeded my advice and took the day off. Hopefully he's sound asleep."

"Poor baby," Maureen said.

"He'll be fine," I assured, "and so will you."

She started to say something but tears interrupted. "It was so awful," she said through her sobs.

"Ayuh, it was that," Seth said, "but try to put it in the past, Maureen. What's important now is the future, get you up and out of here and back to your normal routine."

She managed a smile. "That sounds so good," she said.

I asked Seth to drop me at Mort's office instead of taking me home.

"Don't think our esteemed sheriff followed my orders to get some sleep, huh?" he said.

"There's something I need to run past him," I said.

"Whatever you say, Jessica."

As we passed through town, we saw preparations under way for the next day's fishing derby festivities. Signs and balloons were everywhere. A stage had been set up in the town park, where Mayor Shevlin would welcome the crowd and the prizes would be awarded for that year's winners.

"Maureen looks good considering what she's been through," I said as he drew up in front of headquarters.

"And how about you, Jessica?" Seth asked. "You've been through an ordeal, too."

"Me? I'm fine. Knowing that Maureen is back safe and sound, and that Darryl Jepson is behind bars again, is what counts."

It was no surprise to me that Mort hadn't heeded Seth's advice. Instead of sleeping off a stressful event and resting up from the effects of four sleepless nights, he was talking on a speakerphone to a rapt audience of deputies when I entered his office. He gave me a wave and a thumbs-up.

"Well, you'll hear all of this again at the press conference this afternoon," he said into his phone's built-in microphone. "There's a lady just walked in that I owe a big vote of thanks to. So, let's get back to work, ladies and gentlemen. Good job."

"You don't look any worse for wear," I said as I took a chair in his office.

"Had myself a good sleep, Mrs. F., not a long one but good enough." His deputy Jerry poked his head into the office. "Can you rustle up a cup of coffee for our guest?" Mort said to him. "And one for me, too?"

I thought about declining the coffee but decided this was likely to be a long day. A cup of hot coffee, even the headquarters variety, was appealing.

Mort dropped into the chair behind his desk with a big sigh. "What a triumph!" he crowed. "Look what we accomplished, Mrs. F. We rescued a hostage, captured an escaped prisoner—

and a convicted killer at that—and now I can charge Jepson in Caruthers's murder. Like they say at the track, we hit the trifecta!"

"I'm pleased for you, Mort, and the way things turned out, but I think you might be jumping the gun on one of those races."

I didn't know whether he hadn't heard me or chose to ignore what I'd said, because he didn't respond.

"What I mean, Mort, is—"

"I owe you a big debt of gratitude, Mrs. F. Sure, we would have eventually had the same outcome without that map you found in Kinney's house and the note from Jepson's aunt, but it would have taken a few more days to wrap things up."

"Thank you, Mort. As I was saying—"

Jerry returned with two mugs of coffee and a pitcher of cream. "We splurged this morning to celebrate," he said, "real cream, not the powdered kind."

I sipped slowly, allowing Mort some time to come back to earth. I put my hand in my pocket and felt Jepson's lucky stone, which I intended to return to his aunt Darcy along with my personal account of what had taken place. But first I had to convince Mort to open his mind to the possibility of another killer besides Jepson in the Caruthers case.

"I had a call from Peggy Abelin yesterday," I said.

"Who's she?" Mort asked.

"Wes Caruthers's former secretary."

"Oh, right. Yeah, I interviewed her after we found the body. Nice lady. Don't know how she could have worked for that guy."

"Yes, she told me you'd spoken with her."

"We checked out her story with the bank and she can account for her time."

"Oh, I'm sure she can."

"So what did she say when she called you?" he asked, taking a gulp of the coffee.

"I had asked her if she could look up who might have called Wes the day he died or who he might have called on that day."

Mort nodded. "Good thinking, only it was unnecessary. Caruthers might have talked to a lot of people that day, but so what? Jepson was the one who killed him, and he sure wasn't talking on the phone to anybody. He didn't even have a cell phone. No, Mrs. F., it was Jepson all right who killed Caruthers. He had the motive and he was on the loose at the time of the murder."

I pressed on. "Peggy gave me the name of a caller who'd twice spoken on the phone with Caruthers just hours before he died."

"Not unusual," Mort said. "As bad an attorney as Caruthers was, he had clients who either didn't know better or couldn't afford a better lawyer."

"True," I said, "but I came across another piece of information about this caller that should give you reason to talk with this individual."

"You're beating around the bush, Mrs. F. That's not like you. What would you like me to do? This is going to be a very busy day with wrapping up all the paperwork and state reports, plus the upcoming fishing derby festivities and all. I can't waste time on speculation when it could be postponed to another day."

"I understand that, Mort. Give me ten minutes to lay out for you what I believe happened to Wes Caruthers."

Mort groaned, then sighed, but after going through those indications of his pique he agreed to hear me out and did so without interrupting. When I was finished making my case, he came forward in his chair. "I'm not sure what you say proves that this individual is guilty of killing Wes Caruthers, but you've got my attention, Mrs. F."

"That was what I was hoping for," I said.

Mort stood and grabbed his Stetson from where it hung on the wall.

"Let's go have a chat with this guy," he said.

Chapter Twenty-six

Red, white, and blue triangular pennants attached to the antennas of the hundreds of cars on the lot fluttered in the breeze as Mort and I pulled up in his cruiser. Placards in car windows advertised special pricing on the variety of secondhand luxury vehicles, and signs flanking the front entrance invited buyers inside to see the latest models. A large sign had been strung over the entrance: FISHING DERBY SPE-CIALS.

John Pelletier, who'd been outside chatting with one of his salesmen, greeted us as we exited the car and walked toward the entrance to the sprawling corner property.

"All hail the conquering hero," he said heartily, extending his hand to Mort and nodding at me. "Are you here to look for a welcome-home gift for your wife, Sheriff? I have just the thing, a sweet little sports car she'll just love tooling around town in. Let me show you this baby. It's red. Women love red. Wouldn't you agree, Mrs. Fletcher? That color is my number one seller with the fair sex."

"We're not buying a car today, John," Mort said sternly. "We'd like to talk with you somewhere private about a serious matter."

Pelletier's smile evaporated.

"Okay. Absolutely. You bet. I always have time for our local law enforcement."

Pelletier ushered us into his showroom, a hushed atmosphere, all marble and glass, with classical music playing softly in the background.

"My office is over there," Pelletier said, pointing at a glass-windowed space with a high counter overlooking the showroom. His upbeat tone was less so now, and his wide smile was gone. "Go right in," he said. "I'll be back in a minute. I want to tell my secretary to hold my calls."

"Can't you call her from your office?" Mort asked.

"Oh, sure, of course, of course." His chuckle was forced. "Make yourselves at home," he said, struggling to sustain his cheerful expression as he went behind the counter and picked up his phone. "No calls, Rita," he said sharply. He came around the counter. "If you don't mind, I'd like to close the shades. I get the feeling that this is going to be a serious discussion, although I can't imagine what it could be about."

At Mort's nod, Pelletier picked up a remote and activated blinds sandwiched between two panes of glass that slowly lowered, casting the room in shade. He switched on an overhead light and leaned back against the counter. "Clearly this is not a social visit. What can I do for you, Sheriff? I'm a busy man and I know you are, too. By the way, congratulations on bringing that nut Jepson to justice. He's back where he belongs, behind bars." Then, as though he knew the reason for our visit, he said, "I can't believe that he killed Wes Caruthers. Wes may not have been the best lawyer to come down the pike, but he didn't deserve to die. Jepson really must have had it in for Caruthers because of the way he botched his murder conviction."

Mort nodded at me.

"Mr. Pelletier," I said, "last Friday, when Wes Caruthers was killed, you were the last person he spoke with. Why was that?"

"I was? Really? Well, maybe I was. So what?"

"Were you also the last person he saw before he died?"

"How would I know? The man was a drunk, always looking for a handout."

"And apparently he could rely on you for one," I said. "Wes's secretary tells me that she cashed checks from Pelletier Motors on a regular basis."

"Checks? What checks? What makes you think *I* knew about those checks? My secretary often signs checks in my name."

Mort held up his hand. "I find it hard to believe that a successful businessman like you wouldn't be aware of a sizable amount of company money being given away regularly without your approval. What did Caruthers do to earn such loyalty?"

Pelletier thought for a moment before answering. "He did a little work for me in the past," he said weakly.

"What kind of work?" Mort asked.

Another pause before he replied, "Legal work, of course."

"Peggy, his secretary, says that Caruthers never did any legal work for you," I said. "All the checks from Pelletier Motors to Caruthers—and there were quite a few of them—were labeled 'miscellaneous.'"

"I'm not in the mood for playing games, John," Mort said.

"What's the big deal? He did some work for me. I paid him. And when he was down and out, I helped him out."

"So you're saying it was purely generosity on your part?" I said. "You're sure that he wasn't blackmailing you?"

Pelletier guffawed. "I'm a law-abiding, upstanding citizen in this town, Mrs. Fletcher, as pure as the driven snow." He guffawed again for added emphasis. "What could he possibly blackmail *me* about?"

"How about throwing a case for you?" Mort said, his eyes focused on Pelletier.

"If that's all you have to base this accusation on," Pelletier said, "it's not much."

"Where were you last Friday morning?" Mort asked.

"Right here. Go ask my staff."

"What would you say if we have a witness who will attest that you were somewhere else?" I asked

"And where else would I be?"

"At home, feeding your bloody clothes into the washing machine, and on the boat where Caruthers was killed."

"Your prints were on the boat, Mr. Pelletier," Mort said flatly.

I glanced at Mort. That was news to me. But I'd seen Mort do that in previous cases, make a claim that wasn't true to get a suspect to open up.

Pelletier's face paled.

"Helen was very insulted that you didn't trust her enough with your laundry," I added. "She says that it was the first and only time you did your own laundry. Was it to prevent her from seeing Caruthers's blood on your clothing, to cover up evidence?"

Pelletier's expression changed from defensive to conspiratorial. He gave us the sort of smile I'm sure he used when charming a potential car buyer, leaned close, and said, "You're after the wrong man, Sheriff. Caruthers is the one you should be questioning, not me. He was a swine, a real lowlife, and a nasty drunk to boot. Of course you can't question him because he's dead." He straightened as he added, "Thanks to me. I've saved the town a lot of aggravation, to say nothing of money, by getting rid of Caruthers."

"So you're admitting that you murdered him?" Mort said.

"Murdered him? Come on, give me a break. Look, I went to see him on the boat, but I never intended to kill him."

"What *did* you intend?" Mort asked.

"He was bleeding me dry. I just wanted to stop the blackmail."

"But apparently he wasn't cooperating," Mort said.

"He laughed at me. Can you believe it, after all these years of saving his butt, he laughed at me."

"What did you do?"

"I wanted to punch his lights out. I grabbed him by the collar and socked him in the jaw. I think I knocked a tooth out."

"How did he end up in the water?" I asked.

"He fell backward and hit his head on the railing. I made a grab for him but he fell overboard anyway, and my shirt was full of his blood."

"So you're saying it wasn't your intention to kill him?" Mort asked.

"Kill him? No, of course not."

"But you didn't call the police to report that he'd gone overboard. They might have been able to save him."

"I guess I panicked. I'd never been in a situation like that before."

"Panicked, and lifted him over the side," I said, "hoping he would sink and give you time to create an alibi."

"Come on, you're sophisticated people," Pelletier said. "Don't you understand? I have a reputation to protect in Cabot Cove. And don't forget I have plenty of clout in this town. I voted for you for sheriff every time you ran. As for what happened to Caruthers, I figured the escaped convict, Jepson, would be blamed, considering how much he hated Caruthers, and I'd be off the hook. It's no big deal. Caruthers was a bad guy and I took care of him."

Mort shot a glance at me, the first since we'd entered Pelletier's office.

"What was he blackmailing you for?" I asked.

Pelletier laughed. "For paying him to throw the case against Kinney."

My expression mirrored my confusion.

"I paid Caruthers to make sure that Kinney ended up behind bars." Another laugh. "I'll say this for Caruthers, he did a good job of that. He put up the worst defense for Kinney that anyone could imagine and cut backroom deals with the DA. It worked out for Wes's son, Cory, too. Got the kid off the hook for the grocery incident. Kinney was convicted and sent away—which was exactly what I wanted to happen."

It took me a second to get over the disgust I felt. "Didn't you feel bad that because of you an innocent man spent seven years in prison?"

"Bad? Are you kidding? I wanted that punk out of my daughter's life. I would have done anything to make sure that happened."

"That punk you're referring to saved my life yesterday," Mort said.

"Yeah? He's still a punk."

Mort stood. "You're about to be arrested," he said. "And, by the way, thanks for helping me solve an old mystery."

Chapter Twenty-seven

The culmination of Cabot Cove's annual fishing derby is always a joyous affair, but this year's event had special meaning.

Maureen Metzger was alive! And safe at home.

In a sense the celebration was as much for her safe return as it was for the winners of the derby.

"So Wes Caruthers's murder has been solved, thanks to J. B. Fletcher," Seth said when I told him about Mort's and my confrontation with the wealthy car dealer.

"I really did nothing, Seth. Once I knew that Caruthers and Pelletier had spoken just an hour before Caruthers died and that right after Caruthers died Pelletier came home and washed his own clothes—wouldn't let the housekeeper, Helen, touch them—the rest was easy."

"Easy for *you*," he said.

"I'm beat," I said. "I think I'll take the advice you gave Mort and catch a nap."

"Best medicine there is," Seth said. "I'll see you tomorrow."

I made myself a cup of tea but didn't drink it. Fatigue suddenly washed over me, and I kicked off my shoes and stretched out on my living room couch. I fell asleep immediately and probably would have slept into the night had it not been for the ringing phone. It was Tim Nudd from Nudd's Bait & Tackle Shop, who would be presenting the fishing prizes at the next day's event.

"Hope I'm not taking you from something," he said.

"I'm just getting up from a nap, Tim."

"I'll make it short," he said. "I know that Maureen Metzger is in the hospital."

"Yes, but she'll be—"

"Keep a secret?"

"I'll try."

"Maureen's catch is the winning one in the rainbow trout category."

"That's wonderful. She'll be so pleased."

"The problem is that with her in the hospital she won't be able to come up on stage to accept the prize."

"I don't think there'll be any problem, Tim," I said. "Dr. Hazlitt plans on releasing her first thing tomorrow morning."

"I didn't know that. But in the event there's a complication and she can't be there, I was wondering whether you, as her close friend, would accept the prize on her behalf."

"I'd be willing, of course, but her husband, Mort, is a more logical choice."

"I know, but you know how grumpy the sheriff can be, Jessica. Besides, you're the person who saved her life. It'd be only fitting that—"

"I did no such thing, Tim. Look, if Mort declines to accept on her behalf, then I'll be pleased to do it. Want me to ask him?"

"Would you? He and I—well, he and I don't get along these days."

"I'll be happy to. But this is all probably unnecessary. I have every confidence that Maureen will be out of the hospital and at the awards ceremony."

I slept like a log that night—what an apt metaphor for a sound sleep—and awoke early the next morning. The sun was coming up, which meant good weather for the wrap-up of the Cabot Cove fishing derby.

I made myself an unusually large breakfast—stress invariably makes me hungry—and got ready to join other Cabot Covers and tourists at the festivities. Despite my efforts to focus on what was in store that day, I couldn't help but ponder the sordid aftermath of the past few days.

That John Pelletier had actually killed Wes Caruthers because the unsavory attorney had been blackmailing him was a shocking revelation for the community. Pelletier had been a successful businessman in town for many years; how many citizens had purchased their vehicles from him? Yes, he was known as a dour, even sour man who turned on the charm only when it came to a sale of an automobile, but to think of him as being capable of killing someone was unfathomable. Of course, he hadn't confronted Caruthers with murder on his mind. Striking him and causing the drunken attorney to fall into the water and drown certainly wasn't premeditated. But he had caused Caruthers's death, failed to call for any help, and would be held accountable.

Brian Kinney's decision to shuck his ankle bracelet and take it upon himself to track down Darryl Jepson wasn't the smartest move he could have made, but his motives were pure. After all, his map had led the authorities to where Maureen was being held captive, leading to her freedom. Mort had reluctantly agreed to not charge Brian with any violation of his home confinement. After all, the young man had stepped in front of a knife aimed at our sheriff. I had a feeling that over time, he would soften his view of Brian and accept him for what he was: a troublemaking teenager who'd been mistakenly convicted of murder and was now a law-abiding married man with a child and a second on the way.

But as Seth Hazlitt had told Maureen, all that was past tense. What was important now was to move ahead, put those unfortunate incidents behind us, and enjoy a bright, sunny day in Cabot Cove, Maine.

Seth had intended to drive me to the event in town, but he called to say that he'd been called to the hospital for an emergency and would meet up with me later. I used Dimitri's Taxi Service, and one of his drivers delivered me to the center of town where things were already underway. The high school band was tuning up, a few out-of-tune trumpet players' dissonant sounds like chalk on a blackboard. Hopefully they'd get in tune before the event commenced.

I spotted Mayor Shevlin and chatted with him until he was called away by an aide. Everyone was in high spirits, no surprise. The annual fishing derby was always cause for a heightened sense of well-being, but this year the recapture of Darryl Jepson, the resolution of Wes Caruthers's murder, and Maureen Metzger's safe return home had added an extra dimension to the day.

I was standing talking to some members of the committee when Mort Metzger pulled up in his marked squad car. Attired in his dress uniform, he got out, came around to the other side, and opened the passenger door.

"It's Maureen," someone said.

Sure enough, Maureen Metzger stepped from the vehicle. She wore a pretty red dress, and her smile stretched from ear to ear. Spontaneous applause erupted, and people shouted expressions of joy and relief. Maureen gave everyone an energetic wave, like a popular political figure greeting her constituents.

I joined others who'd formed a line to personally greet our returning heroine. When I reached her, she threw her arms around me, saying in my ear, "Don't let me cry. Please don't let me cry."

Her husband came up behind her.

"She looks pretty good considering what she's gone through, doesn't she?" he said proudly.

As he said it Brian Kinney, his arm in a sling, walked up to him. He was accompanied by his pregnant wife, Alice, and their young daughter, Emma. Mort looked at Brian quizzically.

"Hello, Sheriff," Brian said. "I just wanted to say how pleased Alice and I are with the way you rescued your wife from Darryl Jepson."

Mort seemed unsure how to respond.

I filled in the silence. "Brian's map certainly helped you find and rescue your wife," I said to Mort. "He's to be congratulated, too."

Mort hesitated, his face set in a scowling question mark. Then, to my delight, he extended his hand to Brian. "You're okay," Mort said.

Brian beamed; so did Alice.

"But stay out of trouble," Mort added.

"You can count on it," Brian said with a grin.

The sound of the band playing a spirited Sousa song as its members marched into place in front of the raised platform captured everyone's attention. The band played a second number, a medley of show tunes, which had everyone tapping their toes; some sang along to the music.

But then our beloved mayor, Jim Shevlin, stepped to the microphone and waited for the music to stop. When it had, he asked for everyone's attention.

"What a great day!" he exclaimed. "Not only will the winners of our annual fishing derby be announced, a recent event that had everyone upset and looking over their shoulders is now over. It's a real happy ending for Cabot Cove!" He pointed to Maureen, who stood with her husband in front of the stage. "Welcome back, Maureen Metzger," he said. "You gave us quite a scare."

A chant broke out: "Yay, Maureen! Yay, Maureen!"

"And don't forget our sheriff," Shevlin shouted into the microphone.

"Hip, hip, hooray, Mort! Hip, hip, hooray!"

"Okay," said the mayor, "it's time to award the fishing prizes. We had some great anglers this year who fished their hearts out. I doubt if there's a fish left in Moon Lake that isn't afraid of our hooks."

There was laughter.

"Let me introduce Tim Nudd of Nudd's Bait and Tackle Shop, who'll announce the winners."

Tim replaced the mayor at the mike and ran through a recitation of how the fishing contest was managed and the winners decided. There were a number of categories, which Tim smoothly navigated. Each winner came up on the stage to accept the award, a handsome wood-and-silver trophy with his or her name on it. When the rainbow trout category was introduced, I glanced at Maureen, whose face reflected her interest.

". . . and the winner is . . . Maureen Metzger, whose winning catch was a nineteen-inch beauty."

While each of the winners who'd preceded Maureen to the stage received a well-deserved round of applause, the mention of her name brought about an eruption of clapping and shouted congratulations. The band's leader, a music teacher at the local high school, must have been cued in earlier because when Maureen's name was announced, he led the musicians in a rousing rendition of the old tune "Ain't She Sweet?"

Maureen wiped tears from her eyes as she stepped on the stage and accepted her trophy and cash prize. I looked at Mort, and if I wasn't mistaken, his eyes were misting.

It was a fitting ending to what had been a tension-filled, frightening week.

The mayor took over the microphone once again. "We have one last prize to announce. The winner of the Chamber of Commerce twenty-five-hundred-dollar reward for information leading to the safe return of Maureen Metzger is Brian Kinney."

That night, a dozen of us gathered at Mort and Maureen's house for a celebratory party. To my surprise Maureen had taken the time to prepare an assortment of hors d'oeuvres. Mort was in especially good spirits, bantering more than usual with the guests. Toward the end of the evening Maureen came from the kitchen, took off her apron, and said that she had an announcement to make. A hush fell over the gathered in their backyard and she reined in her emotions.

"First of all," she said, "thank you for coming tonight, every single one of you. To know that Mort and I have so many caring, wonderful friends makes me want to cry—again." She laughed. "But I won't. I've shed enough tears to last me a lifetime. What I want to say is that despite how my first time as a fisherman—I should say fisherwoman—ended up—I mean being captured and all—the fishing was for me a wonderful experience. And catching the biggest rainbow trout makes it even more special. I can't wait for next year's fishing derby and spending a wonderful weekend on Moon Lake with my dear friend Jessica."

All eyes turned to me, and I hoped they couldn't read in my face what I was thinking. As much as I love Maureen Metzger, fishing with her had been a challenge. She looked right at me.

"But this time, Jessica, I'll be a better fishing buddy," she said, reading my mind. "I promise. And as long as no one escapes from prison while we're at the lake, we'll have a blast!"

She shouted the final words.

When I went to bed that night, my mind was filled with thoughts, most pleasant, some not so pleasant. Overall, things had worked out for everyone except for Darryl Jepson, who was now back behind bars in the state penitentiary; and John Pelletier, who was being held in the county jail awaiting his trial for manslaughter; and Caruthers's son, Cory, who was about to face a jury after years of getting away with murder. He had been Jepson's accomplice at the mini-mart.

I had promised myself that if Maureen was found safe and sound, I would welcome her to join me for next year's fishing derby. It was time to keep that pledge. I found myself smiling at the contemplation of another weekend at Moon Lake with her. Maureen is good people, just like most folks in Cabot Cove.

But as I fell asleep, I had one final thought.

Next year it would be Jessica Fletcher who caught the biggest fish.